A PALE REFLECTION

ALSO BY JANE GORMAN

A Blind Eye, Book 1 in the Adam Kaminski Mystery Series
A Thin Veil, Book 2 in the Adam Kaminski Mystery Series
All That Glitters, Book 3 in the Adam Kaminski Mystery Series
What She Fears, Book 4 in the Adam Kaminski Mystery Series

A PALE REFLECTION

BOOK 5 IN THE ADAM KAMINSKI MYSTERY SERIES

JANE GORMAN

BLUE EAGLE PRESS

Copyright © 2018 by Jane Gorman

All rights reserved.

No part of this book may be reproduced in any form or by any electronic or mechanical means, including information storage and retrieval systems, without written permission from the author, except for the use of brief quotations in a book review.

This is a work of fiction. Names, characters, places and incidents are the product of the author's imagination and used fictitiously. Any resemblance to actual events or persons, living or dead, is entirely coincidental.

Cover design by BookFly Designs.

ISBN 978-0-9991100-0-3

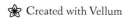 Created with Vellum

To my father, for his unwavering support and encouragement

1

THE LYRICAL SOUND of steel pans filled the air, interrupted occasionally by the breathless gags of the old man. His eyes bulged. The deep red of burst capillaries slowly suffused his cheeks, forehead, and neck as he gasped unsuccessfully for air.

It took only a matter of minutes. His eyes remained open, but eventually his body relaxed, all tension gone from his arms, neck, back. His tongue lolled out of the side of his mouth, spotted with blood where he had bitten it in his desperate gasps.

The killer stepped back, pocketed the murder weapon, and glanced around the bedroom of the first-class cabin. A suite, the best the cruise line had to offer, of course.

Curtains pulled back from sliding glass doors exposed a wide deck, subtle lighting glowing against the table and chairs, chaise lounges, and hot tub. Beyond that, the blackness of the sky and ocean was complete. In the sitting room, a menu of the next day's activities lay neatly on the coffee table, set out by the suite's butler, ready for the old man when he woke in the morning.

Remains of a late night snack marred the otherwise pristine neatness of the room, a small bowl and spoon, two used champagne flutes. The music from cleverly hidden speakers seemed to swell and grow, and the killer's shoulders moved to the rhythm. The killer crossed the room, pocketed one of the glasses, and nudged the cluttered tray with a knee. A snack for one.

No indication anyone else had been there. Just the last drops of champagne and lingering scent of an Amaretto crèmebrûlée.

Shoulders still moving rhythmically, the killer stepped across the room to the door, checked that the passageway was empty, and stepped out, pulling the door closed.

2

ADAM KAMINSKI WATCHED the restless waves with a sense of commiseration. He knew how they felt. Tossed this way, then turned that way, unable to resist an irresistible force. Only the peaks of the waves showed green below the frothy white flecks. The deeper troughs that danced below them were almost black in the dark morning light. It wouldn't be dark for long, though. Flames of deep red and orange lit the clouds that sat low on the horizon, slowly filling the eastern skies.

"Red sky in the morning ..." he said, turning to the woman standing next to him.

"Sailors take warning. Hm." Julia Kaminski turned her lips down into a mock frown. "Should we be worried?"

"Probably." His answer held no humor.

"I'm glad you came on this cruise with us, Adam." Julia leaned into him as she spoke, her slight frame bouncing off his broad shoulders, the curls and waves of her red hair tickling him below his jawline. "It'll be good for you. I'm sure of it."

Adam didn't turn to look at his sister as she spoke, but

the glance he caught of her from the corner of his eye didn't convey the assurances she was trying to give. The light freckles that dotted her face moved in and out of frown lines that slid across her forehead and around her lips.

"That's from the Bible, you know."

"What? What is?" Julia turned to face him.

He laughed at the expression of confusion on her face. "Red sky in the morning. It's in the Bible."

"Is not."

"Is too."

"Is not."

"Is too."

Funny how a simple argument that could have been taken word for word from all the other arguments they'd had as children could finally make him feel a little better. A little less lost.

"It's from the book of Matthew. I swear." He grinned as he held both hands up in front of him in a show of innocence.

"Why would the Bible talk about that?"

"I don't remember." Adam turned back to the gradually lightening seas. "I'll have to look it up sometime."

Julia apparently had no good reply to that, no sly insult or caustic observation. They stood in silence again, watching the sun as it grew before their eyes. Layers of dim yellow and pink ballooned out ahead of it, as if clearing the path, pushing back the purples and reds of the earlier dawn. The sound of a tin drum came from somewhere behind them, a not unpleasant mix of upbeat rhythm and heavy, dark syncopation. Voices carried from somewhere else on deck, though Adam couldn't tell exactly where.

The music matched his mood. He closed his eyes and let the beat soak through him, feeling each pulse like the rhythm of his own heart. Something else he couldn't control. He was truly tired of being jerked around, whether by women or by his boss. Or by criminals, even. He needed a break.

"You'll get better, you know. You'll heal." Julia said the words softly. She spoke as if she were continuing an earlier conversation. And in some ways, she was.

Adam hadn't exactly kept his heartbreak to himself over the past few months. He hadn't talked about it, obviously. No point rehashing the worst. But he'd let it take over his moods, his attitude. His life. His work.

"It's like the world is turned upside down, you know?" he said. "What was right is wrong, what was wrong is powerful."

"I know," Julia answered. "It can be frightening."

It *was* frightening. Hell, it felt like the tumultuous waves had more power than he did. But he didn't want to take his despair out on his sister.

Julia and Pete had been nothing but supportive. Which was only right, since Pete still owed him for not breaking his nose for sleeping with his sister. Pete was his partner on the force, first and foremost. And cops weren't supposed to fall for their partner's sisters. Adam was pretty sure about that.

He took a breath, steadied himself against the rail as if against a high wave, but in reality against the enormity of the words he knew he had to say.

"Thank you."

"For what?" Julia smiled up at him as she asked.

"For this." He looked out over the ocean, then down at her. "For dragging me along on this. You and Pete. It means a lot to me, and I appreciate it."

"Wow." Julia's head moved back over her shoulders and

her eyes widened. "Did my big brother just thank me for helping him?"

"Whatever." He grinned and turned away from her.

"Hey, it's no big deal. What were we going to do, trash the tickets? These cruises aren't cheap, and you know they said no refunds. And we sure as hell weren't going to let you come out here alone."

Adam said nothing at first, just kept staring at the waves, trying to see some sort of pattern in the cacophony of greens and blues and whites, like bruises forming and disappearing on the ocean surface. But no pattern emerged. He saw no sense.

"I shouldn't be here. I mean" — he draped an arm around Julia as she opened her mouth in protest — "I know what you're doing for me. And I'm grateful, I really am. But seriously, what the hell am I doing with my sister and her boyfriend on the honeymoon cruise for a wedding I had to cancel?"

Julia's silence was answer enough. They'd been through this before. Sylvia and Adam had purchased the tickets while they were still engaged. Still planning to get married. Still planning to have a honeymoon. With their breakup, Adam had been left with two tickets. He'd offered them to Julia and Pete, but the two of them had had a better idea: buy a third ticket and the three of them could go together. He'd heard everything she had to say. Enough times that he'd finally agreed to it. Reluctantly.

When she spoke again a few minutes later, it took Adam a moment to redirect his thoughts back to her and her life. "This is just what I needed, anyway. A little time off, a little distance ... it's the best way to get perspective on things."

Adam tried to imagine what problems Julia had in her

life that required distance. Or perspective. As far as he could tell, her photography career was moving along. Not flourishing, exactly, but she was still young, still building her reputation.

"Is something wrong with you and Pete?" he asked.

"Pete?" She laughed and his shoulders relaxed at the sound. "No, not at all. We're still having fun."

Adam smiled back at her, but wondered if "fun" was the way Pete would want to hear her describe their relationship.

He watched her face as she looked out over the ocean, the smile from a minute before drawing down, her brow lowering over her eyes.

"You know I'm here for you if you need to talk, sis. No matter what, I'm always your big brother."

"I know, Adam. Thanks." She gave him a weak smile and bumped her shoulder against him. "I just need to be patient, that's all."

"Ha, you?" Now it was Adam's turn to laugh.

"Oh, you're one to talk, Mister 'Let's-get-married-even-though-I-just-met-you-a-few-months-ago.'" As soon as she said it, Julia clamped her lips shut.

Adam tried to ignore the words. Ignore the fact that she was right. So painfully right. He was saved from responding by a voice behind them.

"Adam Kaminski? Detective Adam Kaminski?" The voice came from a crew member who'd approached from the back of the boat. He was a bear of a man whose rounded shoulders and wide stance suggested years of athleticism, the gut hanging over the top of his beltline and graying hair notwithstanding. A man whose need for physical fitness appeared to have diminished over the passing years.

"Yes?"

The man put out a beefy hand and offered a firm handshake. Firm enough that Adam subtly shook his hand after the man released it. "Wayne Rittle, Deputy Chief of Security. Captain Harding sent me to get you, sir. He needs your help. If you'll come with me?"

"My help? What's this about?"

Wayne's wary eyes flicked toward Julia, then back to Adam. He opened his mouth, shut it again, then nodded as if ending an internal argument. "One of the passengers was found dead, and we think you might be able to help."

"You've got to be kidding me." Adam felt his anger rise. "This is the last thing I need on a vacation." He looked at Julia and shook his head. "I can't believe this."

"Come on." Julia patted him on the shoulder. "You've been summoned, we might as well go and find out the whole story."

Adam lowered his eyebrows and let out a low sigh, but he also recognized that frisson of excitement he always felt at the beginning of a new case. He pushed it deep down and ignored it. This was not a new case.

As they passed single file along the narrow stretch of deck, he heard Julia's voice: "Sailors take warning."

3

Julia followed her brother along the narrow deck, a blaze of color from the newly risen sun lighting the sea to their right. Pale yellow light cast a warmth across their path and she turned her face to the light, just for a moment, before following her brother and his guide through a doorway that led into the dark.

Wayne stopped at the open door to a cabin and waved Adam and Julia in ahead of him. They were in the front of the ship, above the tennis courts and climbing wall. This section of the ship was not available to the regular passengers. To passengers like them. The hallways gaped a little bit wider, portals stood a little bit bigger, letting in more natural light. Unnecessary, really, given the large chandeliers that dotted the ceilings, themselves a little bit higher than Julia was used to from their part of the ship.

This was the first-class section of the ship, a section that provided a private pool, deck, and recreational area for the more important passengers. Or at least, those who could pay for the privilege.

The cabin they entered was not all that different from

hers and Pete's, if you ignored the fact it was about ten times larger. And didn't consider the floor-to-ceiling windows that ran along one wall, opening onto the now bright ocean beyond. Not exactly the same as the two-foot round portal she and Pete could peer out of.

Purple and gold covered every surface, from the deep purple of the sofa and chairs set out in one part of the room to the pale gold curtains that lined the edges of the bright windows to the gold hues of the remains left in a champagne flute and small bowl on a tray on the end table near the sofa.

Music played in the background, the lilting rhythm of Bermudian steel pan. Not quite reggae, not quite Caribbean, but bouncy. The fun little tune didn't match the mood in the room.

Through a wide doorway on the far side of the room, Julia could see a handful of men with somber expressions gathered around a bed. The bed's gold and purple cover was thrown aside, crunched into small balls and hills that reminded Julia of the dark waves they'd been admiring outside. She followed Adam into the bedroom, but stopped at the doorway, leaving a space between herself and the death she knew they faced. As she watched him, Adam's face changed, his expression became guarded, closed off. He became a stranger to her, his thoughts impenetrable. She looked away.

She recognized the captain of the boat. He'd made some comments of greeting when they set sail the day before, welcoming the passengers. By his side, a man holding a stethoscope could only be the ship's doctor. Two more men hovered around them, men she didn't recognize. They turned as one when Adam entered. Three of the men stepped back, away from the bed. The doctor stayed where he was.

Julia pulled out her phone and started snapping pictures. As much as she hated this part of Adam and Pete's work, at least this gave Adam something else to focus his energy on. Maybe she could help.

"Detective Adam Kaminski?" the captain asked. When Adam nodded, he reached out a hand. "Captain Harding. I appreciate you coming. As you can see, we have a bit of an emergency here."

Adam turned to the doctor. "Any information on what happened?"

The doctor was a short man. His hands shook as he gripped tightly the stethoscope around his neck as if drawing comfort from its professionalism. Its symbolism. "I mostly deal with seasickness, you understand. Bug bites, sunburn, that sort of thing."

"People do die, though, don't they? You must have encountered an unexpected death before."

"Yes ..." The doctor drew out the word. "But not quite like this."

"Tell me."

The doctor gestured toward the corpse that lay twisted on the bed. The man's face looked like it had been attacked by a child with a red marker, tiny pinpricks of red spotted around his cheeks, chin, nose, forehead. His body was twisted, as if he had died writhing, his eyes wide open, his silk pajamas coiled around him. The whites of his eyes, no longer white, almost glowed red in the morning light. His tongue hung out of his mouth, blue bite marks along one side.

"Poisoning?" Adam asked.

The doctor nodded. "I believe so. Probably within the

past five or six hours. This isn't something I've encountered before, you understand ... I'll need to do a little research. Look at the body in more detail."

"But you don't have the equipment here to do an autopsy? To run blood tests?"

The doctor mutely shook his head.

Julia took a step further into the room, still snapping shots. The steel pan music trilled in the background, the smell of Amaretto distinctive on the air.

"Almonds," she said.

The men all turned to her.

"Do you smell it?" she asked them.

Adam leaned closer to the dead man and sniffed. "Could be cyanide. Looks like it, anyway. But we'd need blood tests to be sure." He straightened and moved closer to the captain. "What do you need from me?"

In response, the captain turned away from him toward the doctor. "Let me know as soon as you have anything more. Immediately."

As the doctor nodded his compliance, Captain Harding put a light hand on Adam's shoulder. "Come with me, we need to talk."

"I REALIZE how unexpected this must be for you. Thinking you're on vacation and getting called into ... well, whatever this is." Harding spoke softly, his voice just carrying over the shouts and calls from the basketball court on the deck below them.

Adam heard the captain's words, but he also heard the doubt and fear in his voice. At least he thought he did. The boat tilted as it hit a large wave and he shifted his feet to keep his balance. Harding didn't seem to notice the movement. Clearly a man used to working on an uncertain surface. Maybe he should get used to uncertainty, too. Since he didn't seem to be able to trust his gut anymore.

"I still don't understand how I can help."

"You're a detective, correct?" Harding asked.

"Yes," Adam responded cautiously. "Homicide, in fact."

"Even better," Harding said.

"I don't know much about the law on the high seas, Captain, but I'm pretty sure PPD doesn't have jurisdiction out here."

"The Philadelphia Police Department?" Harding laughed. "No, that's very true, Detective."

"So then, how can I help?"

A shout rose up from the courts below them, a group of young men, sweating in their shorts and T-shirts, thumping each others' backs. Adam thought he could almost smell the testosterone, though it was more likely sweat mingling with the salt in the air. He closed his eyes and took a breath, letting the sun fall on his face while he waited for Harding to answer.

"It can be a little complicated figuring out jurisdiction at sea," Harding finally explained. "Though if this is really a murder, it will be the FBI who has the lead in the investigation."

"Because this is an American ship?" Adam asked.

Harding shook his head. "No, we sail under a Bahamian flag. No, the FBI has the lead because we departed from New York — a U.S. port — and the victim, if that's what he is, is American."

"You think he might have died of natural causes?" Adam knew his skepticism showed on his face but didn't bother hiding it.

Harding ignored the question, continuing instead with his explanation of jurisdiction, as if the picayune rules and policies that defined the situation would somehow add clarity. Or comfort. "When a crime occurs outside U.S. jurisdiction, FBI legal attachés work with local officials to conduct the investigations. In this case, because we'll be docking at Bermuda, that will be the Bermuda Police Service. My security team isn't prepared to handle an investigation like this."

"OK. And where does PPD fit into this?"

"It could have been an accident." Harding finally turned to look at Adam. "Without a final cause of death we can't be sure."

"Didn't look like an accident to me."

"No, nor to me." Harding's face was inscrutable.

"What am I missing?"

"I'm concerned the Bermuda police will see an accident."

Adam raised an eyebrow. "Are you expecting corruption? Or incompetence?"

"Neither." Harding paused as another cheer arose from below, another series of fist bumps and chest thumps. "It's the fumigation ..." His voice trailed off, his face now reflecting nothing but confusion.

"You need to tell me what's going on."

"Of course." Harding shook his head as if shaking water from it. "That's why I agreed when Rittle suggested contacting you. I had the whole ship fumigated. Just before we left."

"Sounds reasonable."

"It's not standard. We're only required to do it a few times a year. But we had some complaints on the last voyage, so I took the liberty of stepping up the schedule."

"I still don't see the problem."

"Some passengers, very few, very infrequently, have problems. Particularly elderly passengers."

"With the poisons you use in the fumigation."

Harding nodded, his lips pressed together in a tight line.

"So you think," Adam continued, "the FBI will conclude that this was an accidental death due to a reaction to the fumigation?"

Harding nodded again. "The shipping line will be held responsible. And they will hold me responsible." He turned to Adam with a grim smile. "Now you see my problem."

"You want this to be a murder."

"That's a terrible thing to say. And even worse thing for me to be thinking. But it's not just the fumigation."

"There's more?"

"Arthur Claypoole, the victim, is a very important person. Very important. The government will want this wrapped up as quickly as possible. The police in Bermuda are waiting, I've already alerted the FBI and the BPS. But they don't care about the cruise line, they'll surely jump to the simplest explanation."

"And your job is on the line."

"I didn't want this man to die, you understand. But I most certainly don't want to find that it was my fault."

"Why is this man, Claypoole, so important?" Adam asked. "Because he's rich?"

Harding dipped his head in acknowledgement, avoiding Adam's accusatory glance. "In part, yes. But he's also politically connected. To some very powerful people in our government."

"He's a politician?"

"Him? No, Oh, no. He's a businessman, absolutely. But a donor. A very generous donor, from what I understand."

Adam examined Harding, looking for more answers. "You know an awful lot about him. Do you know the background of all your passengers?"

Harding grinned. "Like you, you mean? It was Rittle who saw on the manifest that you listed your profession as a detective. You and another passenger you're traveling with."

"Pete Lawler," Adam nodded. "My partner."

"Rittle went out to find both of you. Either of you." Harding shrugged. "Neither of you were in your cabins and he found you first."

"Captain."

Adam and Harding turned to see Rittle, Julia trotting close behind him, seething.

"Adam, tell this jackass—"

"Whoa, Julia, what's going on?" Adam cut her off.

"This ...*woman*," Rittle emphasized the word with distaste, "was taking photographs of the deceased's cabin. With the deceased still in it." He almost spit out the words.

Captain Harding glanced at Adam.

"Taking photographs of a scene is standard procedure, Rittle. You should know that."

"Of course I know that." Rittle rolled his eyes. "I am a law enforcement officer. But she is not a member of the investigative team."

Adam blinked in surprise at Rittle's sudden invention of an investigative team. "My *sister*, Julia," — he paused for extra emphasis — "isn't a regular police photographer, but she is a professional photographer. Her pictures could prove helpful."

Harding nodded as he took a breath. "Understood. Rittle, return the camera. But" — he added as Rittle's face grew red — "thank you for your diligence with this. You were absolutely right to ask me first." He cast a look in Adam's direction.

"Fine," Julia huffed as she snatched her phone. "Next time, I'll be sure to ask." She gave them a narrow smile and sauntered off down the stairs to the deck below.

"I don't think I can legally be involved in this investigation, Captain. I'm sorry." Adam almost regretted having to turn down the invitation to catch a murderer. Almost. Feelings of relief and disappointment battled against one another. At least if he didn't take the case, he couldn't screw it up.

"But you're the only person on board who can help." Harding's voice dropped a notch. "Look, I can make it worth your while, anything I can offer. What am I supposed to do, sit by idly until we dock on Wednesday? Knowing there might be a murderer on board?" He glanced at Rittle, who reddened again.

"It's no secret, I don't have experience investigating suspicious death. That's never been part of my remit."

Adam took a breath, felt his lips pulling tight. "I can look around a bit. Informally, that's all," he added as he saw Harding's eyes light up and Rittle's brow lower. "Maybe I can ask a few questions that will point you in the right direction. But if I get involved, it could make things worse for you, you must understand that."

"Where shall we start?" Harding asked.

"Why don't Rittle and I get to know each other." He looked at the other man. "You can fill me in on what you know."

Rittle shrugged. "Sure thing." His eyes didn't convey the same level of affability.

THE OFFICE SPACE Wayne Rittle led Adam to had about as much in common with the public areas of the ship as a sausage factory had to a five-star restaurant. Where public spaces were grand to the point of gaudiness, this office was sparse, with simple metal desks and chairs, no windows, fluorescent lights. And where the rest of the ship was organized to the nth degree, everything held down tightly in its designated place, here files, notebooks, and stray papers vied for space on the few surfaces available. Wayne leaving his personal mark, perhaps?

It clearly wasn't only his office. The number of desks squeezed into the narrow office like a madman's game of Tetris made Adam's cubicle back in Philly look almost grandiose in comparison. But for now, he and Wayne were the only occupants.

Wayne lowered his rear onto a desk — crushing the papers below him without care. He lifted something from the desk next to him and with a quick movement of his chin, he tossed it at Adam. "Catch."

Adam's instincts kicked in and he grabbed at it, but immediately dropped it back on the desk when he realized what it was.

"What the hell are you doing with a grenade in here?"

"Don't worry." Wayne laughed, his smile genuine. "The explosive's been removed. Nothing to be afraid of. Come on, take a seat."

Adam sat. "Seriously, why do you have a grenade?"

Wayne took a breath. "Reminds me of who I used to be. Of what's important to me."

"And what's that?"

"You're the detective, you tell me."

Adam resisted the urge to roll his eyes. What kind of game was this?

Instead of walking out of the room as he wanted to, he took a look around him. The grenade was military issue, as was the folded and framed U.S. flag hanging on the wall behind the desk, a plaque recognizing twenty years of service below it. He let his gaze move back to the aging man in front of him. Twenty years of military service was nothing to sneeze at. He could see why Wayne would want to be reminded of it. But how had he ended up here?

Wayne's eyes narrowed as Adam focused on him. The skin of his face sagged, as much from carrying extra weight as extra years. His spare tire hadn't completely taken over. Yet. He couldn't imagine life on a cruise ship was as active as life in the military, though.

"You were married," Adam finally said.

Wayne grinned and held up his ring finger. "What makes you think I'm not anymore?"

"I have to imagine this type of career choice is more appealing for single than married people."

"You're right about that. And about me." Wayne looked down at his ring. "She died. Just a year ago now. I took it as a sign that it was time for me to make a change."

"Leave the military?" Adam grabbed onto his chair as the ship moved, cresting over another large wave. Was he ever going to get used to this? Wayne hadn't seemed to notice, even through the grenade shifted on the surface of the desk.

The other man shook his head, his jowls moving with the motion. "Did that twenty years ago. I've been working hotel security ever since."

"And now you run security on a cruise ship. But you introduced yourself as deputy."

"That's the job I was hired for. I'll admit, it caught me

by surprise when my chief left after I'd only been on the job a month."

"And left you in charge," Adam said. "So why'd you encourage the captain to contact me? You think you need my help?"

Wayne's expression darkened again. He stood, his bulk shifting the desk underneath him, and walked around to the far side of the desk. He sifted through the papers, as if looking for something, but then sat and looked over at Adam. "I'm not some rent-a-cop."

Adam lifted his face to the flag on the wall. "I can see that. You've got a distinguished record."

Wayne grunted. "And I'm damn proud of it."

"So why'd you contact me?" Adam asked again.

Wayne sucked in a deep breath through his nose, his mouth narrowing. "I'm proud of my accomplishments. Proud enough to know when I'm in over my head. I've never investigated a murder before. I'm man enough to admit it when I need help."

"Even if you don't like it." Adam grinned.

"We understand each other."

Adam shook his head and laughed. "Great. We'll have a perfect working relationship. OK, then, tell me about your security team here."

Wayne shrugged. "Just like any other security. We have limited surveillance, screening onto and off of the ship, we keep an eye on the passenger lists in case we see anything out of the ordinary."

"Like what?"

"Our focus is on smuggling, also terrorism."

"So you work with Customs?"

"With, yeah, but we're not part of Homeland Security. Our role is a lot more limited than that."

Adam tried to read the other man's eyes. He spoke like he didn't care about his role, but his eyes told a different story. It might seem to outsiders like a "rent-a-cop" kind of job, but Wayne clearly took his responsibilities seriously. Adam had never liked the term "rent-a-cop."

"Tell me what you can about Arthur Claypoole, then. You knew he was coming on this cruise?"

Wayne nodded and returned his attention to his desk, finally finding the papers he'd been looking for. Adam might have been impressed by the man, but definitely not by the man's organizational plan.

"We were surprised to see his name on the list," Wayne said, glancing down at the paper. "He had a history with this cruise line."

Adam's attention perked up. "What kind of history?"

"Not a good one." Wayne handed over the report.

Adam flipped through it. "He was suing this cruise line. At least, the parent company. So why was he here as a passenger?"

"That's what we couldn't figure out. He had a pretty good case against corporate, you can see, negligence at one of their resort properties. Why he'd risk that case by coming on a cruise with us beats me."

Adam read through the file one more time and handed it back. "How would that hurt his case?"

"He claims the company is negligent to the point of real danger," Wayne responded, flicking his hand against the pages he held. "A judge isn't going to find his argument compelling if he's willing to place himself 'at risk' by coming on board as a passenger, is he?"

Adam didn't know much about lawsuits, but Wayne had a point. "Maybe Claypoole thought he'd get better treatment here, everyone doing their best to keep him happy?"

Wayne grinned. "Man like Claypoole? Everyone always did their best to keep him happy. You must have heard of him."

Adam shook his head. He wasn't in the habit of reading up on political donors. "All right." He stood up. "There's more going on here than meets the eye."

Wayne stood, too. "So you'll investigate?"

"I'll consult. Advise. That's all. This is still your investigation."

Wayne's expression lifted. "I never said it wouldn't be."

4

"It was his birthday. Tomorrow." Brad Claypoole half-sat, half-lay against the short sofa in his suite, which matched that of his father's in all but size.

Wayne had led Adam to Brad's cabin, a few doors down from his father's, while sharing more details about the ship and staff. Together, they'd broken the news about Arthur Claypoole's death.

Brad Claypoole, for his part, looked surprisingly composed, considering they'd gotten him out of bed. They'd waited in the sitting room of the suite while Brad dressed. He appeared a few minutes later in jeans and a button-down shirt, a thin yellow sweater draped over his shoulders. His brown hair was already perfectly styled, with a hint of gray in just the right places. Adam put him in his mid-thirties, though Brad's confidence — arrogance, really — might be making him seem older than he was.

He strode into the sitting room, his back straight, as if intentionally emphasizing his above-average height, and offered both of them a strong handshake and cocky grin before they'd announced the purpose of their visit. On hearing the news, Brad's posture dipped. He stepped backward and almost fell onto the sofa behind him, slumping sideways against the arm.

"He would've been seventy," Brad continued. "He wanted to celebrate. We wanted to celebrate. No one thought he wouldn't make it …" He shook his head, blinked his eyes a few times. "He was so vibrant. I didn't expect …" He looked up at the bearers of bad news. "He went up to his cabin around ten. I thought he'd just get a good night's sleep. I guess no one ever expects it, do they? Was it his heart?"

"Did he have heart problems, Mr. Claypoole?" Adam asked as he perched on the end of the sofa near Brad.

"No, not that I'm aware of. I just thought … man his age … I guess that's usually what kills people."

Wayne kept silent.

"This is a slightly different situation," Adam explained. "We don't know the cause of death yet. This ship isn't equipped with a full medical lab, as you can imagine."

"Stop!" Brad put the back of his hand up against his eyes dramatically. "Why would I want to imagine something like that? Doesn't really matter, does it? He's still dead."

"That's true. But it's also true that if someone killed him, we need to catch that person."

Brad bolted upright. "Killed him?" His voice rose a few levels. "What the hell are you talking about? You just said he died."

"Yes, sir, that's correct. But there is some evidence to suggest he may have been killed. The captain has asked for my help as he looks into it."

"And who are you?" Brad's eyes narrowed as he asked the question, his hand now fluttering to his neck.

"Adam Kaminski. Detective Adam Kaminski. I'm a homicide detective."

"This ship has homicide detectives working on the security team? What the hell does Harding expect to happen on his boat?"

"Detective Kaminski doesn't work for me, Mr. Claypoole. He's a passenger. But when ... with the passing of your father ... the nature of the situation ..." Wayne seemed to be struggling for words, more uncomfortable than Adam had expected. "I've asked Detective Kaminski to step in and help. Given his particular expertise."

Brad nodded, looking back and forth between the two men.

"I'm going to ask a few questions, that's all. Chief Rittle is in charge of any investigation. Do you mind talking about your father?" Adam asked, wondering if all the first-class passengers knew the captain's name offhand.

"Talking? No ... no, that's fine. He is — I mean, I guess, he was a good man." Brad's voice broke on the use of the past tense but he held up and kept going. "Very altruistic. He supports so many people, groups, through his church and foundations." Brad slipped back into present tense and Adam didn't correct him.

"He was a wealthy man?"

Brad nodded. "Wall Street. Amazing, really, what he did. What he accomplished. Not even from this country originally."

"No? Where was he from?"

"Russia." Brad bit at a nail, then pushed his hand down into his lap. "He came over when he was a child. They lived in New York. He somehow got into banking. I don't really know the details."

"You didn't follow him into the family career, that sort of thing?"

Brad looked at him skeptically. "Was your dad a detective?"

Adam smiled in acknowledgment. "And what do you do for a living?"

"I do work." Brad's response was defensive. "You probably think we're all just layabouts, living off Dad's money, but we're not. I'm an architect. Run my own company, in fact. I support my family quite well, thank you."

"I'm sorry, I never meant to suggest otherwise." Adam rose from the sofa and Brad's shoulders lowered a fraction, as if stretching to encompass the empty space. "Is your family with you on this cruise?"

Brad shook his head. "The children couldn't get away — sports, you know. Grueling schedules they have to keep. My wife stayed back with them."

The suite's butler had left a tray with mugs and a carafe on the low table next to the sofa after going in to wake Brad on their arrival, and Brad now picked up one of the mugs. Steam rose from the cup as he poured and Adam inhaled the scent of strong, black coffee. What he wouldn't give for a cup of that himself. But Brad failed to offer any, despite the extra mug that had been provided, and Adam didn't ask. Though he couldn't help but wonder who the extra mug had originally been intended for, given that he was traveling alone.

"I'll want to talk to the others in your group. People here on this family vacation," Adam said.

"Hm. Some vacation." Brad's fingers tapped out an irregular pattern against his cup as he spoke and his face reflected a mix of loss and confusion.

"I am sorry for your loss," Adam said with complete honesty, "but if we want to find who did this, I'm going to need to ask some uncomfortable questions. You said he went up to his cabin around ten. You didn't see him again after that?"

Brad looked confused. "No. What do you mean?"

"Where were you last night, after your dad went to bed?"

"Me?" Brad shot a panicked look toward Wayne, then back to Adam. "I was here, in bed. I mean ... I guess I came up around eleven."

"OK," Adam said soothingly. "And you were alone after that?"

Brad nodded.

"Can you tell me how many family and extended family members are in your group?"

"Twenty-four, and no, before you ask, I don't know them all well."

"You don't know your own family members?" Adam thought about his own family members, Julia and Pete, and how disappointed they were going to be with this interruption to their vacation.

Brad shrugged without passion. "There are cousins and spouses of cousins. Who can keep track of all that? Well, actually, Dad did. He was pretty good about that sort of thing. Always knew what the family was up to."

―――

"THIS COULD BE A VERY GOOD THING," Pete Lawler said brightly to Julia, then caught himself. "For Adam, I mean. Not for Mr. Claypoole, obviously." He'd just stepped out of the shower after his early morning jog around deck and still had a towel wrapped around his waist. There was only one chair in their tiny cabin, so he lay down on the narrow bed that took up most of the space.

"Obviously." Julia draped herself across him. "But I know what you mean. Gives him something to focus on."

Pete shifted under her, his long legs reaching down to the foot of the bed and even a little beyond. He was thin but wiry, his appearance deceptive. She felt his muscles move and snuggled in deeper, loving how strong he was, both physically and emotionally.

"Instead of the fact that he's on what would've been his honeymoon with his sister and her boyfriend." Pete added his own thoughts in agreement with hers.

Julia sighed and burrowed her head against Pete's chest. She'd been so sure this non-wedding wedding present was a good idea. "I'm worried about him, you know? He seems so ... oh, I don't know what."

She rolled over to swipe through the photographs on her phone, losing her train of thought as she took in what she was looking at. When she could make details out clearly, that is. The purple sheets bunched up around the body; a heavy gold watch that pulled at the sagging skin of a dead arm; the face of death. They weren't terrible photos, but they weren't going to win any awards, that was for sure. Not why she took them, of course.

"Sad?" Pete finished her thought for her. "That's only what we could expect."

"Yeah, but no, not sad." Julia rested her chin on his chest again. "He seems like he's beyond sad. Like there's no hope at all. No future."

"He's dealing with it in his own way. Give him time, he'll get over it."

"I'm afraid for him — but more than that ..." She

pictured Adam's eyes as they spoke this morning, his expression when he saw the victim. "I'm afraid *of* him." She laughed. "That's crazy, isn't it?"

Pete didn't answer the question, instead reaching for her phone. "Whatcha got there?"

"I took some shots of the dead man, his cabin, where he was killed."

"What?" Pete sat upright and Julia had to catch herself from rolling off the bed. "What were you even doing there? Are you OK?"

"Don't be silly, I'm fine. I stayed mostly outside the room, just took some pictures, that's all. I thought Adam might want them."

"He might, yeah. But that's a tough thing to see. For anyone, Julia, not just you." His voice softened and she felt him looking at her, examining her for any sign of weakness, she was sure. He was so kind to her, always, but she'd picked up on his cynical streak early on. His sarcasm often held a note of truth. A little bit of selfishness hid behind his pride in his work. Why didn't he want her to be a part of that? To appreciate what he did?

She shrugged. "No big deal."

"No big deal? A man dies, you see his body, and it's no big deal?"

She propped herself up on her elbows and Pete winced as her bones dug into him. "I'm curious, Pete. About what you guys do. What it's like for you. You deal with this every day and I want to learn about it."

He lay back down and she lowered her arms, her face once again on his chest.

"Not every day, just when there's a murder to solve. Look, I appreciate that you want to learn more about what our job is like, but you need to be careful. Don't throw yourself into a situation you don't understand."

"Aye-aye, Captain." She forced a smile. "You know, you're as hard to understand as Adam sometimes. I know you think you're protecting me, but sometimes it seems like more than that. Like you're hiding something."

"I am, Julia. I'm hiding the hatred, the fear, the despair, the anger that I have to deal with every day on the job. I don't want you to see that. Any of it." He ran his hands through her hair as he spoke, his tone making the words more like a caress than a criticism.

She smiled again, this time for real. "I know, Pete. I know."

"Maybe. I hope you do understand. But I'm all for encouraging Adam to get involved in this investigation. He needs something to do."

"So get dressed, lazy boy, and let's go find him. Tell him what we think." She moved to sit up.

"Why, you think he's waiting for our opinion?" Pete pulled Julia closer to him, running a hand along her cheek.

"No, probably not," she admitted, feeling herself drawn toward his eyes. His smile. His lips. "We could wait just a little longer ..."

The ship bounced lightly on the waves, rocking her as she lay on Pete, back and forth like a lullaby.

5

THE BOWLING ALLEY had to be along here somewhere. Adam put a hand out to balance himself against the wall as the ship crested over a particularly large wave. He heard a crash of silverware and raised voices somewhere behind him, but kept moving forward, walking at an angle to stay upright.

The passageway opened up ahead into a grand lounge, curving staircases leading up on either side to a balcony above. On the main floor, a stage lay empty, but the wall behind it was lit up with a series of pictures, scrolling through one by one, film-like. Passengers dotted the chairs, benches, and poufs that filled the space, watching the screen. Some with awe. Some in boredom.

Most of them were laughing, talking, enjoying themselves. Exactly what Adam was supposed to be doing, but wasn't. Involving himself in this investigation was not the right thing for him. He should be relaxing, taking it easy. The whole point of going on a cruise was to get away from the daily grind, forget the stress and pressure of home.

They'd intentionally chosen a cruise that focused on photography, an opportunity to hear lectures from a former photographer with a major media outlet, to learn how to take better pictures. It was supposed to be fun, educational, and entertaining. A chance to do something different, be someone different.

So much for that idea.

Captain Harding had set aside the bowling alley for the victim's family's use, for the time being at least. To give them a space where they could all gather alone, avoiding the gawking stares and uncomfortable condolences of other passengers. Apparently the first-class lounges weren't sufficient for their needs.

Adam checked the ship map visible along one wall to confirm he was still moving in the right direction, taking in the drawing showing the library, billiard room, spa, tennis courts, theaters — not one, but three theaters — main dining room, buffet, smaller dining rooms ... The list went on and on. It really was a floating city. From what he could see, the bowling alley was still ahead.

"You look like you're lost, young man." The deep, raspy voice cut through his thoughts.

He looked toward the voice and saw a man leaning against a tall stool, propping himself up with an elbow on the coffee bar. His salt and pepper hair was trimmed short. The skin of his face and neck sagged in a few places and its deep brown had turned a little gray around the edges, but his expression was strong, his eyes piercing.

"Thanks, I think I've figured this out." Adam tapped the map.

"That's good. I was thinking to myself, you looked a little out of place."

Adam glanced down at himself. He was dressed casually, jeans, Italian loafers, T-shirt that pulled a bit across the muscles of his chest. He thought he'd packed appropriately. "Why do you say that?"

The old man laughed. "It's not your clothes, son, it's what's in your eyes."

Adam had no idea what that was supposed to mean.

"Adam Kaminski." He took the stool next to the old man as he introduced himself.

"Marcus." The two men shook hands.

"You sound like someone who knows a lot about cruises. And the people who take them."

"I should." Marcus laughed again. "I've been on enough of these."

"You enjoy them that much?"

"I wouldn't say that. I'm the hired help."

"You work on this ship?" Adam looked around at all the other staff busy running back and forth between the bar and the passengers or working tirelessly in the little shops that lined the ballroom or scurrying through on their way to cabins with food, drinks, towels. Marcus leaned silently on his stool watching him, relaxed in casual slacks and a black polo shirt. "You don't look like the other staff."

"That's true." Marcus nodded. "But I'm working right now."

"So what's your role here?"

"I teach." He gestured toward the screen. Adam finally looked more closely at the pictures that were scrolling by. He saw images of old Caribbean buildings, town squares with people dancing, bands performing.

"You're a photographer?"

"No, not me. I teach about music. Alice Murphy is the

photographer." Marcus gestured as he spoke toward a woman walking through the ballroom on the far side.

She didn't look like an internationally successful photographer. Her lips moved as if she were speaking to herself and her hair fell in strands out of a clip that was failing to keep it contained at the back of her head. Her long skirt caught between her legs, tripping her up occasionally as the camera that hung from her neck swayed dangerously close to other passengers.

As if reading his mind, Marcus added, "She was one of the best before she retired maybe ten or fifteen years ago. She was deeply affected by some of the things she saw. She was an international war correspondent. That can't be easy."

Adam couldn't imagine. He had figured out how to distance himself from the death and murder he faced on the job, but the idea of writing about it, of memorializing death in imagery, was beyond him. She was probably even more damaged than he was.

"So this is one of your classes?" Adam brought his attention back to the man in front of him.

"Well, I just finished, but this is a chance for my students to put it all together. Listen."

Adam listened. He'd been ignoring the music playing over the ship's speakers. It had become such a ubiquitous part of his experience since coming on board, he no longer noticed it. But as he listened and watched, he realized the images matched the music. Images of historic structures, World War II soldiers at the Royal Naval Dockyard, performers on bagpipes, and traditionally costumed and masked Gombey dancers accompanied a series of musical compositions that highlighted the melting pot of Bermudian culture and tradition.

"Sounds like a great job to me." Adam chuckled. "Sitting here, listening to music, talking about what you love, sharing that love with other people."

Marcus looked surprised. "Spoken like a true teacher."

"No, not me. Not anymore, anyway."

"Could've fooled me."

"So you work here. Do you know the captain?"

"Harding? A little. We don't work closely. I can tell you he runs a tight ship."

"Micromanagement type, huh?" Adam asked.

"You could say that." Marcus' eyes narrowed. "I gotta say, that's not usually the first question I get from passengers. Why're you asking about him?"

"Just something I'm working on, it's helpful to have a feel for the people on board." Adam smiled and stood. "I gotta get back to work now, too. I hope I'll see you around again soon. I have a feeling I might have some more questions you can help me with."

He moved away from the coffee bar, but turned to watch as a tall brunette approached and greeted Marcus. She noticed Adam, giving him an appraising glance as she passed, but kept her focus on the old man. It might have been the inquisitive look, or it might have been the way her body flowed to the rhythm of the music as she walked, but he was sorely tempted to let the Claypoole clan wait a little longer.

The temptation lasted only as long at it took him to think of Sylvia and past mistakes. He didn't know which was worse, his judgment when it came to the opposite sex or his odds of finding another woman he could trust.

He walked toward the wide hallway that led, he hoped, to the bowling alley.

"Hey, partner, how can I help?"

"Glad you could make it." Adam checked his watch to confirm that Pete had taken his own sweet time to get there. "Julia filled you in?"

"Just the basics. Dead man. Rich man. Possible poisoning. How'd you get involved in this?"

Adam shrugged. "Not entirely sure and I'm not really involved. Captain Harding says his acting chief of security noticed on the passenger manifest that we listed our professions so he asked us to help. And, partner" — he tapped Pete lightly on the back — "he offered to comp our tickets in exchange."

"A free cruise, are you serious?"

"Like I said, we're not really involved. You know there's nothing we can do, legally I mean. We'll just ask a few questions to help point the security chief in the right direction. Maybe it will help the Feds, once they're involved."

"After we get to Bermuda?"

Adam nodded. "They'll meet us when we dock on Wednesday."

"So that leaves us two days to keep things in order here, make sure no evidence gets destroyed."

"And no one else gets hurt."

"And where's this acting chief of security?" Pete asked.

"Wayne Rittle. He's back at the scene." Adam's lips rose into a subtle smile as he spoke. "Taking pictures, I believe. Official photographs."

Pete looked around the room at the muted gathering. "These are the victim's relatives?"

"Meet the Claypoole clan. There are twenty-four of them on the cruise, not all here."

A Pale Reflection

The family had spread out around the room, grouped into small clusters as each naturally gravitated to those they were most comfortable with. A handful of older women whispered together conspiratorially while a group of younger men and women sat looking around morosely. One man stood alone, staring at nothing in particular, while another older man swayed uncertainly toward a few chairs set up against a wall.

"And who's missing?" Pete asked.

"A couple of cousins, apparently. The son. And the adopted daughter, Hope. Too upset to come out of her cabin."

"OK, then, let's get interviewing. Motive, means, and opportunity."

"Why?" Adam asked. "Our job is to keep the crime scene uncontaminated, keep an eye on the family, wait to dock, and hand it over to FBI."

Pete looked at Adam like he'd just sprouted a second head. "I don't understand what you're saying. If there's a murderer here, we need to do more than that. You know that."

"We're supposed to be on vacation. Why is this our problem? Since when do we have to solve all the world's problems?"

"Not all the world's, partner, just the ones we can. And this one we can. Look," he continued as Adam opened his mouth to object, "we don't even know what the murder weapon was. We can't watch all these people 24/7."

"That's true. But without real authority, without support from the lab, what can we do?"

Pete laughed as he shook his head incredulously. "Who are you and what did you do to my partner? As a wise man has said to me many times before, let's start by talking to them."

A shout from the far side of the room cut off the rest of their argument.

"Gerald, not again," a woman complained loudly, followed by the crash of someone knocking over a chair.

"Gerald, you're drunk," came from another woman.

"Again." From yet another.

The man in question had managed to seat himself on a chair — without knocking this one over — and was leaning heavily against a carpeted column to his right. "I'mnot ..." he slurred. "Not my faul ..."

"And this is why I don't want to get involved in a family squabble," Adam muttered to Pete.

Pete gave him an angry look as he crossed the room toward Gerald. Adam followed at a distance, still reluctant to get too involved. He let Pete handle it, hanging back near one of the elderly women who had complained about Gerald being drunk.

"It's standard for him, you know," she whispered to Adam conspiratorially.

"Sorry to hear that," Adam replied. "Do you know him well?"

"I should. He's my brother. I'm Betty Richards." She put her hand out to shake Adam's. "This is the last straw, though. As soon as we get home I'm booking him into rehab. Really, it's barely eight a.m."

"Right, sorry. Dealing with difficult family members is never fun. Particularly at a time of loss, like this one. What is your relation to Arthur Claypoole?"

She dropped her eyes and did a quick sign of the cross. "My cousin, my poor, poor cousin. Gerald should know better." Her eyes narrowed and her moment of mourning had passed. "He does this at the most inopportune times."

"Such as?" Adam tried to look merely polite, but he knew sometimes the best information came from casual conversations instead of official interviews. He wasn't getting involved, he reminded himself, just satisfying his curiosity.

"Well, like when Nancy died. Where was Gerald? At the pub. Or when our beautiful nephew was killed in that tragic accident, what did Gerald do? Throw himself a party." She looked sideways at Adam, to make sure he got her point. "For one. Oh, Gerald." She moved forward as Gerald slid off his chair onto the floor.

Pete was trying gamely to get him to stand. "Gerald, is it?" Pete asked. "I know this can be an upsetting time, but you're not helping. Maybe you should go back to your cabin for a while."

"Not my faul ..." Gerald repeated. "Another one dead ... another ..." Giant, sloppy tears rolled down his face and he ran his sleeve across his nose, then crawled back onto his chair.

"What do you mean, another one?" Pete asked.

Gerald looked up at the sharp tone in Pete's voice, his eyes still watery. "Wha?"

"You said, 'another one dead.' What did you mean?"

Gerald just shook his head and looked down at his feet.

"He's drunk, don't mind him." The man who'd been standing alone approached. "He's not thinking clearly." He lifted his voice as he ended each sentence, making them sound like questions instead of statements.

"Do you know what he's talking about?" Pete asked.

The man shrugged. "We've lost a number of family

members over the years. It could be any one of them." He shook his head sadly. "Death is never easy to accept."

"All right, let's get you back to your room." Pete pulled Gerald up, half-carrying, half-dragging him across the room.

Adam watched Pete maneuver Gerald out of the room. Served Pete right for getting involved, but now that meant Adam was on his own.

"Excuse me." The man who had been speaking with Pete a moment earlier approached him, his expression a picture of helpfulness, eagerness even. "You're the other detective, aren't you?"

"Adam Kaminski, and that was my partner, Pete Lawler."

"Ah, two of you. Good. Great. How can I help?"

"And you are?"

"Bill Langtry." He clasped his hands together in front of him as he spoke, turning to frown back at the other people in the room. "Such a devastating thing to happen. On this trip, of all trips. The family is simply torn apart."

"You're a member of the family?"

"Of course. I'm so sorry, I thought you knew that. Cops, you know, I figured you got all the information about us in advance, right?"

Adam didn't think he was imagining the cynicism in Bill's voice, but didn't respond.

Bill continued, "I'm a cousin. Cousin to Arthur, that is. Well, maybe second cousin. Or something like that."

"I appreciate you coming over to talk with us. Is there something in particular you think we should know about Mr. Claypoole?"

"About him?" Bill looked confused. "Well, I'm not really a people person, not my area of expertise. He was a nice enough man, I suppose. Very helpful, supportive of his family."

Adam was finding it hard to ignore Bill's speaking tone, the feeling that he was asking a series of questions instead of making statements. "What is your area of expertise, Mr. Langtry?"

"I'm an investigator. Like you."

"You're a cop?" Adam asked skeptically.

Langtry made a quick movement of his head, sort of a nod to the right. "Well ... not a cop, exactly. I'm a tech. I analyze crime scenes."

"You're a crime scene technician?"

"I am. And I'm at your service, to help in any way I can. I don't have any of my equipment, of course," he said ruefully. "I was expecting this trip to be a vacation, you know?"

"Sure. But you think you might be able to pick up some things from the crime scene, even without your tools?"

Bill shrugged. "Possibly. I've no idea, really. Until I see it."

Adam felt the ship move again. What the hell, maybe this made sense, a suspect helping with the investigation. Everything else in his life seemed to be backwards, why not embrace it? "Maybe. But first, I need to know where you were when Mr. Claypoole was killed."

"Me?" Bill looked surprised.

"No offense, but you must realize you are a suspect. If this was a murder, that is."

Bill grinned. "Cool! There's a first time for everything. I don't have an alibi, if that's what you're asking. I don't even know what time he was killed."

"I don't have the exact time yet. We know he went to his cabin around 10 p.m. and wasn't seen again."

"Then nope, no alibi. I hung out in the lounge until about eleven, then I went back to my cabin. Alone." He looked sideways at Adam. "If you don't trust me, you can keep me company while I look at the crime scene. I don't need to see it alone or anything. Hey, you guys are working pretty thin on the ground here, right? Don't you think it might be worth the risk?"

6

Julia closed her eyes and turned her face toward the sun, taking a deep, tantric breath. She focused on the scent of salt in the air, the calls of the gulls that circled the ship as it made its way south along the Atlantic coastline.

Pete and Adam were busy digging into this investigation — digging into the past was something Adam always seemed to enjoy. Not her. They were similar, she and her brother, she could admit that. They were both driven by the recognition that life was short and they both wanted meaning. For Adam, that meant understanding the past, knowing why things happened and who was responsible. For Julia, it meant being in the moment, seeing the world around her. Really, truly seeing it.

Opening her eyes, she trained her camera on the group of men playing an enthusiastic, if not overly skillful, game of basketball on the half-court next to the tennis court. Her experienced eye picked out the best images of aggression, teamwork, frustration as she clicked away, intentionally letting her emotions guide her. She didn't try to pick out individual players, though she thought she caught the eye of one player, the only one who seemed to have noticed her. She'd have to go back and check the photos later.

Low shouts and a few claps signaled the end of the game, and the group of six men left the basketball court. They huddled near the gated entrance to the courts, wiping sweat from their necks and shoulders. One man stepped away from the others, waving his thanks.

He walked toward the spot where Julia stood watching the various activities on the recreational deck. As well as the pickup game that had just ended, three young people worked their way up a climbing wall, two pairs of tennis players worked up their own sweat on the tennis court, and a family took their best shots on the mini-golf course — not an easy task on the surface of a boat, even one as big as this one.

The basketball player passed directly in front of Julia, so she smiled and said hello. To her surprise, he stopped to reply.

"Good game?" she asked, trying to make light conversation.

"Sure. We lost." He shrugged, smiled. His face was fairly ordinary, attractive without being beautiful, evenly featured without being perfect. But when he smiled, his eyes lit up, and Julia felt a spark she didn't expect. "But it's about playing the game, right, not winning or losing?"

"I guess that depends who you ask."

He stopped to adjust the laces around one sneaker, his shirt pulling tight against the muscles of his back as he knelt down.

"Is it hard to play on a boat? With the constant motion, I mean?" Julia asked, truly curious.

"Are we in motion?" He smiled as he asked. "I couldn't even feel it." He stood, put both hands out to his side as if testing the surface of the air. "You're right, we are in motion. I guess I got caught up in the game."

"You rolled with the waves, is that it?"

He laughed. "I'm supposed to be getting away from my day job, but I guess some things you just can't forget. You probably do the same thing when you're taking pictures, right?"

Julia tucked her phone into her pocket self-consciously. "I guess so, I didn't really think about it."

"Paul," he introduced himself. "Are you waiting for someone?"

"No, just looking around. Getting a feel for the ship. I'm Julia."

"You're not traveling alone, are you?"

Julia shook her head. "You?"

He also shook his head, but didn't share anything more about who his companions were. The other basketball players had left the area without stopping to speak to him, giving the impression he had just met them on board.

"I recommend the pool," he said. "And the hot tubs. Very relaxing."

"I haven't walked that way yet. I'll have to check it out."

"I'm on my way there now, after a shower. Hot soak is exactly the thing after a game like that. Maybe I'll see you there?"

"Maybe you will." Julia bit her lip as soon as she said it, but the words were already out.

What the hell was she thinking? She felt her cheeks burn as she watched Paul walk away. Why hadn't she mentioned Pete? Her internal alarms were going haywire about this guy — and her reaction to him.

A QUICK SHOWER and change into her bathing suit and cover-up helped clear Julia's mind. Rinsing away the sensory overload, she thought, the same way she focused in on the key image in her photographs. She knew how to do that when taking pictures. Her dilemma now was how to narrow her focus on this ship. How could she best help Adam get through this rough patch in his life?

Her path up to the pool took her past the Sunlight Lounge and she heard the laughter and shrieks as she approached. They were playing some type of adults-only game, she realized, as she saw a crew member chasing a woman around the room as everyone else laughed uproariously. It looked like other passengers were taking the freedom that cruises promised to new heights, grabbing the opportunity to be crazier, happier, different than they really were.

It wasn't much quieter on the pool deck, where more crew had set up a game for kids that involved balloons, bubbles, and cream pies. She swept past the deck and moved into the relative quiet of the covered buffet area beyond the pool.

"Hey, there you are." Julia pivoted to walk toward Pete when she saw him, shifting her towel to her other arm as she wrapped her now free arm around him.

"Hey." He kissed her lightly. "Just handling a sad drunk. It's like another day at the office."

"If only your office could look like this." She let her gaze take in the open buffet, fresh fruit and glazed pastries glistening in the morning sun as if dancing to the rhythm of the music emanating from hidden speakers. Beyond the buffet lay the sunny pool deck, the dark hallway leading to the spa, gym, and library. All surrounded by glittering waves that cast reflections of light throughout.

"You heading to the pool?"

"I was, but if you're free ...?"

"I'm all yours, baby." Pete smiled as he kissed the top of her head. "What do you want to see next?"

"I'd like to see a boat where no one has been murdered. Where you and I could just relax and enjoy a vacation."

"I know, me too. But look, I can let Adam handle it. Mostly. He's got the support of the security staff, anyway."

"You two are partners. You can't abandon him."

"I'm not abandoning him. I'll be here when he needs me. But maybe an investigation is exactly what he needs to take his mind off of Sylvia. Right now he's checking out the crime scene again."

Julia shuddered. "Ugh, don't even say her name. I gotta say, I know this is tough on him, but I also know he's better off without her."

"That's your opinion. He doesn't share it right now."

Julia looked at the pool deck, where the man she'd met earlier at the basketball court stood alone, looking in their direction. "I want to help, too," she said absentmindedly, trying to catch Paul's eye. He looked away, as if looking for someone else. He must have seen her, though it was possible he didn't recognize her. She had changed, after all.

She shook her head, as if shaking away a bad thought. "I want to help, too," she repeated.

"OK. How?"

She pulled out her phone. "By doing the one thing I know I do better than either of you."

"Making phone calls?" Pete joked.

"Ha, ha. No, taking pictures. You never know what the camera will catch that the eye misses. I can keep my eyes — and my lens — open. See what I see."

Pete frowned. "I don't like the idea of you going around

surreptitiously taking pictures of people, and I don't think Adam will either."

"Surreptitiously taking pictures?" Julia laughed out loud. "Pete, honey, that's what I do every single day. How else do you think I get those great candid shots? Calm down." She wrapped her arm around him again. "Let's go check out some of the programs going on. The activity list for today was huge, there must be something going on we'll enjoy."

She glanced back toward the pool as they walked away, but Paul wasn't there anymore.

7

ADAM SWIPED THE KEY CARD, pulled the door open, and stepped into Claypoole's cabin. The music that had been playing early that morning had been stopped, thank goodness, and the room was unnaturally quiet. He hadn't realized how accustomed he'd become to the music that always played in the background on the ship. He stood to the side to let Bill in, then pulled the door closed.

This was a long shot, he knew. Not to mention a bit crazy, letting one of the witnesses — possibly a suspect — investigate a crime scene. But he was tired of being jerked around. It was time for him to take control, even if that meant taking steps that weren't exactly kosher. Who knew, maybe he still had some luck left. Maybe Bill could find a clue.

The cabin was exactly as Adam remembered it. The dirty glass and bowl on a side table next to the list of the day's activities. Curtains pulled back from the long, sliding doors to the balcony. Unlike this morning, the sun was high in the sky now and bright beams of light highlighted tiny dust motes dancing in the air. Whatever was leftover in the dirty bowl had started to rot and Adam caught a whiff of rancid milk as he passed by. Better than the smell of death, he thought.

"So, what can you do?" he asked.

Bill looked around the space, hands on his hip. "I can look, anyway. See if anything catches my eye."

Adam pointed to the dirty dishes. "How about those? Can you get some useful fingerprints off them?"

Bill leaned over them, his hands still on his hips. "If I had my tools, sure. A fingerprinting wand would be perfect, cover it with some cyanoacrylate fumes."

"You still use those wands?" Adam asked, surprised to hear Bill talk of a tool the PPD had stopped using a few years earlier. Not useful enough, apparently, to warrant the safety risks it posed.

"Sure." Bill took a step closer to the tray with the dishes.

Adam didn't respond. He knew from experience how much the crime scene technicians with the PPD resented when cops tried to butt in on their collection of evidence. Whatever worked for him.

"It works in a closed space," Bill continued. "But I could create one using ... well, like that lampshade, even. With a little plastic wrap over the top. Sure. If I had my tools, that is."

"How about an informal method, in the meantime?"

Bill laughed. "A little lead shaving from a pencil or something like that? No." He shook his head. "You said the Feds have jurisdiction over this investigation. If they show up and find out we've screwed up their crime scene, they'll be royally pissed. Uh-uh, I'm not doing that."

Adam took a breath. Of course, Bill was right. He stepped closer to the glass doors to the deck, then turned to get a full view of the cabin and the bedroom beyond. Bill had pulled on a pair of thin plastic gloves and was working his way slowly around the room, examining every detail.

Adam watched him as he peered into drawers, smelled the dirty plate, ran a gloved hand over sheets and clothes. He didn't make any comments at first, just looked. And touched. Adam felt his hopes rise with each item. The hope that the item in his hand might be the one that held the clue he needed.

"Why are these dishes still here?" Bill asked.

"I guess the captain didn't want to remove anything that could be evidence."

"Yes, obviously," Bill said impatiently. "But they shouldn't just be sitting out here. They need to be protected ... covered at least. Not just sitting out here."

"I'll let the captain know," Adam said, chagrined he hadn't thought of that himself.

Bill was looking back and forth between the sitting area and bedroom, where the sheets remained bunched and twisted.

"What are you thinking?" Adam asked.

"Just that if the poison was in the food, it's odd that he had such violent convulsions on the bed." He glanced at Adam. "I'm no expert on poison, so I could be wrong, just seems weird to me, that's all."

Bill turned his attention to a collection of devices piled up on a long table that seemed to have been used as a makeshift desk. He picked up and identified two smart phones, a tablet, a laptop. They were all safely ensconced in plastic protective cases, some with bright colorful stripes, some somber black, one made out of a photograph of a smiling family.

Voices passed in the hallway and Adam tensed. The captain had invited him to investigate; after all, he'd given him the key card to Claypoole's cabin. He had no reason to think he'd be stopped. But he nevertheless felt like they were doing something illicit and he relaxed when the voices passed by.

He'd forgotten how good it felt to be taking a risk, following a hunch. Bill would find something, he was sure of it. It was high time Adam's instincts started paying off again.

Bill straightened up, pushing his hands into his spine as he did so. He pulled off the plastic gloves and shoved them into his pocket.

"So?" Adam asked.

Bill shook his head. "Sorry. I don't see anything here. Without my equipment, I can't tell you any more than you already know." He smiled apologetically.

Adam's hopes sank. What had he been thinking, anyway? Clearly, luck — and good instincts — had abandoned him long ago.

ADAM LEANED against a wall and watched the passengers milling about in the main hall. The slide show had stopped, the music class over. People lingered in their seats, sipping morning cocktails and coffee, chatting, generally enjoying themselves.

"Interested in that lecture now?"

Adam turned to see Marcus sitting at the coffee bar. He stepped next to him and ordered an espresso from the barista.

"Not today, sorry. Got other things on my plate right now."

"Want to talk about it?"

Adam considered the offer. Pete was off with Julia, as they should be, not spending their time on this romantic cruise digging up evidence in a murder investigation. Bill hadn't found anything helpful in his examination of the crime scene. Wayne was pulling background information on their victim.

"What's that saying about doing the same thing and expecting a different result?" Adam asked.

Marcus sipped his coffee, his eyes narrowed into a thoughtful expression. "Einstein, right?"

"Someone like that."

"You been doing the same thing over and over again?"

Adam let out a light laugh as his espresso appeared. "I guess so."

"In music, we use *da capo*. A valuable technique, if you use it right."

"That right? And do you always expect the same result?"

"Oh, no." Marcus shook his head slowly, frowning. "You never expect the same result, within the piece or from one piece to the next. Music has personality. Passion. Character."

Adam laughed again. "I get enough characters in my day job."

"I see."

A waitress carrying a tray loaded with dirty cups and glasses stepped up to the bar across from them, resting the tray on the bar as she leaned in to speak with the barista. Adam looked at the collection of cups, smears of pink and red lipstick along the rims of coffee cups and champagne flutes. The boat rocked and the waitress put a hand out to steady the tray without breaking eye contact with the barista, as if it were an unconscious reaction. A well-coifed middle-aged woman farther down the bar didn't handle the boat's movement as gracefully, grabbing the edge of the bar with an involuntary yelp, then placing a perfectly manicured hand over her bright red lips in embarrassment.

"I listen to them, too," Adam said. "I watch. I learn. Figure out who's not who they seem. Who's hiding something."

"Ah, the hidden strain. Like a polyrhythm in jazz. It frequently appears, but not always as expected. Surprising. Toying with us."

"So are you going to come up with a musical equivalent for everything I say?" He looked at Marcus, amused.

"Sorry." Marcus grimaced. "Occupational hazard, I guess. Tell me, what is it that you're working on that's got you so upset?"

"It's nothing. I'm not working on it. I mean, I was asked to ..."

"But you don't want to."

Adam tipped his head in agreement as he downed the remains of his espresso. "I was recently on a futile search," Adam admitted. "It didn't go well."

"Didn't find what you were looking for, huh?" Marcus said. "Sometimes it's as much about the search as about what you find, you know."

Adam frowned. "I suppose. I was prompted by some old family letters I came across a couple of years ago. I didn't have to pursue it, I guess, but I've always been curious."

"I know the type." Marcus grinned. "Reminds me of my younger son. Always poking his nose into things to figure out how they work."

"Turns out, you don't always want to know how it works." Adam took a breath. "I thought I'd learn a little bit about my great-grandfather. Some family history, you know? Now it turns out he was working with the Nazis during the Second World War."

"He was German?"

"Polish, but in western Poland. A school teacher, if you can believe that."

"Interesting." Marcus looked away as he spoke, as if he were losing interest.

Adam's anger flared at Marcus' attitude. "I guess not. Sorry I brought it up."

"No, no." Marcus waved a calming hand toward Adam. "It's just, I don't know if you knew this, but if you're looking for hidden histories from 1940s Europe, you're going to the right place."

"What're you talking about?"

"Bermuda," Marcus said. "Bermuda Station, as it was during the war, has all the best-kept secrets of that time."

"How so?" Adam tried to resist his curiosity. He was supposed to be moving on. But a little history talk couldn't hurt. Could it?

"Almost all of the transatlantic mail passed through Bermuda back then," Marcus explained. "So the Brits turned the Hamilton Princess Hotel into a censorship station."

"Censorship? How does that relate?"

Marcus shrugged. "That's what they called it, but don't be fooled. They were doing counterespionage, plain and simple. If you're looking for stories from the war, the librarians there are sure to have answers."

Adam laughed as he shook his head. "So tell me again what kind of music you teach, that you know all this?"

"Oh, quite a variety. On this trip, I'm sharing what I know about Bermudian music. And the music is part and parcel of Bermuda's complicated past, its complicated relationship with Europe, with other islands."

Adam nodded, trying to recall some of the details he'd read, trying to figure out how much he should care — or not — about what Marcus was telling him.

"Do you always adapt your lectures to the cruise destination?" Adam asked.

"Always. That's kind of the whole point, isn't it?"

Adam shut his eyes for a moment. "To adapt. To offer a service people want. Maybe that people need. Yeah, I guess that is the whole point."

"And do you think your help is needed?" Marcus asked, following Adam's train of thought.

Adam nodded. "Sadly, I'm beginning to think it is." He pushed himself away from the coffee bar. "You'll have to excuse me. There's someone else I need to talk with."

8

Adam found Hope in her cabin. She'd been crying; her eyes were still red, wads of tissues piled up in the wastebasket.

Unlike Brad's, Hope's suite was as big as her father's. But substantially neater. Every cushion was perfectly fluffed, every scarf folded neatly or draped artistically, nothing out of place. Hope sat tucked into the corner of her sofa, her legs curled up, caressing a silver picture frame. When Adam entered, she ran a finger along the picture, then placed it carefully on the table next to her.

"I'm sorry to have to bother you, Hope. I know how upset you are. I'm just trying to gather some information, and I think you can help me."

"Information about what?" Hope sniffed and held a tissue to her nose. She was a fragile-looking woman, blond, willowy, with pale blue eyes and clear white skin. The type of skin that looked like it would burn easily.

"Well, that's kind of hard to answer. About your father. Your family."

"My adopted father, you mean."

Adam nodded and settled into a chair facing her. "How old were you when you were adopted?"

"Young. An infant. Dad was my dad my whole life." Hope looked confused. "Why did he have to die?"

Adam nodded, offering a sympathetic smile as Hope dabbed at her eyes. There was no good answer to her rhetorical question. "I'd like to hear your opinion of your father — who he was, what kind of work he did." Adam let the question trail off, hoping she would step in to fill the void.

"I can't ..." She looked around vaguely. "I wasn't involved in his work at all."

"But you knew him well. Better than most."

"Of course." With that, Hope broke down into tears, sobbing into a new wad of tissues.

Adam waited, the sympathetic expression tacked to his face. He hated doing this, but he had to persist. "Hope, when was the last time you saw your dad last night?"

"When he left the group." Hope sounded confused again. "I don't know what time it was. He went up to his cabin."

"And what did you do then?"

Hope sucked in a loud breath. "You think I killed him? I was here, in my cabin. Asleep. How could you ..." Her voice trailed off into another sob.

Adam let her cry, turning his attention to the picture she'd been holding. It was an image of Hope and her father. Smiling, arms wrapped around each other. She wore fashionably large sunglasses, and sunlight reflected off the windows of the building behind them. The photograph was too close-in for Adam to tell where it had been taken, but the yellow-brown stone of the building hinted at somewhere in Europe.

He tried another approach. "Why Hope?"

"What do you mean?"

"Your name. Do you know why your father named you Hope?"

She shrugged. "He chose me, you know? He didn't have to adopt me, but he did. Because he wanted me. He had dreams, I guess. For himself and for me. He had hopes."

"From what I hear, he achieved all he ever wanted."

"I suppose." She sniffled, but her tears had stopped as she considered Adam's question and a hint of something other than sadness ran through her eyes. "Don't we all have unfulfilled dreams, though, really?"

He didn't know what that look had meant; it could be nothing. Fond memories of her father, for instance. Or confusion as to the nature of his questions. Whatever it was, Adam had a sense that she was stronger than she looked, not nearly as fragile. And that she was being evasive. Or maybe he was looking for evasion where there wasn't any.

Hope looked the picture of innocence. She wore the light-colored, draped clothes that rich women on beach vacations seemed to favor. A large floppy hat lay next to her on the sofa. A champagne flute stood nearby, half-full of an orange beverage. Or half-empty.

Hope must have seen him looking at the glass.

"I was out on deck when they found me. I figured, it was a cruise, why not start with a mimosa. Then I learned what happened."

"Tell me about yourself, Hope. What do you do, for work or for fun?"

"I'm an artist. At least, I want to be an artist. That's one of the reasons Dad chose this cruise, because of the art and music classes." Her hand drifted toward the photograph, then fell back onto her lap.

"Are you and your brother close?"

"Not really." Hope frowned at the photograph. "He doesn't like ..." Her voice trailed off.

"What doesn't he like?" Adam prompted her.

A grin crossed her face, only for a moment. The first smile she'd offered since he arrived. "He doesn't like the same things I do. The same things my father likes."

"I see," Adam replied, though he didn't really. "And where is Brad's family now, why aren't they here on the cruise?"

Hope shook her head. "Some tournament. The kids, you know. They always have some league or game or something they have to do. They couldn't get away, so Madeleine stayed home with them. Brad came alone." That hint of a grin came back. "I don't think he minds."

Adam waited, hoping for more. None came. "He doesn't like his family?"

Hope blinked and turned toward him, her eyes wide. "I didn't say that. I would never say that. He's a good father. A good husband."

Adam let the subject drop. "You said your father chose this particular cruise because it was something you wanted. Did he always give you what you want?"

"Almost always." Her bottom lip shook. "But he was good to everyone, not just me. He gave so much, to so many ... organizations that support education, travel, churches, things like that. But he was a tough businessman, too, he was nobody's fool."

"What do you mean by that?"

She lifted one narrow shoulder, causing a cascade of linen and sheer cotton. "He took care of himself, his family and his business. That's all."

"Isn't it unusual that he chose this particular cruise?" Adam asked.

"I told you, he wanted a trip that would be good for me. He knows I want to be an artist. He's even sending me to study art and sculpture in Paris. Oh! I mean, he was." She squeezed her eyes shut as tears spilled silently down her cheeks.

"I'm sorry, I really am. It's just that he's suing this cruise line. For business reasons, I understand. But why would he want to travel on it?"

Any answer Hope might have given was cut off by the knock on the door.

A man stuck his head around the door. "Am I interrupting anything?"

Hope's eyes lit up. "Oh, Paul, come in." She smiled, a different smile this time, this one bright, welcoming.

The man approached, hugged her, then sat next to her, carefully sliding the floppy hat aside. She inched closer to him as he sat down.

"Are we done, Detective?"

"Just one more thing. Can you tell me about your mother?"

"I don't have a mother." Hope dragged her eyes away from Paul to look down at her hands.

"How do you mean?"

"Dad's wife died and he never remarried. For me, it was always just him."

"And your brother."

"And Brad, sure. And all the cousins and uncles and aunts." She smiled shyly at Paul. "Some very distant cousins I never got to meet before."

Paul made an expression that Adam had heard described as an "aw shucks" look but that he'd never actually seen on a grown man before. He took another look at this newcomer.

"Adam Kaminski." He put his hand out.

Paul shook it. "I'm a cousin — a distant cousin. Paul Burke. Just here to help. To offer my condolences and support, that is." Paul's voice seemed weak, his handshake limp. But the arm he draped around Hope was firm and she settled onto his shoulder with apparent comfort.

"I'm asking Hope a few questions about her father, trying to get a picture of who he was, what kind of relationships he had, that sort of thing."

Paul kept his eyes on Hope. "I didn't really know him. Not really. I mean, I met him a few times, here and there. I have very good memories of him. He was a good man. It's just too bad, Hope."

She nodded, starting to sniffle again. "I know," she said on a long, drawn-out breath.

"About your fight, I mean," Paul continued. "You said you had that argument the day before the cruise."

Hope sat up slowly, a flicker of annoyance clear in her eyes. She turned to Paul. "I told you that in confidence."

A bright red blush crept up Paul's face. "I'm sorry ... I didn't realize ... I mean ..." he stammered, turning to Adam. "I shouldn't have said anything."

Hope waved a hand at him, then settled back onto his arm. "It was nothing," she said to Adam. "Just another of our quarrels about father-daughter stuff."

"I can't claim the privilege of ever having had a father-daughter conversation." Adam smiled kindly. "What kind of stuff is that?"

"Oh, you know" — Hope smiled at Paul again — "What kind of men I'm dating, when will I get married, things like that."

She was clearly throwing her best moves Paul's way, though Adam couldn't understand it. What did she see in him? He seemed boring, shy, even nervous. But Adam wasn't here to play matchmaker. He excused himself as Hope stared dreamily into Paul's bland brown eyes.

Adam felt conspicuous waiting in the hall, so he followed the light to where the hallway opened up onto the overlook at the front of the ship. From here, he could breathe a little easier but still keep an eye out for his quarry. He leaned back against the railing, closing his eyes for a moment to enjoy the feel of the sun against his face, the wind against his skin. Waves continued to break against the ship, as they had all night and all day. It promised to be another rough day at sea.

Adam focused his attention back on the pool deck on the next level below as he waited. Unlike at the main pool, guests here weren't worried about keeping an eye on their kids or hiding their bags under the towels on their lounge chairs. Hell, these passengers didn't look like they were worried about anything. They should be, though, Adam thought.

A perfectly bronzed woman let her arm dangle into the pool to her right, a bracelet that surely cost more than Adam's annual salary — a lot more — twinkling below the water's surface. Another passenger flicked through screens on his tablet, then set it carelessly down on the small table beside him as a waiter brought him a cocktail.

A pickpocket or thief — and Adam immediately thought of a few he knew — would have a field day here. But that was one of the perks of traveling first class, he guessed. Not having to worry.

Ten minutes later, he saw the man he was looking for.

Adam strolled after him, following Paul into the relative darkness of the hallway and catching up to him as he stood waiting for an elevator.

"Good morning, again," Adam said, stopping next to him.

"Hm? Oh, yes, good morning."

"Good conversation with Hope?"

"I'm sorry, have we met?"

"About half an hour ago, in Hope's cabin. I'm Detective Kaminski."

"Of course, I'm so sorry." Paul slapped his hand against his forehead. "I'm terrible with faces, and this whole tragedy ...well, it's knocked me off sorts. It was not a good conversation, no. Of course not. I'm just going to get changed for lunch."

He gave Adam a quick smile and nod and turned toward the wide staircase behind them, perhaps intending to leave Adam by the elevator. Adam followed him.

"I'm curious how well you know the rest of the family," Adam said, falling into step next to Paul.

A look of irritation crossed Paul's face but was quickly replaced by his usual bland expression. "Oh, not well at all. I'm quite a distant cousin. In fact, I met a number of them on this trip for the first time."

"And how did you get included in the party, to begin with?"

Paul pulled his head back in affront. "I *am* a member of the family, detective. The invitation was sent far and wide. To celebrate old man Claypoole's birthday."

Adam switched tacks. "Do you enjoy cruises? Have you been on a cruise before?"

"I don't think I will again, after this one," Paul answered in a flat voice.

"No, I suppose not." Adam hadn't missed the fact that Paul had avoided a complete answer. But hadn't lied, either.

"And do you plan to stay in touch with the family, now that you've had this opportunity to meet them?"

They'd come to Paul's floor, apparently, as he paused with a hand on the doorframe that led to a wide hallway interspersed with a few cabin doors. "I have no idea what the future holds, Detective. How could I? I have a family like everybody else. We do our best to stay in touch. Sometimes we succeed, sometimes we don't."

Adam grinned. This man was a slippery one, never refusing to answer a question but never answering directly. He should be a politician. Why had Hope been so happy to see him? What did she see in him?

"I won't keep you, I know you need to change, but just one more question." Adam spoke quickly as he saw Julia and Pete heading their way.

"Yes?"

"You said you'd met Arthur Claypoole before this trip, is that right?"

"I had," Paul answered, and Adam was surprised at such a direct response. "I've had some work involvement with him."

"You worked together?"

"Something like that." Paul turned to Julia, and the features of his face shifted. From bland and boring, he suddenly looked eager, interested.

Julia's face lit up as well, Adam was sorry to see. What did women see in this guy? His features were regular. Square. Flat. His eyes brown, not hazel or chestnut. His hair a dull brown. He was forgettable, at best. But he did show expression when he smiled. When he let himself.

Pete must have noticed Julia's smile as well, because he

stepped a little closer to her and grabbed her hand. "Adam, we were just looking for you. Julia's gonna take a class and I gotta check some messages, but we have time for lunch later. Want to join us?"

"Sure—"Adam's attention was caught by Captain Harding stepping out of a cabin up the hall.

Harding glanced around as he straightened his shirt and he saw Adam, Pete, and Julia. At first he turned away, as if to ignore them, but he must have changed his mind. He spoke as he approached them.

"I'm glad I found you. There's something I thought you should know. One of my crew — Chef Guzeman — used to work for Arthur Claypoole."

"You're kidding," Pete said with a laugh. "Yeah, that is kinda good for us to know."

Adam didn't think he'd be able to hide his anger at this sudden revelation as well as Pete, so he kept his mouth shut, focusing instead on Paul slipping away down the hall.

Harding continued, "When he was fired from the Claypoole household, there were hints about drug use, but nothing was ever proven. My chief steward hired him because he was honest about his past, he didn't try to hide it, but he denied it completely."

"And you have no indication of anything improper in his activities since he started working for you?" Adam asked, wondering why the hell Wayne hadn't included this nugget of information in his earlier debrief.

Harding shook his head. "No. And believe me, I know how big a problem drug smuggling is on these cruises. I'm not a fool. My crew are thoroughly searched when they come on board." Harding took a breath, his mouth a narrow line, and turned his eyes away from them. Adam got the impression his attention had turned away as well. "No one sneaks anything onto my ship."

Adam frowned at Harding's arrogance. "So that's what you're doing up here, looking for us?"

"That's right." Harding cleared his throat and once again adjusted his shirt collar.

Even as he processed what Harding had told them, he couldn't ignore the fact that the cabin Harding had just come out of belonged to Brad Claypoole.

He might not have asked about it. He might have found a less intrusive way to dig into it. But as Harding sauntered away from them, Brad chose that exact moment to exit his suite.

The two men barely glanced at each other and Brad swiveled to walk in the opposite direction from Harding, his left hand swinging across his body to cover the heavy gold watch wrapped around his right wrist.

Adam chased down the hall after Harding. "What's going on, Captain?" He couldn't keep the edge out of his voice.

"What do you mean?"

"I don't like being lied to. That's never a good sign."

Harding shook his head. "I agree. If you know who's lying—"

"You are."

"What? What are you saying?"

"What else are you not telling me, Captain?" Adam took a step closer to the captain, who took a step back and hit the wall behind him.

"I ... I don't know what you're talking about."

"Adam, calm down. I'm sure there's an explanation." Pete's voice was calm. Rational.

"An explanation for what?" Harding was clearly confused.

"For why you're sneaking around up here with Brad Claypoole, for starters. For why you decided to fumigate this ship when you did. For why you failed to mention that Arthur Claypoole has a bad history with this cruise line."

"I did mention those things, or made sure you found out," Harding said. "I told you why I was worried about this death."

"But you thought you could just tell me half of it, is that it? Because you needed me to get you off the hook for Claypoole's death."

"No, that's not true. I wanted you to find the truth."

"I will find the truth, Captain. But you should know, in a murder investigation, all the truth comes out. All of it. Whether you want it to or not."

9

The photography lecture had already started, so Julia tiptoed over to the closest chair. She smiled at the willowy blond woman next to her, then turned her attention to the instructor.

The woman leading the group stood at the front of what might ordinarily be a dance floor. From the list of activities scheduled to take place in this room, Julia knew it was used for everything from dance classes to bingo games. For this lecture, the instructor had a series of color blocks showing on the screen behind her as she talked to her students about the potential uses of color in photography.

"I love this stuff, don't you?" the blond woman leaned over and whispered.

Julia smiled back. "Sure do. I studied uses of light and color in college. It's fun to revisit the basics sometimes."

"You're a photographer?"

Julia nodded. "You?"

The woman shrugged. "Well, I want to be an artist, anyway. Call it an aspiring artist."

"Do you create art?" Julia asked with raised eyebrows.

When the woman nodded, she added, "Then you're an artist. Not aspiring. An artist."

"Hope Claypoole." The woman put out her hand.

Julia's mind raced as she shook it. "Claypoole? You …"

Hope's smile faltered. "You heard. I thought the captain was keeping it under wraps." She turned back to the instructor.

"I'm so sorry," Julia whispered. This was a definite opportunity for her to help. Not just by taking pictures, but by talking to a witness. Or suspect. Or whatever. What would Adam do in a situation like this? Julia laughed to herself under her breath. He'd tell her to leave it alone. Let him and Pete do their jobs.

She tried to focus on the class again. The instructor was really getting into her act, her loosely draped wrap flying around as she waved her arms, moved her shoulders, even wiggled her hips while she talked. She was doing everything she could to keep this class interested, including snapping a few shots of the students as they grinned for her camera.

Julia looked at the audience. A few were entranced, certainly. But others were reading, playing on phones, or just chatting. One group of women was more focused on their cocktails and gossip than the class.

"That's what you get for trying to teach a class on a cruise," Julia thought. She couldn't blame the passengers; they were on vacation, after all.

The instructor, who had introduced herself as Alice Murphy, didn't seem fazed. Her exuberance never waned as she focused her attention on the few students paying attention, ending her lecture with an exhortation for all the students to go out and explore the ship with an eye to color.

"Sorry if I was rude." Hope surprised Julia by speaking to her again. "I'm just … you know."

"I do. I'm so sorry. It must be terrible for you."

Hope nodded. "It's been good to have family around. We're on a sort of family vacation, so I'm not alone."

"I'm glad to hear that," Julia commiserated. "I'm here with some family as well, but if something happened to one of them ..." She shuddered.

"My cousin Bill — he's been so kind, he's always been there for me, ever since cousin Nancy died, really. Plus this trip has been a good opportunity to meet more family members."

"There were some you didn't know?"

"Can you believe it? Yes. Like Paul. A distant cousin I met on this cruise."

The sound of a glass sliding across the table caught Julia's attention. Turning, she noticed a carefully made-up middle-aged woman sitting alone at the next table over. The woman's eyes shifted away. Had she been listening to them? Julia leaned closer to Hope, lowering her voice.

"Weird. I guess I have some family I've never met, too. My brother met some of them a couple of years ago. He visited Poland, where they live."

"So you're a photographer? Do you love it?" Hope seemed eager to change the subject.

"I do. I really do. Not a good way to pay the bills, I'm afraid."

"Oh." Hope's smile faded. "I never really thought about earning an income. I never had to. Now, who knows?" She sat up taller in her seat. "But I can manage, I know I can."

Julia regretted raising a potentially upsetting topic. "It is a great career, though, you're right. I get to focus on things like bright, gorgeous, tempting colors like we just heard about. But sometimes when you take the color away, you can see even more."

"What do you mean?"

"The color can be a distraction, you know? From the form. The shape. The texture. Look at those things, and you can see even more. Imagine a red rubber ball, right? You look at it, and you see a red ball. But photograph it in black and white, blow it up, then really look at it. Now, you see the ridges etched into the rubber. Some of them are from the production — you know, straight, perfect lines. Others are scratches, from use. Now you're seeing kids playing with that ball, you're seeing that ball bounce along the rough pavement, picking up a nick or a scratch, before the kid scoops it up again. And is it really round? No, it's not. It's a little flat. From being used. The side against the ground has an edge to it, just a little bit. That's the real ball. Now you're seeing the real thing. Not just red."

"Wow. I hadn't thought of it that way. Funny, when I see things I assume I'm seeing the real thing. But not you." Hope started to leave, but then paused. "Hey, maybe we could meet for drinks? We could get to know each other, I could meet the family you're traveling with."

"Oh, right." Julia felt her face turn red. "Actually, I think you've already met my brother. Adam Kaminski. I'm Julia Kaminski."

"That detective? He's your brother?" Hope's eyes widened in surprise, then narrowed. "He sent you here to spy on me? That's horrible."

"No, I promise. I just came to enjoy the class. I had no idea you'd be here," Julia pleaded desperately.

"Sure. Right." Hope grabbed her bag and stormed away.

10

Marcus was back at his regular seat at the coffee bar in the main hall. Another of his lectures must have just ended, as passengers milled about gathering bags and sunglasses, looking at schedules. Adam heard snippets of conversation about music. About rhythm. About history.

"I missed another one, huh?" Adam approached him. "I'm sorry to hear that."

"There are plenty more, don't you worry. Pull up a stool."

"I can't stay long." Adam sat anyway.

"What is it you're doing that's taking you away from what you want to be doing?"

"I'm not sure it is — taking me away, I mean. I like what I'm doing."

"But I still don't know what that is."

Adam grinned and took a sip of coffee, then coughed as the beautiful woman he'd seen earlier approached them. She was tall, strong, but with curves that Adam couldn't ignore. The kind of taut fitness that came from hours on the tennis court, not in the gym. Long waves of brown hair framed her face, a face filled with joy and laughter — though the laughter might have come from her recognition that Adam was entranced. He tried to focus on the flecks of gold dancing in her brown eyes instead of letting his gaze wander over her body.

"Ah, Karen," Marcus greeted her. "Adam Kaminski, may I introduce you to Karen Sigelman. Karen, Adam Kaminski."

Adam felt his pulse speed up as they shook hands. It was not a bad feeling. Not bad at all.

"I'm surprised you two haven't met yet," Marcus said. "Seems you have a lot in common."

"Oh?" Karen smiled. "Are you sitting in on all of his lectures, too? I hadn't noticed you — and I think I would." Her mouth raised into a half-smile as one eyebrow went up.

Adam felt a goofy grin spread across his face and self-consciously tried to stop it. He hated it when his dimples showed.

Marcus thankfully intervened at that point, leading them into a discussion of various activities available to them in Bermuda. Adam let himself relax, but not too much. He wasn't sure why, but he didn't want his new friends to know about the investigation. The murder. He felt like he was channeling Paul — being honest without being forthcoming. It wasn't hard. Maybe he was better at keeping secrets than he realized. Isn't this what the cruise was supposed to be all about anyway, pretending to be something he wasn't?

"Adam, there you are." Pete's voice carried ahead of him.

Adam dragged his gaze away from Karen. "Pete, buddy. Let's go over here." He put a hand on Pete's arm to direct him to the far side of the room, ignoring the questioning stares from Karen and Marcus. "Sorry to have to run, I'll meet up with you for lunch?" he said to Karen, who raised her glass in a parting salute.

"D'you have any news?" Adam asked once they were a sufficient distance away.

"I do." Pete settled into a deep golden couch with his back to the coffee bar. Adam sat facing him, occasionally letting his gaze drift back to Karen, who still sat talking with Marcus. "Our friend Captain Harding is right to be worried."

"I'm not surprised to hear that. He's not telling me everything, I'm sure of it."

"Well, he is telling the truth about the fumigation."

"In what way?"

Pete pulled a folded piece of paper out of his shirt pocket and shook it to straighten it out. "I got this from our friend Rittle, he directed me to this website. Easily available information, in fact."

"What does it say?"

"Cyanide is still used in some fumigants on sea vessels. Not always, but it's not so uncommon, either. And poisoning by cyanide would fit the scene you described: the petechial hemorrhaging, his bitten tongue."

Adam nodded as he glanced at the paper Pete handed him. "And cyanosis. Death by lack of oxygen, as if he'd suffocated. But how would they permit that, isn't it too dangerous?"

"It shouldn't be. As long as passengers, crew are kept away from the affected area for enough time, there's no risk."

"Did the captain keep everyone away for enough time?"

"According to the ship's records, yes, he did."

Adam tried to figure out what this meant, and what it had to do with whatever secret Harding was keeping from him. As his thoughts wandered, Karen stood, shook hands with Marcus and turned to leave. She caught his eye as she moved and gave him a quick nod. He felt his face burning.

Pete glanced at him, then over his shoulder toward the coffee bar. "Something I should know about, buddy?"

"No. I mean ..." Damn, why was he getting so flustered? "You've got enough to worry about. Focus on your own love life, leave mine alone."

"Love life?" Pete smiled, then frowned. "Wait, what do I have to worry about?"

"Nothing, sorry. Look, I was just thinking, could Harding have fudged the records?"

"About when the fumigation happened? When passengers were allowed on board?"

"Yeah."

"I guess it's possible, but he'd have to deal with records not only from the ship but also the contractor who did the fumigation and the port that managed it."

"So not easy. But he could do it. Particularly since we're at sea, not a lot of law enforcement running around looking over his shoulder."

Pete considered. "I suppose. But I'm not sure I like it. Plus, if he did it, why'd he get us involved?"

"To cover his tracks. A double blind. Maybe he thought two cops out of Philly couldn't do any real harm."

Pete grinned. "Shows what he knows. I did confirm what he told us about the jurisdiction."

"FBI?" Adam asked.

Pete nodded. "And typically they'll work in cooperation with the local police."

"The Bermuda Police Service."

"That's it. If they saw the need, the Feds could fly out and take over the investigation now, before we dock."

"But if they think it was an accident, they won't feel any urgency to do so."

Pete shook his head. "Exactly."

"So do we have any good news?"

"Not yet. Rittle put in a request for a full background on Arthur Claypoole. I'm still waiting on that. Maybe something will show up."

"And until then, we keep talking to people, asking questions."

"It's your game, Adam. Have at it. I'm going to see where Julia's got to."

Adam thought about cyanide and fumigation as Karen and Marcus passed out of the lounge, on their way to lunch.

"Adam." Bill slid onto the sofa next to him, shifting him forward.

"Bill." Adam didn't pretend to be happy to see him.

"What?" Bill held up his mojito defensively. "I'm sorry I didn't find anything at the crime scene; I did try. You were there, you saw."

"Pete and I were just having a conversation. A private conversation. I hope you weren't eavesdropping."

"About the case?" Bill asked eagerly, keeping his eyes on Adam as he sipped his drink. A drop spilled from his straw and ran down his chin, leaving a slimy, citrusy streak.

"Yes, and like I told you before, you're still a suspect. I can't bring you into this. I'm sorry."

Bill looked down at his glass and ran a hand along his chin, smearing the streak. "I get it. I'm just not used to it, you know, being a suspect."

"Believe me, I know," Adam said, thinking about his experiences in Warsaw, where he'd faced that very problem.

"But listen, there's something I thought you should know." Bill's eagerness was back.

"What's that?" Adam asked, tucking Pete's cheat sheet into his pocket.

Bill's eyes followed the paper as he answered. "Arthur had a history with this cruise line. I don't know if Captain Harding mentioned that, but I thought you should be aware."

"Ha." Adam blew out a laugh. "There are all kinds of things I should probably know about Captain Harding. Yeah, I'd heard something about that already. Why are you telling me this now? Why didn't you mention it earlier?"

Bill shrugged. "Sorry, I guess I should have. But when I overheard you arguing with Harding, I realized he might not have told you himself."

"You overheard ...? What did you hear?"

"What?" Bill leaned forward to put his glass down on the low table in front of them. Condensation ran down the glass and Bill wiped his hands along his legs. "Nothing. I mean, I heard you telling him you'd take on the case, that's all. You didn't seem to be happy about it. Which I get, believe me." He held up both hands in front of him. "You're on vacation, you don't need this aggravation."

"I didn't see you around, didn't realize you'd heard that," Adam said quietly.

"You were in the hallway, near the stairs." Bill looked quizzical. "Lots of people must've heard."

"So what do you know about Arthur's relationship with the cruise line?"

"Just that he sued them. And won a lot of money, too."

"So the case is over? I didn't realize it had been resolved. What was the outcome?" Adam asked.

Bill shook his head. "All I know is that Arthur got a lot of money. And then he gave it all away."

"He gave it away?" Adam's voice rose in surprise. "Man, the things rich folk do."

Bill laughed. "He gave it all to an art and sculpture school. Hope's school. He was like that. He liked to help good causes, whenever he could."

"And it sounds like he liked to help Hope, in particular."

"But that's not a motive for murder," Bill responded quickly. "He helped her. She wouldn't want him dead."

Adam took a breath and thought about that. "Motive works in really surprising ways sometimes."

11

"Ms. Murphy?" Julia approached the instructor tentatively as Alice Murphy gathered together the detritus of her instruction tools.

"Alice, please. What can I do for you?" Alice dropped the colored notecard she'd been holding to stick out her hand and didn't seem to notice when the notecard fluttered to the ground.

"Julia Kaminski." Julia shook her hand with a smile. She knew she was running late — she was supposed to be meeting Adam and Pete at the lunch buffet — but she had to introduce herself. "I just wanted to say how much I enjoyed your class. It's been a few years since I studied photography."

"Ah, you studied photography. In college?" Alice had pulled on a pair of tortoiseshell half-glasses and was now looking at Julia over the top of the frame.

"That's right. I'm a photographer now, full time. I haven't found the time to go back to keep up my studies, I'm afraid. I was so excited to see the types of classes that were offered on this trip."

"Oh, you should, you should." Alice glanced down at a sheet of paper in her hands. "Ah, what a schedule. They do drive us, don't they?"

"Who's that?" Julia asked with a smile.

"The cruise line. You sign up to teach a few classes, and next thing you know you're working ten-hour days, running from one assignment to the next."

Julia took a step back. "I'm sorry to keep you, then."

"Not at all." Alice removed her glasses to smile at Julia. "It's always a pleasure to meet a fellow photographer. Most of the passengers take the classes for a lark, you know. To pretend to be photographers. They don't think I'm serious, I suppose."

"Or they're just not in the mood to be serious," Julia added. "They are on vacation."

"Of course, of course. My mood will improve after I've had a break. Or two. But no rest for the weary right now." Alice finally noticed the colored note card on the ground and bent to retrieve it. "I believe the captain has allotted me a lunch break at 4 p.m. this afternoon." She rolled her eyes before shaking Julia's hand once more and trotting out of the room.

So Captain Harding was a taskmaster. That fit with everything she'd experienced so far. Why Wayne Rittle had been so rough on her for taking pictures in Arthur Claypoole's cabin, for example. And why Adam seemed to have taken a dislike to the captain.

Would someone that much in control of his own ship really make a mistake with fumigation? Get the timeline wrong? It seemed unlikely. So either the captain was right and the fumigation wasn't responsible for Arthur Claypoole's death ... or it was the fumigation, and there was nothing accidental about it.

12

Adam looked for Marcus and Karen in the buffet. He figured he had a few minutes before Pete and Julia got there, which meant a brief opportunity to get to know Karen a little more. And a chance for her to get to know him — not the cop Adam Kaminski, but the man. The longer he could keep her away from his real life, the better.

He saw his new friends making their way through the buffet, looking over the cheese and fruit selection that came after the smorgasbord of pastas, meats, and vegetables. Other passengers milled around the food, the tiki bar in the middle of the room, the tables, laughing, eating, enjoying themselves. How many of them, Adam wondered, were enjoying the opportunity to let their workaday selves go, to be someone else for this trip? He loved that, for at least a few days, he had the chance to be a man who didn't chase killers, who hadn't had his heart broken by his fiancée. He could really get used to this cruise life.

Keeping an eye out for Pete and Julia, he helped himself to a glass of seltzer water and some fruit to tide him over and caught up with Karen and Marcus in the middle of a conversation.

"Now that is interesting," Marcus was saying, his finger pointing skyward.

Adam saw nothing but the overhang of the deck above them, beyond that the blue and gray sky.

"Not up." Karen laughed. "Listen."

Adam listened. Above the chatter of the other guests at the buffet and the sounds of games from the deck above, he heard the familiar lilt of the music that had been playing throughout the cruise so far. Of course, Marcus was back on his favorite topic.

"It's beautiful. Fun. Why do you say interesting?" he asked Marcus as they took seats at a table along the rail, looking out over the still raucous waves.

"The steel pan. It was a late entrant to the diversity of Bermuda music. Post–World War II." He shut his eyes as he listened. "But the Bermudian version is so distinct from the original Trinidadian."

Adam closed his eyes, tilted his head to one side, and listened. His attempt to hear what made the music so distinct to Marcus was interrupted by a giant of a man who loomed over their table. "Excuse me, Detective Kaminski?" The soft rolls of the man's Spanish accent hung over them as Marcus and Karen both turned to Adam with surprise.

"*Detective* Kaminski?" Karen almost mouthed the words, her voice was so soft.

Adam stifled a curse and stood, dropping his napkin onto the table. "May I help you?"

"Chef Guzeman. Security Officer Rittle pointed you out, said you might want to talk to me."

Marcus and Karen shared another look. Damn, Adam

thought. "He did? OK, then, perhaps we should talk. But not here."

"No." Guzeman looked down at the two other people staring up at him, his expression dark. His hands fell at his side in loose fists, his pockmarked face gave the impression of a lifetime spent fighting, not cooking. "No, I see. Find me when you can, then. I'm always in one of the kitchens."

With that, he turned and stomped away, dispensing frowns and complaints to the staff as he walked.

"So, Detective Kaminski, what was that about?" Marcus asked.

"It's nothing," Adam answered as he regained his seat, only to jump up again as he saw Pete. "I'm a detective back in Philly, that's all."

"And that's what's had you so preoccupied. But why, on a cruise?" Marcus asked.

Adam glanced down at them. "I'd really rather not talk about it." He saw Karen frown and relented. "Maybe later, OK?"

"OK, no big deal." She picked up a fork, but her cheeks had a touch of red in them and she toyed with her food without picking any of it up.

"Thanks for your understanding." He lowered his voice as he touched her shoulder. "I'll find you later." He was used to this kind of reaction by now. People always got nervous when they found out he was a cop.

He caught Pete by the buffet, before he felt obliged to introduce him to his new friends. He'd keep that conversation at bay for as long as possible.

"Pete, where's Julia?"

"She's on her way, but I wanted to catch you." He glanced back in the direction Chef Guzeman had taken.

"There's something you should know about Chef Guzeman."

"I got some more information about the ship's crew," Pete explained as Adam pulled him off to the side of the buffet. "No thanks to our security chief."

"He wouldn't share his info?" Adam asked, surprised.

"He didn't have anything to share," Pete said. "He's off digging through the crew's background info now, to see what he can find. But I've been in touch with the Feds in Barbados as well. To let them know we're here and available to help however needed."

"And they were OK with that?"

Pete grinned. "OK with me assuring them we weren't getting involved, just keeping the crime scene safe and keeping an eye on the suspects. You know the thing, making sure everyone else is safe, consulting with the on-board security team."

"So not investigating."

Pete shook his head. "Not investigating."

"Then how'd you get the background on the crew?" Adam risked glancing around as he asked his question. He could see Marcus and Karen from where they stood — which meant they could see him. He grabbed Pete's arm as he spoke, pulling him closer to the tiki bar, hidden from Karen's view. No point looking even more suspicious than he already did.

Pete looked confused by the movement, but kept talking. "I have a friend at the FBI. He called in a favor, got this sent through. And check it out: Guzeman has a past."

"I know he used to work for Claypoole," Adam said. "Harding mentioned that."

Pete nodded. "Six years as head chef to the Arthur Claypoolehousehold, then let go. Quite suddenly. No charges ever filed but there was an accusation of drug use."

"Like Harding said. So he might hold a grudge."

"He shouldn't," Pete said. "From what I've learned, he got off easy. Guzeman's name pops up on too many DEA lists. He's a known associate of a number of people suspected to be part of a smuggling ring."

"What kind of smuggling?"

"Some prescription drugs, some harder. Before this ship left New York, Guzeman met with a guy suspected of distributing ketamine, among other things."

"Special K. Great." Adam shook his head.

"The Feds have been effective at breaking a lot of these smuggling rings recently, so they're not interested in exposing their hand to catch a small-timer like Guzeman."

"I get it," Adam said. "Using their intelligence to best effect. Makes sense."

"What makes sense? That we're not eating yet?" Julia approached them with a plate laden with breads, cheeses, meats, fruit, and pastry. "Come on, I'm starving."

Adam and Pete followed Julia's lead, loading up their plates — both with more meat and fewer vegetables — then following her to a table. A nod to the bartender staffing the tiki bar that divided the eating areas into cozy nooks got them a round of mojitos to go with their lunches.

"After we eat, we find Guzeman, right?" Pete asked, after he had filled Julia in on what he'd found.

"Right." Adam's answer was wary. "Unless *he* has something new to add."

Pete and Julia looked up to see what Adam had seen. Wayne Rittle was working his way through the tables toward them, and the excitement on his face made it clear he'd found something he wanted to share.

WAYNE CAREFULLY SETTLED his bulk into the empty chair at their table, slapping a file down in front of him. "I got something." He grinned, his eyes gleaming.

"Sounds big. What'd you find?" Adam asked, letting his fork drop onto the plate.

"Oh, just who's gonna inherit. Everything." Wayne raised an eyebrow. "Everything."

"I thought you were looking through the crew's background?" Pete asked, clearly irritated.

Wayne's eyes widened. "Seriously? I find what's probably the clue that's gonna break this case wide open, and you're complaining?"

"Calm down," Adam answered him. "Tell us what you found."

"Hmph." Wayne sniffed and picked up the file, handing it to Adam. "It's Claypoole's will. Faxed over from New York."

Adam flipped through it, feeling Pete and Julia's eyes on him. He whistled, then handed it to Pete. Julia leaned over his shoulder and they read it together.

"Oh, no," Julia muttered as she read. "Poor Hope."

"Poor Hope?" Wayne's voice rose. "That's how you react to this?"

"All right, we get it. Brad inherits the bulk of the fortune." Pete handed the document back to Wayne. "That's a motive."

"Damn straight it is," Wayne said.

"If he knew," Adam added.

"What?"

"If he knew," Adam repeated. "Arthur Claypoole had two children. It would have been reasonable for them to assume they'd split the inheritance."

"And that's enough money for a strong motive already," Pete continued Adam's thought.

"Well, how am I supposed to know?" Wayne said. "He's the guy's son and only real heir. Yeah, I'm willing to bet he knew."

Julia shook her head as she finished chewing a piece of banana bread. "I feel so bad for Hope. She gets such a small inheritance. This is going to shock her."

"You think she thought she was getting more?" Pete asked sharply.

Julia looked at him. "What do you mean?"

"It's no big deal." Adam spoke kindly to calm his sister. He recognized the flash of anger in her eyes. "Just, if Hope knew she wasn't inheriting, that would mean she didn't have a motive to kill him."

"Oh." Julia sounded surprised. "But she didn't kill him. I'm sure of it. She was so upset at his death." She looked around the table as if seeking support. None of the men offered her any.

Pete changed the subject. "Why didn't you tell us about Guzeman?" he asked Wayne.

"The chef? What about him?"

"Are you telling us you didn't know your head chef has a criminal record?" Adam asked.

Wayne shut his eyes. "Not this nonsense again. No, he doesn't."

Adam felt his frustration rising and looked over at Pete,

who picked up the questioning.

"Guzeman has a connection to drug smuggling. You should have known that."

Wayne turned to look out across the room, his eyes darting from table to table. "Yeah, I know. I didn't mention it because I didn't want to prejudice you. I told him he should find you and tell you himself. To clear everything up."

"That's bullshit." Adam couldn't hide his anger. He didn't even bother trying.

"Look, he's not involved in this murder. I know." Wayne looked them each in the eye this time, his hands flat on the surface in front of him. "I know he wasn't. Not any of our crew. Everyone who works on board this ship is carefully vetted."

"Yeah, how carefully? Guzeman made it through."

"Yeah, well. He was charged, never convicted. You can't punish a man for an accusation." Wayne's eyes narrowed as he answered Adam. "Even a low-level security guy like me knows that."

"No one is saying you're to blame for this, Wayne." Pete's voice was soothing.

"Since you're so well-informed about Guzeman's past, I assume you know that Arthur Claypoole served as a reference for him to get this job?" Wayne looked pleased with himself as he dropped this news.

"Why would he do that, since he's the one who accused him?" Adam asked.

"Beats me. Maybe he felt guilty, maybe he just really liked the man's cooking. In his letter, he said he'd never had a better cook, he missed his specialty desserts most of all." Wayne looked back and forth between them. "I'm telling you, Guzeman had nothing to do with Claypoole's death. You're barking up the wrong tree."

"If you know anything else about any of the other crew members, you need to tell us."

"I don't need to take this." Wayne stood abruptly. "I'm telling you now, it wasn't a member of our crew. Are you going to look into this inheritance or not?"

"We'll look into it." Adam turned his attention back to his plate to avoid saying anything that would upset Wayne even more. He still needed his help and couldn't afford to antagonize him.

Wayne huffed a little, then walked away.

The other two must have needed some time to process this information, too, because Pete and Julia stayed as silent as Adam for a few minutes, each focusing their attention on the food in front of them. Wayne was right, money was definitely a motive. And if Brad knew he was getting it all, that was even more of a motive. But then why kill his father now? Surely he'd have plenty of other opportunities — easier opportunities — when the old man was at home.

Guzeman, on the other hand, had a really good reason to hold a grudge, and this would have been a rare opportunity for him.

He finished his meal and looked over at his partner and sister. "They do a good job with the food on this ship, you have to admit."

Pete nodded. "Maybe Guzeman really knows his way around a kitchen."

13

"It's quite an operation they have here."

"It should be. They've got five thousand passengers to feed."

"That many! I don't believe it."

"Well, all right, I made that number up." Pete laughed. "But it's a lot. Just look around."

They all let their eyes roam over the kitchen and the staff that scurried around them.

"This is just one of the kitchens, remember. They've got food operations on every level of the ship," Pete explained. "I got a crew manifest from Wayne, along with a brief explanation of how the ship operates. This" — he gestured again — "could be ground zero for the fumigation problem."

"The poison that Captain Harding's worried could have killed Claypoole."

"The poison he insists didn't kill Claypoole."

The kitchen didn't look anything like Adam had expected a working kitchen to look. Crew members gathered around giant stovetops, grills, and steaming basins, cooking whatever concoctions were on the menu for today.

But he saw no chopping, no prepping, none of the frenetic back and forth he was used to seeing on those cooking reality shows.

Julia ran a hand along a stainless steel countertop. "What are they cooking?" she asked, echoing his own thoughts. "I don't see any food being prepared."

Pete shook his head. "Food storage, preparation, and cooking are all done in separate rooms to prevent any cross-contamination. No prep work happens in the kitchen."

"Kaminski."

Even though he'd just met the man, Adam started when he turned to see the chef looming behind him. Guzeman barked out a command to a crew member, who scurried off to obey.

"Chef Guzman, thanks for agreeing to talk with me." He introduced Pete and Julia. "I need you to tell me about your relationship with Arthur Claypoole."

"Claypoole." Guzeman's lip lifted into a sneer. "I had no relationship with Claypoole. Not anymore."

"You were mad at him for firing you?" Pete asked.

Guzeman's eyes slid toward Pete, then back to Adam. "I was. Once. I'm a good chef. I had no problem finding other work."

Adam stepped aside as a crew member in a white chef's coat brushed past him carrying a huge vat of something hot. "On a cruise line. Perhaps not what you were used to."

Guzeman smiled, exposing large, yellow teeth. "It's not so bad."

"I heard you had a vermin problem."

"No way!" Guzeman slammed a hand down onto a countertop, his face turning red. "No, not in my kitchens and not because of my food. I run a clean operation. Always."

"But there were vermin, weren't there?" Pete asked.

Guzeman glared at him. "I saw none. No evidence — no droppings, no chewed bags. Nothing." He looked back at Adam. "But Harding says he wants to fumigate, so he fumigates. No skin off my back."

"You accompanied the contractors as they did the work?"

"Of course. Here and in all my kitchens. Not in the public areas or private rooms."

"You've got a record, Chef Guzeman," Pete pointed out.

"That's a lie." Guzeman turned on him and the anger in his eyes made Julia reach out and put a hand on Pete's arm.

Pete ignored her gesture of warning. "You've been accused of drug smuggling."

Guzeman's face shut down, as if a window blind had been pulled shut. "Accused. Not convicted. Not even charged. I think it is time for you to leave now."

"Just one more question," Adam said. "Tell me about Harding's relationship with the crew. How is he to work for?"

Guzeman shook his head, his face still a mask. "No. You must go. Now." He pointed them toward the door.

"He's hiding something," Adam said as they found their way back to the main hall.

"Sure seems like it," Pete said. "We need to talk to some of his staff. Find out what's really going on. Too bad we don't have someone on the inside besides Wayne."

"He's not going to help with Guzeman," Adam agreed.

Julia perked up. "I might be able to help with that."

ALICE MURPHY HAD JUST FINISHED another lecture. She

bent over her table, hair flopping about her face as she gathered her camera and teaching supplies. Julia grabbed a seat at a table in the back of the dining room that was serving as Alice's classroom this time. Alice could definitely offer some inside knowledge about the ship and its crew. And its captain.

"Hi. Julia, right?"

Julia jumped up at the light touch on her arm to see Hope standing close behind her.

"Yes, that's right." She smiled, not sure why Hope was talking to her now but willing to hear her out. "Listen, I'm really sorry about earlier. I didn't mean to mislead you."

"No, it was my fault. I overreacted. It seems like everyone knows about Dad and our family." She shuddered and glanced over her shoulder. Julia recognized the well-dressed woman who was watching them, arms crossed in front of her chest, tapping blood-red fingernails against an empty cocktail glass in her hand. An enthusiastic photography student, apparently, since she'd been in Alice's class earlier as well.

"Do you know her?" she asked.

"She said she wants to talk to me, but I don't want to meet anyone. Not now. Everything is wrong right now, every little thing seems off, somehow."

"I know what you mean." Julia leaned back against the table she'd been sitting at. "When you lose a loved one, it's as if someone had made a terrible mistake and you're just waiting to wake up and find out that it was all wrong, that it's been fixed."

"That's exactly right." Hope smiled sadly and sat down. "I keep waiting for everything to be fixed."

Julia looked down at her notebook. She'd been drawing while waiting, doodling really. Just a few pencil drawings.

"You're pretty good," Hope said, her gaze also falling to Julia's notebooks.

"Nah, like I said, photography's my thing. How about you, did you try any of the exercises she recommended?"

Hope held out her own drawings for Julia to examine. An outdoor scene portrayed a mountain river, Hope's use of dark and light capturing the velocity and turbulence of an out-of-control force. A cityscape was calmer, though Julia recognized signs of poverty and despair tucked between stately houses. Her attention focused on a closeup of a face. It was an old man's face, full of sadness, exhaustion, even pain. "Wow. These are amazing."

Hope's eyes lit up a bit, the first time Julia had seen her make a true smile. "Do you really think so?"

"Absolutely. You have real talent."

"Dad said that, too. I don't just draw. I love working with metal, too."

"Really? In what way?"

"Mostly little things, like jewelry. But I've tackled some bigger works as well. I love it all. Dad wanted to send me to art school, to really study it, maybe make a profession out of it."

Julia couldn't hold back a dry laugh. "Yeah, well, good luck with that."

"Oh, well." Hope blinked in surprise. "I know I'll never be a great artist."

"Oh, no, no, I'm sorry. That's not what I meant at all. Your drawings are wonderful." Julia shook her head at her clumsy word choice. "It's just a hard career to make a living in, that's all."

The expression of confusion lingered in Hope's eyes, but she nodded. "I expect I'll be more of an art patron, anyway. Knowing about art — even being able to create it —

will be helpful. But still, you're making a living out of it, aren't you? As a photographer."

"Kind of. But it's not a safe career. And not a great living. What I told you earlier, it's worse than I made it seem. I can barely afford my rent, and each month my debt gets a little bigger."

"I'm so sorry, I thought ..." Hope shrugged again. "I don't know."

"Don't feel bad," Julia assured her, "this is my choice. It's what I want to do. And hey, I'm not above taking a handout from my mom or dad, or Adam, every now and then."

"You're lucky you have them. I mean, I guess I'll have enough money to support myself anyway, now that Dad's dead. At least, I hope I will. It's not too much money for me to live in Paris for a few years, to study there, and Dad did promise."

Julia suspected she and Hope had very different conceptions of what "too much money" entailed, but she bit her tongue before spouting off anything else insulting. "It's not just family. I have a boyfriend now. Pete was a godsend. Not only is he this handsome, successful, caring, generous man, but he's willing to help me out without making it seem like he's giving me a handout. He always pays when we go out to dinner, or pays for the cab, or if we're grocery shopping together. He doesn't make a big deal out of it."

Hope's eyes widened. "That's exactly how I feel. I plan to marry well, too. I don't mean to sound spoiled, but I know what I like. I like having beautiful things. I like having a certain lifestyle. I wouldn't be happy living in a New York walk-up, not being able to serve on boards or support museums." Her face was a picture of innocence.

Wow, is that what she sounded like, Julia wondered? It

seemed like everything she said was coming out wrong. Or Hope was twisting her words.

"I don't like being dependent," Julia explained. "But for me it's temporary. I'll get a break at some point, I know I will. And meanwhile I work weddings, birthday parties, dull events that help pay the bills. And I always keep an eye out for opportunities, like part-time gallery work."

Hope closed her eyes and took a breath, clearly imagining a future life. "Working at a gallery." She opened her eyes. "Ooh, or an auction house! Can you imagine? It sounds fabulous."

Julia laughed. "It is fun. I won't take a full-time job, though. That wouldn't leave me enough time for *my* photographs."

"I like your attitude. Now with Dad ..." Hope paused, then shook herself. "I need to start thinking about how I'm going to take care of myself. I need to be practical."

"Hey, it's way too soon for you to be thinking about that," Julia chided her. "Your father just died. Don't give up on your dreams yet."

"What dreams are those?"

Both women looked up at the question. Julia hadn't noticed Bill Langtry approaching.

"Oh, things we want to do with our lives," Julia answered vaguely. She wasn't sure how much personal information Hope was willing to share with her cousin and she certainly wasn't willing to share her own.

"Ladies, I hope you were here for the class." Alice Murphy had finished gathering her supplies into a large canvas bag, a camera once again hanging from the strap around her neck. "I have another one in the early evening. And you're welcome to bring a cocktail along," she said with a smile.

"We'll be there. Don't worry." Hope said, trying to smile.

"Art classes, huh? Maybe I should try one of those. You guys seem to be enjoying them." Bill spoke cheerfully, as if trying too hard to boost Hope's spirits.

"Oh, no," Hope responded quickly. "They wouldn't interest you."

"Oh." Bill looked away from them, his attention apparently drawn to something across the room. "That's fine."

"Of course you're welcome to join the class," Julia said quickly, confused by Hope's reaction.

Hope shook her head and sighed. "Bill, I'm so sorry, I wasn't trying to put you off. I really didn't think it would interest you." She tried to smile again, but it didn't reach her eyes. "We can be friends and still have different interests, can't we?"

"Friends?" Bill asked. "Sure. Why not."

Alice chuckled at some internal joke. "Well, I hope I see you all in my evening class."

"Alice," Julia said, "If you have a minute, I'd love to chat with you. I just have a few questions you might be able to help me with."

Bill patted Hope on the shoulder. "Look, I'm going to find a quiet place to relax. You coming?"

Hope looked confused, glancing back and forth between Bill and Julia. "I guess I'll hang out here, if that's OK?" She looked at Julia, though Julia couldn't tell what question Hope was trying to ask with her eyes.

"I'm happy to talk, dear," Alice was saying, "but not right now, I'm afraid. Too much going on, as always. Can I find you later? Maybe tomorrow morning?"

"Of course, that's fine," Julia responded to Alice, but her

focus was still on Hope. And Bill, who hovered nearby, clearly waiting to see if Hope would join him.

Hope finally dropped her gaze from Julia and turned to Bill. "Hold on, I'll come with you."

Alice Murphy kept a curious gaze on Bill's back as they left.

"You think there's something going on between those two?" Julia asked, trying to interpret Alice's expression.

"Oh, yes! Oh ... I mean." Alice laughed at her own words. "Of course I have no idea. It is a cruise, after all. People get to relax onboard, do things they might not otherwise do."

"True," Julia agreed. "He seems to be interested in her, anyway."

Alice gave Julia a sideways look. "You think it's a one-way romance, do you?" Her eyes sparkled with laughter.

"Why, what do you know?" Julia nudged Alice as she asked the question.

"Don't look at me. Staff must never reveal the secrets they see on board."

14

While Julia was pursuing her inside source, Adam and Pete searched out Brad Claypoole. They found him lounging in a wooden pool chair, one hand hanging loose, the other balancing a frosted glass on the arm of the chair. He sat separate from the other bathers, though there weren't that many of them. Adam's eyes lingered when he saw Karen Sigelman sunbathing in one of the loungers, her bathing suit covering just enough skin to let his imagination run wild. He dragged his attention back to the man in front of him.

"Brad, d'you have a minute?"

Brad raised a limp hand to shield his eyes, though his dark sunglasses looked like they would have done the trick. "If you must. I'm just taking a few minutes to collect myself."

"Yeah, I can see that," Adam said, looking around the well-tended pool deck. Music played softly from hidden speakers, that familiar lilting sound of Bermuda. No kids shouted or splashed in this pool. Well-dressed waiters passed from chair to chair offering to top up glasses or bring sustenance.

"Look," Brad muttered, lifting himself into a sitting position and swinging his feet down to the ground. "I know I look like I don't give a damn about my father, but that's not true."

"Of course not, and I apologize if we gave that impression," Pete chimed in. "Everyone grieves in their own way, and I know better than to judge."

Brad's expression was severe, but its severity was undercut as he took a sip from his glass and had to blink when the wedge of pineapple dislodged his sunglasses.

"Brad, we have to ask," Pete continued. "Did you know you'd inherit your father's fortune?"

"Yes, of course I knew. I'm his only child." He looked confused and glanced at his watch.

"Nice watch," Adam said with surprise. "Where did you get that?"

Brad pulled his head back defensively. "It was my dad's. That means it's mine now. Harding made sure I got it."

"He shouldn't have done that."

Brad waved a hand, dismissing the criticism. "It had sentimental value for me. Besides, anything that was my dad's belongs to me now."

"What about Hope? Isn't she also his child?" Adam asked.

"Well, yes, of course. But she is adopted, you know."

"Adopted as an infant. Raised as his own," Pete pointed out.

Brad shrugged. "Still. She'll get a decent amount. The old man didn't leave her with nothing, don't you worry."

"Enough to keep her in the life she expects?" Adam

asked. He'd noticed the level of luxury evinced in Hope's cabin.

"Maybe, maybe not. I know she wants to go to Paris. To study art." Brad snorted. "I would have to pay for that for her. I don't think she'd be able to support herself in *that* way."

"What does that mean?" Pete asked sharply.

"Oh, you know, flitting about, painting and drawing. Traveling the world. No, she would need to settle down. Get a job, get married if she wants to live on the money she has now."

"But being an artist is something your father encouraged in her, isn't it?" Adam asked. "Isn't it what he would have wanted?"

Brad's eyes shifted and Adam followed his gaze to see Captain Harding passing among the passengers, smiling, shaking some hands. He looked toward Karen and smiled, but she turned away without a sign of recognition. Harding moved instead toward another woman in a bikini, kneeling down next to her to massage lotion into her back.

Brad sniffed and swung his legs back up onto the chair. He took another sip of his drink — without injuring himself this time. "Perhaps, perhaps not. I'll need to think about that. I'll need to think about a lot of things now."

"Now that you have the money?"

Brad let his head fall back against the chair. "Now that I have the money."

THE MUSIC from the first-class pool faded away behind Adam as a similar rhythm from the buffet deck beckoned him. Pete had gone back to the computer room to check for more messages, then on to find Julia. They planned to meet at the Starlight Lounge. Adam thought he had time to drop by the buffet for a quick snack — he hadn't decided yet between some of the fresh cut fruit or one of the sweet pastries — when a glance at the basketball court made him change directions.

He continued down one more flight of stairs and turned left toward the court. A game was going on at one end, a solo player practicing at the other. Adam stopped just outside the court and watched Paul toss ball after ball through the hoop. Making every shot.

"That's quite impressive," Adam called out when Paul paused to take a sip from a plastic bottle. "You do this a lot?"

"Basketball? It's my game." Paul laughed and came over to Adam. "I play whenever I can."

"You've been taking advantage of the free courts on board, I've noticed."

"Sure, why not." Paul shrugged. "Just put your name on the schedule and the court is yours for thirty minutes."

"Sorry, I don't want to interrupt."

"Nah, it's no big deal." Paul glanced at his watch. "Those guys look like they won't object to getting on the court five minutes early." Paul waved to a group of five young men pacing along the other edge of the court. They waved back and trotted out to start their game.

"Doesn't anyone else from your family want to play with you?" Adam asked as they slowly made their way along the edge of the court toward the railing.

"I don't know, I didn't ask." Paul tossed his towel over his shoulder. "I like practicing alone. I don't always need a competition."

"It's not about winning or losing, huh?"

"Sure. No. I just enjoy throwing the ball." Paul's mouth

was a straight line and Adam couldn't tell if he'd picked up a trace of humor there or not.

"What do you do for a living, Paul?"

"I'm in business. I work for Breston Miller."

"Never heard of it."

"Hm." Paul laughed lightly. "That's funny. It's one of the biggest multinational corporations in the world, but so few people have heard of it."

"And what do you do there? At Breston Miller?"

"Oh, I work in underwriting long-term loans."

"So they're a bank?"

"No, no, nothing like that. We underwrite loans made by other corporations. We analyze and assume risks that others may not be willing to take. I tend to focus on potential additional collateral or credit enhancements for small or large businesses."

Adam examined Paul's face while he talked. His expression stayed neutral, bland. Even when he smiled it didn't make it to his eyes. His eyes were kind of brown. Kind of hazel. Hard to describe. His hair was neutral, too, not blond, but not dark brown, just something in the middle. He was of middling height, middling weight. In fact, if Adam was ever called to describe Paul in a court of law, he'd find himself struggling to come up with an accurate description. Eminently forgettable was probably the best.

"You can see why I don't talk about it much. Not as interesting as being a cop, anyway," Paul wrapped up his explanation.

"Eh, it's not always that interesting. Lots of paperwork." Adam leaned forward over the railing, his eyes on the dark clouds hanging on the horizon.

"Sure, sure. I get that. Even the exciting cases, right?"

"I'm not sure what you'd consider exciting. Working in

homicide means with every case, someone has died. And someone else is suffering."

Paul nodded, his eyes downcast. "There were those poisonings in New York, you heard of them?"

"What?" Adam turned his gaze back to Paul. "What poisonings?"

"Oh, well." Paul raised one shoulder, pulled his towel down in front of him and wrapped it around his hands. "I'm sure you know more about it than I do, just can't talk about it, right? Ongoing investigation and all that."

"I don't work in New York. I'm not involved in any investigations there," Adam said.

"Right. No, I guess not. Sorry I brought it up."

"Why did you? What made you think of it?"

"Well, it's just — I read about it. Not too long ago. There have been a few deaths by cyanide poisoning. Not connected that anyone can tell, or anything like that. Just unsolved."

Adam took a deep breath and let it out loudly. "It bugs me how many cases go unsolved. I hate that."

Paul nodded, looked back out at the sea trailing behind the boat.

"Did you mention those because you think there's a connection?" Adam asked.

"Me? No, I don't pretend to understand how murderers work. Or murder investigations. It's just, the old man being poisoned, I was reminded of this article. That's all. You could look it up if you want to. I read it .... Oh, where did I see that?"

Adam didn't expect Paul to remember. He knew the type. Boring job, boring life, looking for excitement where there wasn't any. Trying to insert himself into the investigation just for the thrills. Or, worse, committing a murder just for the thrills. Adam took another look at Paul.

"Nope." Paul shook his head. "Don't remember where I read it. Well, maybe you don't care anyway."

"I care very much," Adam corrected him. "I appreciate you sharing your thoughts on the case. That's how cases like this get solved, you know."

"By people remembering old articles?" Paul grinned. It didn't reach his eyes.

"No, by witnesses speaking up when they see something that confuses them. Or that reminds them of something else. It's all about making those connections. And figuring out what they mean."

15

Julia started moving to the beat as soon as she and Pete entered the Starlight Lounge to meet Adam. The music blared — not the lilting rhythms she'd been getting used to hearing on the boat, either. This was dance music for the middle-aged crowd. Music that promised to get you up on the dance floor and shaking your booty if you were a teenager in the 1980s.

Pete made a beeline for the bar. Julia arrested her movement toward an empty cocktail table when she noticed Hope and Bill across the room, just vacating a similar table. Julia sidestepped an elderly couple gingerly shifting their weight on the dance floor and made her way over to where the other couple was engaged in a serious-looking conversation.

"Hope? Hi." Julia stepped close enough to be heard by Hope and Bill. "Sorry to bother you. I don't want you to think I'm following you around or anything, I just saw you over here."

Hope visibly jumped at Julia's voice, but her tension released when she saw Julia.

"Oh, hi." Hope's response was even more despondent than Julia had expected and particularly jarring in this jovial atmosphere. As if to underline Hope's depression, a bright "whoop" carried from the dance floor.

Bill glanced at a woman hovering a few feet away, then put a hand on Hope's arm and guided her through the cocktail tables that lined the dance floor, away from the speakers and toward the long wall of windows that looked out over the turbulent ocean. Julia followed. She'd recognized the well-dressed woman immediately. Who was she and what was her connection to Hope?

"I think you need to take your time, that's all." Bill seemed to be continuing a thought he'd started before Julia interrupted them.

"I know." Hope's face was downcast. "I know."

Julia hesitated, not wanting to interrupt but happy to offer condolences or support if she could. "Anything I can help with?" she finally asked.

"No, Bill's just watching out for me, that's all." She smiled up at him. "Like he always does."

"It's good you have family around you, Hope. People who care about you. But ..." Julia hesitated, knowing it was none of her business, knowing that sticking her nose in could make things worse. And knowing she had no choice. "Hope, who is that woman?"

Hope gave a strangled sob and almost fell into Bill's arms. Bill put his arm around her shoulder and held her up, saying, "You'll do the right thing, I know you will."

"I guess you have some tough decisions to make, now that your father's gone," Julia said softly. "But Bill's right, don't rush into anything."

Bill smiled at Julia with a nod. "That's exactly what I'm saying. Right now, you need to focus on taking care of yourself. And mourning your father, not worrying about some stranger with crazy stories."

"What stories?" Julia asked, even more convinced that she needed to know.

Bill shook his head at her, clearly wanting her to drop it. But she couldn't. "What's going on?" she repeated.

"That woman," Hope said softly, so softly Julia had to lean in to hear her, her hand resting against the bar that ran along the window. "She claims she's my mother."

Julia's hand slipped from the bar and she almost lost her balance. "Oh."

"Let me help," Adam said.

Pete had turned from the bar balancing three cocktails in his hands. Adam took one. "What's going on over there?" He gestured to the far side of the lounge. Hope slouched against a window, holding onto Bill's hand with both of her hands. Julia stood next to them, concern all over her face as she rested a hand on Hope's shoulder.

"Julia? You OK?" Pete asked as they approached the group.

"Pete, Adam, sure, we're fine. Just ..."

"I think I better go." Hope stood, running her hand down the front of her pants, smoothing away invisible wrinkles. "I need to get back to my cabin."

"I'll—" Bill started but Julia cut him off.

"Come on, I'll walk you." Julia draped a protective arm around Hope. "Let's take a break." Turning to Pete, she added, "I'll fill you in later."

Bill, Adam, and Pete watched the two women walk

away, Hope seeming to stand a little taller with Julia's supportive hand still on her back.

"What was that all about?" Adam asked.

"Nothing," Bill muttered. "Hope's just dealing with the sort of problems only rich people have. And trying to figure out what she wants to do next."

Adam was pretty sure Bill was leaving a few details out. "What kinds of problems are those?"

"Oh, you know." Bill shook his head roughly and turned his back to the window, his eyes roving over the dance floor. "People who want things from her. Money, I suppose. Then she doesn't know if she should still take that trip to Paris."

"Right." Adam nodded. "She wants to study art in Paris. She mentioned that."

"But she needs to wait." Bill's brow lowered over his eyes, his mouth turning down into a frown. "She's in no condition to go traipsing around the world right now."

"She needs time to mourn, is that what you're saying?" Pete asked.

Bill shrugged. "Maybe. Maybe that's all it is. But she's not as strong as she looks. I think her father knew that."

"That's not what she told me," Adam said.

"Like I said, she needs to figure out what she really wants."

Adam frowned, thinking. "I can relate to that feeling." He turned to the dance floor, where the music was playing again and a group of women had claimed the dance floor. Hips and arms waved in beat — or not — as they laughed and joked with each other.

"That's what we should be doing, partner." Adam nudged Pete.

"Really? Then I'm glad we're stuck with this case." Pete laughed.

"Are you stuck? I mean, do you feel like you're stuck?" Bill asked.

"Nah, it's fine. We're just asking questions. That's the way investigations always work." Adam spoke more confidently than he felt.

"I see. And who've you been talking to? Asking questions, I mean?" Bill asked.

"The usual suspects." Pete smiled and turned back to the dance floor.

"Like?"

"You're very curious, aren't you?" Adam asked Bill.

"I just want to help if I can. I'm sorry I don't have my kit, that I couldn't find any evidence in Claypoole's cabin."

"That's OK." Adam watched Bill closely. "Look, I appreciate you want to help, but you know we can't discuss our investigation with you, right?"

Bill laughed aloud. "You can't think ..."

He stopped when he saw that Pete and Adam weren't smiling. "It's just, well, I'm usually on your side of the investigation, that's all."

"I know. Look," Adam pressed him, "if there's anything else you can think of — about Mr. Claypoole, or about your family — I'd appreciate hearing it."

Bill shrugged. "Not really. I mean, you know Brad inherits. I guess everyone knows that now."

Pete nodded. "Did everyone know that before?"

"I don't know. I think we all assumed Brad and Hope would split the inheritance. Not sure why the old man made his will the way he did. Honestly, it seemed like Arthur was closer to Hope. They're so similar, in lots of ways." A narrow grin spread to Bill's eyes. "Arthur Claypoole was a man of steel. Brad is a floppy noodle."

"Blood will out," Pete muttered under his breath.

"What's that?"

"Hope's adopted, right? So, maybe in the end Mr. Claypoole saw his real son as more important to him."

"That bastard."

The anger in Bill's voice surprised Adam. "It doesn't really affect you either way, though, does it?"

"Me? No. It's just, I care about Hope."

"More than you care about Brad?"

"Does that surprise you? Have you met Brad?" Bill laughed. "He's an architect, you know."

"Yeah, he mentioned that."

"Well, have you considered that means he has access to cyanide?"

Pete stepped closer to Bill, and Adam leaned in to hear over the music. "How do you mean?"

Bill looked from one to the other. "Blueprints, you know?"

"I've heard of blueprints, yeah. What about it?"

"There's a reason the process for producing blue prints is called cyanotype." Bill spoke like he was pointing out the obvious, but this was the first Adam had ever heard of it.

"Are you kidding? Shouldn't that be banned?"

"Not banned. But regulated, sure. It is. But he has good need for it."

"Is it enough cyanide to kill someone?" Adam asked.

Bill shook his head. "No. It's not."

Pete held up a hand as if to stop them. "I've heard of this. But it's an old technique. Nobody uses it anymore, certainly not most architects. They all work from computers now. Printouts, you know?"

Bill shrugged. "True. But it is still used sometimes, for more artistic designs or to create particular effects."

"So how is that relevant then?" Adam asked.

"Well, the normal ink isn't enough to kill anyone. But if it was used in enough quantity. And with enough intensity."

"You mean turning the ink into poison."

"Exactly. It could be inhal—" Bill coughed, interrupting himself. "Well, inhaled, or swallowed maybe. Who knows? I haven't really thought about it before."

Adam raised an eyebrow. "You seem pretty knowledgeable for someone who hasn't thought about it before."

"I'm a crime scene technician. I stay up to date on this kind of stuff. It's my job."

"So you don't think it's likely."

Bill shook his head again. "No, I don't."

"But it could be done."

"It could be done."

16

"What did you find?" Adam asked.

He and Pete had left Bill behind in the Starlight Lounge, walking through the plush hallway, past the broad staircase, and out a narrow door to a side deck. A shuffleboard court drawn onto the deck lay empty, a few chairs stacked near it.

"I looked into those poisonings like you asked. Checked with PPD and NYPD." Pete handed Adam a few printed pages.

"And was Paul right? Were there a series of unsolved cyanide poisonings?" Adam asked impatiently, folding the papers into his pocket.

"In a way." Pete hedged his response.

"What does that even mean?"

"It means, my guys checked the records and there were five unsolved murders — death by cyanide poisoning through inhalation — in New York over the past few years. It wasn't easy to dig up, though."

"Why not? You'd think they'd be worked up, looking for a serial killer."

Adam hadn't realized how loud his voice had risen until he heard the sharp inhale from the white-haired woman passing by with her husband.

"Sorry." Adam lowered his voice. "Just talking about that movie. You know, that movie."

She tucked her arm more firmly against her husband.

Pete laughed. "There's no serial killer. The deaths aren't connected."

"They were all killed the same way, right?"

"No, they weren't. I mean, it was all cyanide poisoning, but do you know how many deaths by poisoning there are in the U.S. in a decade?"

"No idea."

"Over four hundred thousand."

"You're kidding."

"I kid you not. And New York is one of the top states, going by stats. So a few go unsolved. It happens."

"Yeah, but the connection?"

"No connection." Pete shook his head. "Different people, different places. There's really no connection. You might as well say everyone who's shot was shot by the same killer."

"All right, don't make fun." Adam leaned against the railing. "So where does this leave us?"

"Nowhere. Except ..." Pete bit his lower lip.

"What? What are you thinking?"

"Where did Paul say he read about these killings?" Pete asked.

"He couldn't remember."

"It's just, if no one is linking the murders, I find it hard to believe anyone wrote an article about them. If nothing else, that would've got the NYPD's attention, you know?"

"Yeah. I know. It's weird."

"You know what else is weird? When I tried to find some background on Paul, I hit some kind of warning button — our precinct actually got a call from the State Department telling us to drop it."

"Wow. He is *not* who he says he is."

"But what I want to know is, what does he know about a series of murders in New York?"

"And why did he bring it up with me?" Adam pushed himself up. "Julia's busy with Hope. I say you and I find Paul."

"Pete!"

Both men turned toward Julia as she ran up the deck toward them. "I'm glad I found you." She paused and took a moment to catch her breath. "I just took Hope back to her cabin, but there's something you need to know about her. And her mother."

"SHE'S NOT HERE." Julia shook her head as she scanned the lounge. "I don't see her."

"Well, I see someone else I want to talk to." Adam felt his anger rising and didn't care. This was more than a small detail Bill had chosen to not tell them.

The Starlight Lounge was still rocking, groups and couples jiggling their way across the dance floor. Windows lined three sides of the wide space, but the weak late-afternoon sunlight couldn't penetrate the translucent window shades. Bright neon lights kept the dance floor from feeling gloomy while individual lamps created cozy pockets of light on each cocktail table.

Adam skirted the dance floor, trying to avoid the bulk of

the crowd as he made his way around to Bill. The pulsing rhythm of the music was stronger now, and he twice had to extricate himself from tight-knit groups that surrounded him as they lost themselves to the music. Bill's attention was on the dance floor, but he noticed Adam heading his way and pushed himself up off the window. At first he turned to Adam with a smile on his face, but something about Adam's appearance must have warned him, for his smile dropped, and as Adam approached, he stood with his legs wide, his arms folded across his chest.

"Hope's birth mother is on this boat. And you didn't think I needed to know that?" Adam started talking while he was still twenty feet away, raising his voice to be heard over the music. A few people close to them turned at the sound, but Adam lowered his voice again as he stepped close to Bill, their faces only inches apart. "Why'd you try to hide that?"

"I'm not hiding anything." Bill's voice carried its usual questioning whine. "We don't even know that that woman is who she says she is."

"We can find out. We need to find out. What the hell were you thinking?"

"Calm down." Bill took a step back but Adam matched the movement. Bill leaned back into the window in an awkward lurch. "I had just met the woman myself. Hope was still processing this ridiculous story. It was personal."

"Nothing is personal in a murder investigation." Adam's brow was still lowered but his anger slowly receded. "Tell me everything. Who is this woman?"

Bill's eyes were wide. "I have no idea. She claims to be Hope's birth mother. Said she came on this cruise when she heard old man Claypoole was having this family reunion.

She said she found Hope years ago, but was afraid to approach her before now."

"So what changed?"

"Really?" Bill straightened his shoulders. "She just inherited a fortune, of course the wackos are going to come out the woodwork. You can't be taking this story seriously."

Adam took a deep breath. "Bill, I'm looking for a murderer. If this woman has some way of proving she's Hope's mother — whether she really is or not — then she might be expecting to benefit from that inheritance. That makes her a suspect."

"Oh." Bill's shoulders slumped again. "I hadn't thought of that." He looked away from Adam, chewing on his lip. "I don't know who she is. She didn't tell us her name."

"She tells Hope she's her long-lost mother but doesn't bother introducing herself?"

"You have to understand, as soon as she started in with that story, I cut her off."

"You cut her off? How did Hope react?"

"I'm not sure." Bill hunched his shoulders, tucking both hands into his front pockets. "She was shocked, I guess. She didn't really say much."

Adam thought about this. "So how do I find this woman?"

"I'll recognize her when I see her. Oh, and Julia" — Bill gestured with his chin to where Julia and Pete waited across the lounge — "Julia would recognize her. She said she's seen her before."

Adam sucked in his cheeks and took another deep breath. He'd got all he could out of Bill, no point in antagonizing the man more. But what an idiot for not saying something sooner. Like while the woman was still there. "OK, I guess that will do for now. You see her again, you find me, got it?"

"How can I do that? This is a big ship." The whine was back in Bill's voice.

"I don't care how you do it, just do it."

17

Bill was right about one thing. It was a big ship. Not an easy place to find people.

Adam and Pete finally tracked Paul down, after a number of wrong leads, in the bowling alley. The room was no longer reserved for the grieving family — apparently half a day was all they needed to grieve — and a number of bowlers were taking their turns, laughing and cursing each time the ship hit a large wave.

Paul stood up against a far wall, his back to the room, a cell phone to his ear.

"How does he have cell reception out here?" Adam muttered. "We get nothing."

"I think you have to have a satellite phone, or something like that," Pete said.

"And why does this guy rate?"

Adam stopped about five feet from Paul, their presence blocked, he hoped, by a wide, purple-carpeted column that stood between them. Paul had one hand to his free ear, his features furrowed in concentration. Perhaps it wasn't as good a connection as he'd been hoping for.

"Why is he in here? The other family members we asked expected him to be joining one of the other groups," Adam wondered aloud.

"And who's he talking to?" Pete added.

The two men stepped back behind the column, confident that Paul hadn't noticed them yet. They listened.

"Cheronsky Lab, sure, I know it. Russian research firm ... I've heard that, too many connections to be comfortable ... Payments from who?" Paul's hand moved as if he was holding a pen, but whatever he was focusing on, he was committing it to memory, not to paper. "Same amount from each firm? Cheronsky and Carpathian Air ... too much of a coincidence, got it ... Right, unspecified ... No, I'm taking care of that ..."

"Did you understand any of that?" Adam asked Pete under his breath.

"A bit. Not all. Sounds like business."

"Business as usual?"

"Well, he wasn't that closely related to the victim, was he? I guess he can't be expected to put his life on hold."

"No, I mean, is it regular business talk? Sounds off to me."

Pete laughed quietly. "What are you basing that on?"

"Listen, he says he's an underwriter of long-term loans. But he's asking someone else about Russian labs and airlines?"

Pete raised his eyebrows. "I see your point. I mean, he could be looking at them as potential loan opportunities. Right." Pete nodded once as he saw Adam's face. "We need to find out what kind of business he's really in."

"Exactly."

They waited a few more minutes, but Paul seemed to have finished sharing his information or asking his questions, and was now just listening. One more minute and he hung up the phone.

Pete stepped forward to approach him, but Adam held him back. "Let's see where he goes next, shall we?"

Crowds of passengers filling the lounges and moving from attraction to attraction within the ship made it relatively easy for Adam and Pete to follow Paul without being seen. Though Adam could've sworn Paul noticed them at one turning in the corridor. If he had, he gave no indication. Perhaps his mind was on the call he'd just had. Whatever that was about.

Paul led them through the main lounge, past the smaller dining room, through the dark glass door into the private, front section of the ship.

"Is Paul traveling first class, too?" Pete asked as they swiped their own keycard to access the area.

"Yeah, at least I think so. I kinda stalked him as he was going back to his cabin earlier. But this doesn't look right." A warning was going off in Adam's mind. He recognized the hallway they were following. He knew he was right when Paul paused in front of a wooden door, looked up and down the hall, swiped a keycard over the lock, and entered.

"Why did he look guilty going into his own cabin?" Pete asked.

"Because that's not his cabin," Adam said. "That's Brad's cabin."

18

"We could interrupt them. Just knock on the door," Pete said, his eyes still on the cabin Paul had entered.

"Yep," Adam said, glancing up and down the empty corridor. "But why did Paul have a key to Brad's cabin?"

"That, I cannot say."

"And do we even know Brad's in there?" Adam asked.

Pete glanced at his watch. "He's supposed to be having tea with some of his cousins, according to one of them."

"So what's Paul doing in his cabin?"

Adam and Pete shared a look. Pete finally said, "Let's give him two minutes, then go in."

They didn't need to wait two minutes. Paul slipped out the door again, pulling it closed behind him.

"Come on." Adam waited only until Paul had turned a far corner in the hall, then jogged over to the door before it clicked shut.

Both men stopped just inside the door, closing it softly behind them. Adam didn't know how long they had before Brad returned, but he knew Brad would not appreciate having his cabin searched. He also didn't know what he was looking for.

"If Paul was looking for something, he was pretty neat about it. No evidence of a search." Pete walked around the room, touching a pillow that looked recently fluffed, picking up, then dropping a newspaper that was neatly folded, running his hand over a cell phone covered with a familiar picture of a smiling family. "He didn't want Brad to know he'd been in here."

"So either looking for something. Or planting something," Adam said firmly. "Let's do our own search."

Adam and Pete had been involved in enough searches of suspects' homes to know exactly where to start. And what to look for. Adam wasn't used to having to hide the evidence of his activities, though. He pushed a drawer in the bedroom shut when Pete stuck his head in.

"The drawer's askew."

"A-what? Seriously?" Adam looked, and Pete was right, one end of the drawer was ever so slightly higher than the other. He fixed it and moved on to the next.

Adam finished with the bedroom as Pete came out of the bathroom.

"That's all three rooms. Nothing."

"Or we saw it and didn't realize it."

"I did keep an eye out for any of his work equipment."

"Like blue ink, you mean?" Adam asked. "Yeah, me too."

"But why would he bring drafting tools along on a cruise anyway? That alone would look suspicious."

"Agreed." Adam nodded. "So if Paul wasn't planting something incriminatory, what was he looking for?"

"Brad's got exactly what you'd expect: vacation clothes,

a few magazines and newspapers, an iPad, hats, sunblock." Pete tossed his hands in the air.

"No drafting tools, like you said. How about work papers?"

"Yeah, there was something that could've been related to his architecture firm." Pete walked over to a table against one wall and pulled open a small drawer. "Looks like a few memos about a current project."

Adam looked over his shoulder. "Running over budget. Looks like he's got some tough choices to make."

"That's hardly incriminating though, is it? Pretty standard business experience, if you ask me."

"And why would Paul be looking for that? Doesn't make sense. Can you access the iPad?"

Pete shook his head. "Password protected. Can't get on it."

"So there could be something there."

"But we'd need a warrant to access it."

Adam considered. "Not likely we'll get one. That'll be up to the Feds once we dock."

Pete shrugged. "At least it's something we can give them."

"Along with the fact that Paul was sneaking around in here. Come on, let's go. He could be back soon."

He turned toward the door, when a light tap made him freeze. He put a finger up to his lips and stepped back toward Pete. "Someone knows we're here," he whispered.

"Or they're looking for Brad. Give it a second."

A second tap made them both jump. The person outside the door coughed, then called softly. "Detective Kaminski?"

"What the ..." Adam flung the door open. An embarrassed steward stepped back from the door, pulling his hands behind his back as he stood up straight.

"I'm sorry to bother you, sir, but I was told to find you."

"How did you know I was here?" Adam asked.

The steward actually blushed. "I saw you earlier, sir, following the other gentleman."

Adam laughed and shook his head at Pete. "Not as subtle as we think we are, are we? Who else saw us?"

"No one, I'm sure," the steward replied. "We're trained to keep an eye on the passengers, that's all. I would never tell anyone else what I saw."

"The crew really are everywhere, aren't they?" Pete asked. "Too bad there isn't a nice steward stepping forward to say he saw who killed Arthur Claypoole. So why did you need us?"

"Bill Langtry is trying to find you. He says he has the person you want to meet."

———

JULIA WRAPPED the towel around herself a little more tightly as she reached for the moisturizer. She could hear snatches of conversation from the spa's lobby, which was just on the other side of a very thin door. I bet the spa at the first-class pool has thicker doors, she thought, turning red at the thought.

Hope hadn't been interested in joining her at the pool. Julia had suggested a dip in the pool or hot tub, or even a session in the sauna to help her relax. But Hope had been more interested in going back to her cabin alone, she'd said. Julia could admit now that when she'd invited Hope to join her at the pool she'd been hoping that Hope would agree — then instead invite Julia to join her at the first-class pool.

But Julia had been on her own. A few minutes in one of the hot tubs around the pool had been enough. She'd chosen a tub that was occupied only by other adults, which was nice. In fact, she enjoyed watching the kids running and screaming as they went down the slide into the pool or dipped a toe into one of the other hot tubs. But after a while she realized she'd prefer something a little quieter.

The spa was divided into a ladies' area and a men's area, which met around the sunroom (complete with sun lamps) and the indoor hot tubs. Julia skipped another dip in hot water, instead taking some time to breathe deeply and relax in a dry sauna. She could feel the heat working its way through her bones. She took another deep breath.

When she realized she was sweating a little more than comfortably, she headed back to the locker room for a shower. She tapped in the key code for her locker without too much thought — she always used the same code — and leaned forward to drop her towel on the bench as she reached up to grab her stuff. Then froze as she felt nothing.

She straightened to stare into an empty locker. No pool bag. No change of clothes. No key card, phone, or camera.

"What the ...?" Julia looked frantically around. Had someone broken into her locker? To steal her stuff? That made no sense. She had nothing of value. At least not to anyone but her.

"OK, Jules. Calm down, think rationally." She took a breath, then perched on the stool in front of the lockers. As she stared at the wall of small wooden doors, a blue piece of fabric caught her attention. It was caught in the door of the locker next to hers. She reached a hand up and pulled at the door, expecting it to be locked.

The door swung open at her touch, revealing her bag, its blue strap still hanging over the edge of the locker.

Julia felt her arms go weak with relief as she let out a loud laugh. She'd locked the wrong locker! What a fool. She'd clearly needed her time in the spa more than she'd realized.

"Miss, everything all right?" A spa attendant, dressed in bright whites, stuck her head around the door.

"Sorry, yes." Julia let out another giggle. "Everything's fine," she said as she shuffled to the showers.

Wrapping her towel around herself now, she grabbed a stool at the vanity table in the ladies' dressing room. And listened to the men and women chatting in the spa lobby.

"We do styling, makeup, massage ..." a saleswoman was reading off the spa's offering to someone, whose responses sounded less than enthusiastic. Julia was glad they'd chosen to buy the full package as soon as they boarded, that way she didn't have to feel guilty about using the spa, like she would if she were paying by the day. In fact, she felt guilty if she didn't use it.

Wiping in the last of the moisturizer, Julia grabbed a hairdryer, flipped her head so her hair hung down toward the floor, and gave it a good going-over with the blower on high.

When she turned the air off, she heard new voices in the lobby.

"I don't mean to suggest anything." She recognized Alice Murphy's nervous chatter.

"No, no, of course, completely understandable." Julia couldn't hear the other voice clearly, it must have been muffled by something.

She grabbed a round brush and turned the blow-dryer back on, doing her best to tame the unruly curls her hair insisted on, trying, perhaps in vain, to urge it into smooth waves. Not an easy task.

With a humph, she turned the blow-dryer off while reaching for a different brush.

"I have to know, that's all. Just who else. No big deal." The same person was still speaking. It sounded like a woman, but so low she couldn't even be sure of that.

"No one, I'm sure." Alice Murphy was still in the lobby. "I'm sorry, I am. I should have thought better."

Julia got a firm grip on the larger brush and set to work with the blow-dryer. After a few more futile minutes, she gave up. She turned off the blow-dryer and stashed it back under the counter.

As she reached for her clothes, she heard another woman's voice in the lobby.

"You must take the makeover, then, it will be perfect for this evening." The saleswoman was back, hounding yet another potential customer. Maybe Alice Murphy? Julia giggled to herself at the thought.

She tied her skirt around her waist, pulled down on her T-shirt to straighten it, and headed back into the lobby, expecting to see Alice. But the room was empty. Whoever had been holding conversations there was gone.

19

The smaller dining room was small only by comparison with the main dining hall. Colorful cubes of modern art dotted the walls, movable screens and brightly colored low walls divided the geometrically shaped space. Each blocked-off area seemed small, but they added together to create dining space for several hundred people at a time.

Bill stood as they walked through the room, waving his arm at them.

"You happy now?" He grimaced at Adam. "Here she is. Ms. Molly Gerson."

Bill waved a hand toward the middle-aged woman sitting stiffly at the table. She didn't look at Adam or Pete as Bill introduced her, instead keeping her gaze fixed on the wall across from her. She sniffed, though Adam couldn't tell if she was trying not to cry or frustrated at being required to wait. The table in front of her held an empty plate, dirty silverware placed neatly across it. The half-empty glass of white wine had a red lipstick smudge along one side, the color of her lips matching her nails perfectly — the nails

Adam couldn't help but notice as she tapped them against the glass.

"Ms. Gerson." Adam pulled out the chair next to her while Pete sat on the other side. "I'm Adam Kaminski. I need to talk with you about Arthur Claypoole."

Molly Gerson finally looked at Adam. She had not been crying and didn't look like she was close. She shot an angry glare at Bill, but said nothing.

"I'll leave you alone," Bill said, backing away even as he said it.

"I understand you approached Hope Claypoole earlier today," Adam continued. "You told her you were her birth mother."

Molly raised one perfectly painted eyebrow, showing off the blue-gray shadow that covered her eyelids. She moved her lips to rub them together as if reapplying her lipstick. Her eyes ran over Adam, up and down, then turned to take a similar look at Pete. She picked up her glass, took a long drink, then replaced the almost empty glass in front of her. She raised one hand and a waiter appeared almost immediately to refill her glass from the bottle cooling in an ice bucket beside the table.

She took another drink, a sip this time. Finally, she spoke.

"Yes."

Adam waited a moment, but she said nothing more. "Yes?"

Molly smiled thinly. "Yes, I approached Hope Claypoole and told her that I am her birth mother."

"And are you?"

"Yes."

This was turning into a very monosyllabic interview. Adam looked over at Pete, who seemed to be enjoying this.

"Ms. Gerson, do you have any proof of your relationship to Hope?"

"Yes," she said again, but this time added, "please call me Molly."

"Fine, Molly. What proof do you have?"

Molly lifted one shoulder in a shrug, a movement that struck Adam immediately as familiar. He'd seen Hope make the same gesture, with the same expression. But that meant nothing.

"I have her birth certificate, of course. The copy Arthur has is just a copy. I have the first. The original."

"And why did you wait until now to see Hope?"

"I didn't."

This time, Adam waited her out. She took another drink, eyed him coldly, then continued. "I decided about a year ago that I wanted to meet her. I hadn't planned to, originally. When Arthur adopted her, we agreed it would be better for everyone if I was not part of the baby's life."

"So you stayed away? But you knew about her?" Pete finally chimed in.

Another lopsided shrug. "I knew. And I stayed away." She picked up her glass, looked at it, then put it down without drinking. "I realized recently that I need to meet her. I need to know her. I hadn't expected to feel so ... so strongly about it. But I do." She glared at Adam again, as if challenging him to question her need.

"I understand," he said instead. "So what happened?"

Molly pursed her lips, as if recollecting a bad memory. "I found her quite easily, obviously. The Claypooles don't exactly hide their wealth, do they? They flaunt their presence wherever they are." She blew out a soft breath. "I wasn't sure how to approach her. I knew Arthur hadn't told her about me — it's what we'd agreed to, after all. So I couldn't exactly pick up the phone and call her, could I? Hello, dear," she said in a mimicking tone, one hand acting as a phone against her ear, "it's your long-lost mother. How are you?"

"No, I guess not. You could have found a way, though," Pete said.

"I tried," Molly said. "I knew I couldn't call or email. A letter, maybe, I thought about that." She laughed softly. "I started going out to places where I thought she'd be, hoping to run into her, maybe even strike up a friendship." She shook her head. "How stupid of me."

Adam and Pete both stayed quiet as Molly drank more wine, signaled to the waiter for more.

"Then you heard about the cruise," Adam finally prompted her.

"Yes." She looked at him. "It seemed perfect. The perfect opportunity. I mean" — she waved one hand airily — "I couldn't let Arthur see me, of course. He might have recognized me and put a stop to my plans. But that wasn't as hard as I'd feared, with them all tucked away safely in first class." She gave another thin smile before sipping more of her wine.

Adam wondered if she always drank this much, this fast. It didn't seem to be affecting her, at least not as far as he could tell.

"So you avoided Arthur and kept an eye out for Hope."

Molly nodded. "I did. He didn't seem to be coming out around the ship much at all. I had a few opportunities to see Hope, but none seemed the right time. I finally saw her in the lounge with that young man, so I approached her. I introduced myself."

"That didn't go so well, did it?" Pete asked.

"Hadn't you wondered where Arthur was all this time?" Adam added.

Molly's eyes flashed and she put both hands flat on the table in front of her. "Of course I didn't," she said, her voice high and tight. "Why the hell would I wonder that? I was just glad he wasn't around. I assumed he was spending time in his gold-plated cabin or something." Her voice had dropped again, her eyes moving back and forth around the room.

"You didn't know he was dead," Adam said.

"I didn't know. How could I? It wasn't public information."

"So you approached Hope. What happened?"

"What happened?" Molly almost laughed. "That man — the one who practically kidnapped me at knifepoint to make me stay here and talk to you ... he ran me off, sent me away like a ... a ..." She moved her lips as if looking for a word she couldn't find.

"Tell me about yourself," Adam said.

Molly looked up at him, surprised. "What do you mean?"

"I want to know more about you. What do you do for a living? Where do you live? Are you married?"

"Oh... Oh." She looked at Pete. "He asks a lot of questions, doesn't he?"

Pete nodded. "It is our job."

"Hm." Molly turned back to Adam. "I am a lawyer. In New Jersey, just outside New York. And no, I am not married. By choice. I always put my career first."

"And what changed?" Adam asked.

"Changed?"

Adam raised both hands, as if apologizing for asking the

question. "Why did you realize you needed to know Hope?"

"Ah." Molly nodded, pursed her lips again. "Yes. Things did change."

Adam dipped his head, his eyes questioning.

Molly took another sip of wine. "Cancer." She whispered the word, the way so many people did. It wasn't a word people liked to say too loudly, as if it would call the wolf out of the forest.

"I see," Adam replied.

"Yes. Breast cancer." Molly took another deep breath. "So that was two reasons I needed to see her. She has a right to know her medical history. This sort of thing is hereditary," she explained, looking back and forth between the men, who nodded their understanding.

"And you were afraid you might die," Adam added.

"Yes." Molly looked down again. "There is always that fear."

"Ah, Adam, finally here to take a class?" Marcus waved across the lobby. "I'm sorry to break it to you, but this isn't one of my classes."

Adam saw Julia and Hope sitting near each other at the front of the group, Alice Murphy flipping through slides.

"I'm going to make it to one of your lectures, you'll see." Adam made his way across the room.

Just as he squatted down next to Julia's seat, the slide show dimmed.

"For those of you interested in owning your own copies of some of the works of art I've shown this evening, the art auction will be held tomorrow morning in the Manchester

Dining Room." Alice Murphy turned back to her class. "And for those of you who want to follow this progression of European art into the twentieth century, please join me back here again after the auction."

A few people applauded, others simply rose from their seats, chatting with their neighbors. The lounge didn't empty as much as dissolve, small clusters of people forming around some of the sofas, near the coffee bar, in the benches along the windows.

Julia and Hope stood, but instead of moving away from their seats, Julia raised a hand to Alice. Alice waved back and, shoving a notebook under her arm, squeezed between the disorganized chairs to come over to them.

"Another wonderful class, Alice, thank you." Julia shook her teacher's hand. Hope nodded, though without enthusiasm.

"That's very kind, thank you. And is this your boyfriend?" Alice turned to Adam.

Julia shuddered exaggeratedly. "Oh, no, this is my big brother. Adam Kaminski, this is Alice Murphy."

"Oh, yes, the detective." Alice cast a furtive glance at Hope, then looked back at Adam. "How nice to meet you. Your sister is quite talented. I've looked at some of her photographs and they're stellar."

"Thanks. We're pretty proud of her."

"Hope, I hope my lecture helped bring a little beauty to your mind." Alice spoke softly to Hope, who offered a small smile in return.

"Thanks Alice, it did. You've been very kind. Everyone's been so kind."

"You've got a lot of family here with you, that must be good for you," Adam said, trying to make the comment natural, subtle. Her family, in reality, seemed more like a den of vipers than a web of support.

"Sure. Yes." Hope's response was distracted.

"Are you close with them?" Adam asked.

"With who?" Hope looked confused.

"Well, for example, Paul?"

"Paul? No, not really. Actually, I just met him this trip, he's kind of a distant cousin, I guess. But Bill's been great. He's always been so supportive of me. It seems like whenever something goes wrong, Bill is always there for me."

"That's nice, dear." Alice smiled. "He seems like a very nice young man."

"He's disappointed he can't help more. With the investigation, I mean." She looked at Adam. "Can't you use his help?"

"His help? Oh, yeah, of course. I appreciate that he wants to help. It's just ..." Adam didn't want to say anything to set Hope off, but wasn't about to make promises he knew he couldn't keep, either.

"Because he doesn't have his work kit with him, I know." Hope looked down.

"Yeah, that's the thing." Adam said, relieved.

"Life is funny that way, isn't it?" Alice added. "You think you know one thing, but then it's another."

"What do you mean, Alice?" Julia asked.

"Well, it's like your photographs. What you see isn't always what you see, is it?"

"That's true, the camera catches so much more than the eye."

"Or maybe it's because we see things so quickly, but when we go back and really examine a photograph, we see so much more." Alice nodded. "It helps to talk about it. To share it with others, of course. I mentioned this just the other day—"

"Adam!"

Adam turned to see Marcus and Karen waving in their direction.

"Excuse me." He maneuvered his way across the lounge to them.

"Adam, would you please join Karen and me for dinner? We're just going to eat in the main dining room, nothing fancy."

Adam had seen the main dining room and didn't entirely agree with the assessment that it wasn't fancy. But it certainly offered good food.

"Thanks, I'd love to. I had planned to eat with my sister and partner, though."

"Perfect, it's settled, then," Karen said. "You'll all join us. It will be fun company. I suspect you need a little fun after the day you must've had."

She smiled mischievously at him and Adam couldn't help but agree.

THE BLACK-SUITED WAITER hovered behind Adam as he took his order, then moved on to Pete. Adam hadn't realized how hungry he was until he'd caught a whiff of the food being served in the main dining room tonight. The heady, spicy scent of a grilled steak served with a red wine sauce, the sweet smell of dill over grilled salmon, even the onions in the omelets smelled tantalizing — though not tantalizing enough to stop Adam from ordering the steak.

Some of his fellow diners had dressed up for the evening, a few women in sparkly dresses, men in dark suits and ties. The group at his table had kept it casual, as he had, changing out his khaki pants for trousers, his T-shirt for a button-down.

It wouldn't have mattered what Karen wore, she'd still have looked gorgeous. As it was, her silky golden shirt brought out the highlights in her hair, the yellow flecks in her otherwise dark brown eyes. She smiled when she saw him looking at her and raised her wine glass in a mock toast. Adam reached for his pre-dinner whiskey and returned the look.

"I feel like we uncovered too much today." Pete, sitting next to Adam, kept his voice low so the others across the table couldn't hear. "We need to sort through it all."

"OK, let's talk it through," Adam agreed.

"The bulk of Claypoole's family were together until the early hours of the morning, playing that card game they kept going on about," Pete said. "Without knowing the exact time of death, it's likely that gives them all an alibi."

"I know, it's frustrating," Adam agreed. "I also want to know why Arthur Claypoole chose this cruise."

"For Hope?" Pete suggested.

"Or because he expected to get something out of it."

"A payoff?" Pete asked, his expression one of surprise. "That would implicate Captain Harding, wouldn't it?"

Adam laughed bitterly. "Like you said, there's too much going on here. We're on a floating City of Gotham." He downed the rest of his whiskey. "Look, we're just supposed to be keeping an eye on everyone though, right? Keeping the rest of the passengers safe."

"Hm," Pete mumbled, "if you set the bar that low, then we're doing fabulous."

"Yeah, I guess. Brad inherits everything, that makes him a prime candidate."

"Yeah, but how the hell'd he do it? Where'd he get his hands on cyanide and how'd he get it onboard? Doesn't make sense."

"You two are talking shop, aren't you?" Julia leaned forward to speak around Pete. "I thought this evening was supposed to be a chance to get away."

"It is." Adam smiled, then glanced at Karen when he saw that she and Marcus were listening in as well. "It's just that sometimes it helps to hash things out, talk them through. You know."

"Paul's got something he's hiding," Pete continued. "That much is clear."

"Paul? But he's so sweet," Julia chimed in again.

Pete's frown deepened and his eyes narrowed as he recoiled from Julia's comment. "Sweet? We don't know what his real business is. No one in the family seems to know him well."

"Pete's right, Jules. And why do you think he's sweet? He seems kind of boring to me."

Julia raised a shoulder as she dipped her spoon into her crab bisque.

"Hope has to be a suspect, too," Pete continued. "She may've expected to inherit a little more on her father's death."

"Hope?" Julia put her spoon down. "You must be kidding. Have you seen how heartbroken she is?" She glared at Pete. "Do you have to be suspicious of everybody?"

"Sorry, Julia. It's the nature of the job. Everyone's a suspect until they're cleared."

"Or the real killer is found," Adam added. "It makes sense. She might not've known about the will."

"Then what about Bill?" Julia asked. "He's a suspect too, right?"

"Bill?" Adam asked. "Absolutely. Though I don't see a motive for him. Do you know anything I don't know?"

"No." Julia shook her head lightly. "He's in love with Hope. Would that be motive?"

"I suppose it could be." Adam frowned and took a last sip of his whiskey as his dinner was placed before him. "But why? How?"

"And now we have to add Hope's mother," Pete said.

"The problem we come back to with all the suspects," Adam said, "is means. How'd they do it?"

"Am I a suspect?" Karen asked from across the table.

"I don't think so." Adam laughed. "Did you know Arthur Claypoole?"

"I did say hello to him when we came on board. We sat near each other during the champagne toast at launch."

"There was a champagne toast?" Julia asked. "How did I miss that?"

"Ah." Marcus made a face at her. "That was for the first-class passengers. I believe there was a gathering for the rest of the passengers as well, wasn't there?"

Julia laughed. "You mean the pink cocktails in plastic cups at the pool deck? Yeah, I was there for that." She stopped for a moment. "I wonder if I met any of the family then. I don't think so."

"Most of them are in the first-class section, aren't they?" Adam asked.

"Not Paul," Julia answered.

Pete gave her a look. "How'd you know that?"

"I don't know." Julia shrugged. "I guess it came up in conversation."

"Do you hear the music?" Marcus jumped in before Pete could respond. "This is a wonderful piece. Actually an important part of Bermudian history."

Karen relaxed into her chair as Marcus explained the history of the song, then added a bit of her own opinion of the music. The conversation gradually turned to less murderous talk and Adam felt his shoulders relax, the frown lines on his face go away.

Pete and Julia sat leaning in toward each other, shoulders touching, sharing smiles. This is what life was supposed to be like. Eating, drinking, sharing stories with friends. Not murder. Not investigations. Not complicated relationships that hid more than they revealed. He forced himself to stop thinking about death. Or Arthur Claypoole.

By the end of the meal, when Karen stepped up next to him as they were leaving the dining room and invited him back to her suite for after-dinner drinks, he saw no reason to decline.

20

"Where were you, man? I had crew looking all over the ship." Wayne couldn't hide his anger, pacing up and down the narrow corridor outside the cabin, glaring at Adam. Pete stood beside him, silent.

"Shit, sorry." Adam was still tucking in his button-down shirt as he approached. "I just heard about it. Who found her?"

Pete gestured with his chin toward a young woman slumped on one of the tiny bunkbeds in the cabin, a cabin even narrower than Adam's own. "Bunkmate. All the crew share quarters. Tina here chose to share someone else's last night" — Pete paused to look Adam up and down and narrowed his eyes — "which happens on cruise ships, I guess. She came home early and found Alice."

The two bunk beds meant four crew members shared this cramped space. Though judging by the number of hours they worked, they probably didn't spend too much time in their cabins anyway. Adam looked to the other bunk. The ship's doctor had come and gone, and the body was covered in a thin sheet. Adam pulled back the sheet. He needed to see the face of the woman he'd failed.

He looked down at Alice Murphy.

"Our job was to keep an eye on things. Make sure everyone stayed safe," he said through gritted teeth.

"Yeah," Wayne responded.

"We failed."

"Yeah." Wayne put a little more emphasis into the word this time and shoved his hands into his pockets.

"What'd the doc say?" Adam asked.

"Suffocated, most likely. Not strangled. No ligature marks."

"Suffocated ..." Adam looked around the miniature cabin. A narrow closet held a handful of clothes, a washbasin, shower, and toilet were barely hidden behind a folding door. Each bed had two pillows, two blankets. "Any indication of poisoning? Maybe to knock her out before she was suffocated?"

"Doc said he didn't think so. He took blood samples to send to the police lab in Hamilton, but said he saw no indications."

Adam shrugged. "There aren't always visible indications."

"But it's quite clear she was suffocated," Pete added. "Something held over her face. No marks left at all."

"So something soft. Maybe a pillow. But you know how hard that is to do to a healthy person. She would've fought back, there would've been a struggle."

"And that would've left evidence. But no, no signs of a struggle. She just lay there and let the guy suffocate her."

Adam glanced at Pete. "I don't buy it."

Pete shook his head and shrugged. "Either way, it's a completely different MO."

"So you think we've got two killers on board?" Adam asked, surprised.

"Of course not. But I think this means we can stop looking at the other deaths by cyanide that I'd pulled up."

"Ah, right." Adam looked back at Alice, then pulled the sheet up over her face. "I guess that's good. I didn't like that idea, anyway. Not here."

"No," Pete said softly. "Or anywhere. I hate the wackos."

Adam shook his head at his friend. They both knew they were all "wackos," everyone who killed another human being. "We really screwed up here. We need to figure out what's going on, and fast."

"Yes, you do." Wayne spoke again, his voice low with anger. "Two people are dead on my ship and you two are nowhere near figuring out why."

"Does that mean no more nights of evening cocktails in Karen Sigelman's suite?" Pete was already heading out the door of the cabin.

"Look, I'm sorry, man. I just wanted to relax. Enjoy myself. I had no idea."

"Calm down." Pete looked back at him. "It didn't matter where you were, it's not like you were going to stake out Alice Murphy's cabin just in case. We have to sleep sometime. I wasn't here, either."

"I know, but we should've been focused on the case. From now on we will be."

"We'll catch him, Adam, and fast." Pete pulled the cabin door shut behind them with a bang.

21

"Clearly, it wasn't helpful. I see no point in continuing your involvement in this." Captain Harding barely looked up from the clipboard in his hand. Adam and Pete had followed Wayne to find Harding huddled with a handful of crew in an airy room lined with windows looking out onto the bridge. Wayne visibly cringed at Harding's words, but didn't speak up in support of the detectives.

"No point? Our involvement?" Adam felt his anger rising and fought to keep his voice under control. "You've got a second person dead on board your ship, Captain. I'd say that's a very good reason to investigate."

"I'm well aware of the status of my passengers and crew, Detective." Harding finally looked up. "It's quite clear now that we have a killer on board the ship. You don't think I'm concerned about that?"

"Then why tell us to stop investigating?" Pete asked, placing a hand on Adam's arm as Adam opened his mouth to speak.

"I'm not stopping the investigation, gentlemen. I'm

simply telling you that *your* involvement is no longer necessary."

"But who else on board this ship can handle this?" Adam asked, baffled. "Your own security chief asked for our help."

Harding glanced at Wayne, who'd turned crimson. "And he will continue to monitor the situation. The FBI and BPS have been alerted. They're waiting our arrival and will board the ship the moment we dock."

"And until then?" Adam asked through gritted teeth. "We just wait around for someone else to die?"

Harding's grip tightened on his clipboard, his knuckles whitening. When he spoke, his voice was low. "You exaggerate, Detective. This is not some kind of floating death ship. We clearly have a very sick person on board. Someone willing to murder other human beings. All of my crew are on high alert. If you would let me do my job, I'm in the process of putting steps in motion to revise the ship's schedule to better be able to manage the passengers' safety."

"Then why tell us to stand down? We can help."

"Detective Kaminski, I appreciate your concern. And I will certainly appreciate any help you can offer to keep my passengers safe. You have training and skills that I do not discount ... though they weren't sufficient to help Ms. Murphy," he added under his breath. Then more loudly, "I simply believe we must leave the investigation to the proper authorities."

"You weren't so concerned about waiting for the proper authorities yesterday morning," Pete pointed out.

Adam saw a hint of a smile cross Harding's face. "You're in the clear now," Adam said. "Now that someone else has been killed, the first death was obviously not an accident or caused by the fumigation."

"That's true," Harding admitted. "It's no less tragic."

"But a lot less tragic for you. You're not worried about what they'll find." Adam paced, infuriated. "OK, fine, I get that. But why call us off?"

"As I said, I'm not calling you off the case. I appreciate any help you can offer to keep my passengers safe. I simply want to ensure that you do not complicate the investigation unnecessarily. My job is to preserve the safety of my passengers and crew and to preserve any evidence that may remain on board. That's it."

"That's it?"

Harding nodded and returned his attention to his crew members, leading his team away from Adam and Pete.

"That's bullshit," Adam fumed.

"I know. But he's right. We were never officially on the investigation anyway, you know that."

"He only agreed for us to be involved because he thought we could save his skin — to show that Arthur Claypoole didn't die because of his mistakes."

"But we still have a duty to offer our help, Adam. We don't just walk away, do we?"

Adam thought about what they'd done so far. Which boiled down to not much, really. Now they had a choice to make: let Harding push them around or push back in the only way they could. "No way. We've already got statements from the main suspects. We know who has motives."

"Too many of those."

"We don't know how the killing was done. Maybe this second death will help us with that."

Pete shook his head. "The ship's doctor already said there was no evidence at the scene."

"Let's get Bill in here as well. Maybe he can see something the doctor missed."

"I guess it's worth a shot," Pete said skeptically. "I'm not thrilled getting him involved."

Adam kept pacing. "This was our fault, Pete."

"We've been through this. There was nothing we could've done."

"I don't blame Harding for not trusting us with the case anymore. We did nothing to help. And now another person is dead." Adam slammed his hand into the wall and stormed out of the room.

Adam paid no attention to his path, striding through empty hallways back to the public area, then pushing through the narrow doorway onto the outer deck, ignoring the group of passengers trying to enter. He saw nothing but the water in front of him, his vision narrowed by his rage. He was angry at the captain for claiming his help wasn't needed. He was angry at Pete for trying to be rational. But most of all, he was angry at himself. For letting Alice Murphy die.

"Watch it."

Adam looked over at the sharp voice. Paul Burke stood in front of him, rubbing his arm.

"Watch where you're going, will you?" Paul repeated.

"Who are you?" Adam snapped out the question.

"Me? We met. You interviewed me, remember?" Paul's voice carried more than a note of sarcasm. "You know exactly who I am."

"I know what you want me to know," Adam said. "Want to tell me again about your job? What is it exactly that you do?"

"I work for Breston Miller. I already explained all of this to you."

Paul tried to push past him toward the door, but Adam grabbed his arm, turning him back around.

"Yeah, you underwrite long-term loans. So why did I overhear you on the phone talking about Russian labs?"

"Why? Because you were eavesdropping, obviously." Paul's eyes narrowed. "Who the hell do you think you are?"

"I'm a cop. And I'm investigating a murder."

"Yeah, and what does that have to do with me?" Paul turned again, as if to walk away.

This time Adam grabbed him with both hands and flung him against the railing. "Don't walk away from me, buddy."

"You're out of control, you know that?" Paul snarled. "You're pissed because someone else died on your watch. I get that. But don't take it out on me."

Adam took a step back. "How did you hear about that? The captain isn't alerting the passengers."

Paul shrugged. He looked down at his arms as he adjusted the sleeves of his light jacket. "News travels fast, I guess."

Adam shook his head. "No. It doesn't. Tell me again about your job."

"Why the hell are you so interested in my job? So I don't underwrite loans, is that what you want to hear? Yeah, you caught me. I'm only at Breston Miller to dig up corporate secrets. You think I'm going to go broadcasting that around? Might as well have expected Arthur Claypoole to admit why he gave his money to certain charities and not others."

"What does that mean?"

"That we all have secrets, Detective, and mine is what my job really is."

"You're a corporate spy? Who do you really work for?"

"Kuznetsov Banking Group. They're a competitor. It's no big deal. It happens all the time."

"Then why didn't you tell me?"

"Seriously?" Paul looked appalled. "It's not the kind of thing I tell anyone. Ever."

"Then why tell me now?"

Paul took a deep breath. "You pissed me off. I assume that was intentional."

Adam laughed sharply. "I find it helps sometimes. In digging out the truth."

"So now you have it. What are you going to do about it?"

"Me? Maybe nothing. We'll see if Pete can confirm it."

"Confirm it? You think I'm on the Kuznetsov payroll or something? This is big business, buddy, it's not something you can Google."

"You let me worry about how to do the detective work."

"Yeah, 'cause you're doing such a bang-up job so far." Paul grimaced. "Can I go now?"

"What did you mean about Arthur Claypoole?"

Paul shrugged. "You think he was the type of man to give money away just to be a good citizen?" He laughed. "Maybe you need to learn a little bit more about what kind of man Arthur Claypoole really was."

Adam felt his anger rising again. "So why don't you tell me."

Paul shook his head. "Not me, I didn't know him that well. Just rumors. Hearsay. You want the truth? You need to talk to his family. His close family. Now, are we done?"

Adam nodded and Paul sauntered off, back in the direction he'd come from, hands in his pockets.

Corporate spy? Maybe. That would explain why he was putting Adam off, but not why the State Department would care about him. Adam sure as hell wasn't going to just take his word for it. About Paul or about Arthur Claypoole.

———

ADAM DIDN'T HAVE the patience to wait for the sliding door, pushing his way through into the main lounge before it was fully open. He knew Paul was lying to him. But he needed to prove it. And find the truth.

Of all the family, Hope seemed to know Paul the best. She said she'd just met him, but she might have picked up a few things about Paul that he'd missed. Hopefully she was in a better emotional state than last time he'd seen her, after meeting a woman who claimed to be her mother. He couldn't imagine what it was like to be adopted. She'd had a great life, sure, but she also knew that her own mother hadn't wanted her. Or perhaps hadn't been able to support her. He could understand why she wasn't interested in starting a relationship with her.

On the other hand, he also couldn't imagine how hard it must have been for Molly to give up her child. When he and Sylvia were still together, he'd started imagining himself as a father. He smiled now, just thinking about it, then caught himself and lost the smile.

He would've been a good father, he was sure of it. Not typical, perhaps. Not a lot of dads spent their days with drug dealers, thieves, and murderers. But at least he had his head on straight, he knew what was right and what was wrong. Those were qualities he could have passed on to a son. Or a daughter.

"Young man! You!"

He twirled around toward the voice that had interrupted his thoughts and saw the rotund figure of Betty wiggling toward him, waving a beefy arm in the air, loose folds of skin flapping as she waved.

"Betty, yes. Are you looking for me?"

"Why, no, are you looking for me?" She'd made it all the way to his side by now and smiled up at him sweetly.

Adam clenched his jaw and tried to smile. "You were calling me."

"Oh, yes. I saw you come in, and thought I'd say hello. Such a tragic situation, this. So sad." She tsked and shook her head as she looked around the lounge.

"Are you looking for someone in particular?" Adam asked. When she didn't respond, he repeated, "Looking for someone?"

"Well, who could know?" she replied incongruously. "But that he died before he could say, really."

Adam put a gentle hand on her shoulder and turned her to face him. "Betty? What are you talking about?"

She smiled up at him again and Adam saw the tears in her eyes this time. "Come over here." He guided her to a nearby chair and made sure she was sitting comfortably before perching on the chair opposite. "Are you OK, Betty? I know how upset you must be at your cousin's death."

"Well, we all must go at some point, you know." She waved away an approaching waiter and turned her attention back to Adam. "I suppose it must have been Arthur's time." She frowned and clamped her lips together, letting only a whimper slide out.

"I'm very sorry for your loss." Adam resorted to the phrase he seemed to use more often than any other. "You said something just now, about not saying anything?"

"Not saying what?"

"I don't know, you didn't say. But I'm very curious, especially if it was about Arthur."

She looked at him in confusion. "You're a very strange young man," she finally said.

Adam looked down at his folded hands, trying to figure out how best to dig out whatever thought had been so close to the surface of Betty's cluttered mind just a moment before.

She reached into her handbag and pulled out what looked like a wallet. "You don't need to pay for anything ..." he started to say, then saw her flip the wallet open with a flick of her wrist. A string of photographs cascaded down from the wallet like a plastic waterfall.

"You have pictures," he said helplessly.

"We never know, do we?" She looked over her photographs, then back at him. "I always keep these with me. We never know who we will lose next." She pulled the plastic-covered pictures through her fingers like a rosary, mumbling names under her breath as each picture passed through her gaze. Finally she stopped and held one up for Adam to see. "Arthur and me, when we were younger."

Adam took the photograph, pulling it out of its plastic casing despite the unhappy look Betty gave him. "You look very happy." He wouldn't have recognized Arthur or Betty from this photograph. It must have been at least fifty years earlier, a group of young people who stood around what looked like the Horseshoe Falls. "Niagara Falls?" he asked.

She nodded. "That one's Arthur. That's me, of course."

"Of course," Adam mumbled, refusing to admit that he couldn't have picked either of them out.

"And Sarah, Martha, John." Betty went on with a few more names. "Arthur had just finished business school, we were celebrating."

"You were very close with your cousin?"

"Oh, yes, our whole family."

"I understand Arthur was born in Russia? Claypoole doesn't strike me as a particularly Russian name."

"He was." Betty nodded. "And no, it's not. My parents were the first to come to the United States, and when they did, they changed their name. It used to be Klasprot. Arthur was the last of the Klasprots to be born there, and his parents changed their name as well, as soon as they came to the U.S. The rest of us didn't arrive on the scene until the family was settled in the New World, as they say." A smile played on her lips.

"Do you keep in touch with family back in Russia?"

"Still there? Oh, no, there's no one there. Not anymore." Betty looked like she was about to cry again, so Adam changed the subject.

"What else can you tell me about Arthur?"

"He was such a good man. A good, good man," Betty said as she replaced the photograph and went looking for another. "Always helping others, always doing the right thing. Like with his children."

"His children?" Adam asked.

Betty had found the photograph she was searching for, and held it out for Adam to see, this time keeping a firm grasp on it and not letting go. "Here he is with baby Bradley."

Adam looked at the photograph. He recognized Arthur in this one, it was only thirty-odd years old, the man in the photograph at least recognizable as the old man Adam had seen lying dead just the day before. He was hit with a wave of sadness and blinked, shutting his mind to emotions. "Who are the other people?"

"Well, that's Bradley, of course." Betty pointed to a bundle of blue blankets, in which a face might just have been visible.

"And who's holding him?"

"That's his mother." Betty's voice was wistful.

"Arthur's wife."

"Oh, no, she was infertile. Unable to have children." Betty shook her head. "Poor Angela."

"I don't understand." Adam let go of the photograph to look at Betty. "Who's Brad's mother?"

"Ah ... Natasha, I think her name was. I'm not really sure. My memory is not what it used to be."

"Arthur had another wife?"

"Don't be ridiculous. He loved Angela. Very much. And they both wanted children."

Adam took a moment to absorb this information. "Brad is adopted. As well."

Betty nodded as she tucked her line of photographs back into her wallet. "It was all very hush-hush. This was in ...well, perhaps not the most open circumstances. The mother couldn't keep the baby... Arthur and Angela wanted him so badly. They made ... well, they made arrangements."

"It was an illegal adoption?"

"Don't look so shocked, young man. It happens more than you realize. And everyone came out better for it, didn't they?"

"Does Brad know?"

Betty pulled her lips into a tight line. "Arthur was afraid to tell him, you see. At first. And then after they'd waited, it seemed too late. When they adopted Hope, so much later, there was really no way to tell Brad then."

"So Brad doesn't know?"

Betty looked up at Adam again, but seemed to have been cheered by her walk down memory lane. "We all have to go at some time, don't we? It's just such a tragedy he didn't get to tell him. Such a tragedy."

22

Alice's class had been scheduled for a smaller room this morning, not far from the auction that was still going on in the Manchester dining room. Perhaps they had been prepared for a smaller group. Perhaps they had known something would go terribly wrong.

Julia stopped at the door before entering, a shiver of fear running through her. This was silly, she told herself. Get a grip.

"Julia!"

Thank goodness, Adam. He waved as he moved toward her and she jogged to close the distance, hugging him close as soon as she could.

"Hey, are you OK? What's wrong?" He squeezed her back as he asked the questions.

She shook her head, held on for a second longer, then stepped back. "I'm not. I'm really not."

He lowered his head to look her in the eye, his expression a picture of concern and love. "Talk to me. Tell me what's going on."

She looked back into the dining room, where passengers

were slowly meandering in. "What happened to Alice?" she asked.

Adam took a breath and looked away. "I don't know. I'm sorry. I should've realized how upset you'd be. This isn't normal, seeing people die like this. Especially someone you'd become friends with."

"She was a friend, you're right. But it's not just that."

"Then what?"

"I'm afraid ... that is, I think it's possible ... ugh, I don't know." She threw her hands up in frustration and stepped away from her brother. "Why did she die? Can you tell me that? Why'd they kill her?"

"They?"

"I don't know, whoever's doing this. Was it because ... because of me?"

She could tell from the look on her brother's face that he thought she was being ridiculous. She'd seen that look enough times to know it well. "I'm serious," she continued. "I think it's possible."

"Why would you even say that?" Adam asked, pulling her close to him again, hugging her once more. "Of course it wasn't because of you. Any more than it was because of me or Pete."

"I told her I wanted to talk to her. To ask her questions. About the murder."

Adam straightened his arms, pushing her away to look her in the eye again. "Why did you do that?"

"Why?" Julia felt like she was going to cry. "Because you said you needed someone on the inside. And she's on the inside. Why'd you think?"

"Oh, Jules." Adam sighed as he said her name. "But why would that cause her death? You're not being logical."

"We weren't alone when I asked her." She looked up at Adam. "Bill was there. He heard me ask."

Adam dropped his hands from her arms. "You think Bill is involved? Why?"

"Like I said, he heard me telling Alice I needed to talk to her."

"That's not enough reason to suspect someone, Jules."

She stepped back from him, feeling her own anger rising. "You've suspected people for a lot less, Adam. I know that for a fact."

"OK, OK, you're right." He rubbed a hand across his chin, then through his hair. He looked tired and stressed. "What did Pete say when you told him?"

She smiled. "The same as you. He's gone off to dig up information on cyanide poisoning." She put a hand on Adam's arm. "I just need to know if I was responsible. I need you to find the truth. If anyone can, you can."

"Thanks," Adam muttered. "I wish I had as much confidence in myself as you do."

Julia shook her head. If only Adam could tell how other people saw him: his kind nature, his quick intellect, his willingness to do anything to see justice served. She wasn't helping him by giving in to her own fears. She needed to be the strong one. At least for now.

"So." She smiled up at him. "Pete says things between you and Karen seem to be going well."

Adam scrunched his face into an expression of bewilderment. "Why would Pete tell you that? You're my sister, for God's sake."

"He only mentioned it, that's all." She patted his arm again. "Just be careful, OK? I know you're still hurting."

Adam's face went blank. "Don't worry about me."

"I always worry about you. You know that. And I'm just

saying, take it slow. You know how you are. Flings are not your style. It's not who you are."

"Hey, we're on a cruise, right?" Adam raised his hands as if flinging something away. "We can all be someone different. That's the point. That's why you get away."

"But you could get hurt."

"Maybe the old me would've got hurt. Maybe the old me deserved to. For now, I'm going to be a different man. And Julia" — he looked down at her, his expression serious — "Don't worry about me. You just take care of yourself. I'll be fine."

He gave her a quick peck on the cheek and walked away. Julia watched him go for a moment before turning her attention back to the dining room.

The chief steward stood at the front of the room in a quiet conversation with the captain and a number of other staff members. Including Chef Guzeman, Julia noticed. As each expectant student came into the room and looked for a chair, a member of the staff would approach them and tell them something.

Julia wondered what they were saying. Simply that class was cancelled? Or the truth: that the teacher had been brutally murdered on board this very ship.

Probably the former.

She took a few steps into the room, moving toward the cluster at the front. Captain Harding had his back to her, but Guzeman caught her eye. He said something to Harding, who turned to see Julia. As he did so, Guzeman walked in the other direction, leaving the room by a different door.

"Julia, I thought you would've heard."

"I did. Of course," Julia acknowledged. "I'm not sure why I came. I guess ... I just wanted to do something. This is such a tragedy."

"Shh." Harding put a hand on her arm and pulled her away from another woman who had entered. With a jerk of his head, he sent another crew member over to the newcomer.

"What are you telling the other passengers?" Julia asked.

"Just that the class is cancelled. That Ms. Murphy is no longer available to teach these classes at all."

"So, you're not telling passengers about the murder?" Julia wasn't sure if she was surprised or not.

"We'll have to tell them something, of course. But you understand that their safety is my top priority. The last thing I need is people running amok out of fear."

"No, of course." Julia looked down as she nodded her agreement. "Is there anything I can do to help?"

"I already told your brother, I appreciate his help keeping the rest of the passengers and crew safe, but that's all. There's nothing more to be done until we dock tomorrow morning and the FBI come onboard."

"FBI?"

"They'll take over the investigation in Bermuda." Harding's response was distracted as he gestured to a crew member, who left the room.

"But what about until then?" Julia asked, confused.

"Hm?" Harding turned his attention back to her. "We'll keep everyone safe. I promise. My crew and I will be working around the clock, keeping very close tabs on all our passengers. No one else will be hurt on my watch."

Julia had no problem believing him. Which made it all the more odd that Alice's killer didn't seem to have had any difficulties. "So will you be cancelling all classes, then?"

"Cancelling? Of course not. On the contrary, I'm hoping to add some extra. To keep people busy, and in large groups. The last thing I want is everyone slinking off on their own. Alone."

"Ah. Then I can help." As soon as she'd said it, she regretted it. She'd let the words slip out as soon as the idea crossed her mind.

"You? How?"

"Well, I can teach the photography classes."

"Oh." Julia had been expecting a polite dismissal, perhaps even a sarcastic one, so she was caught off guard by Harding's tone. "Yes, I see."

"You do?"

"Yes, Alice had mentioned you to the chief steward. Said you were a photographer of some skill."

Julia felt herself blush and almost started to cry. "She said that about me?"

"You know, that's not such a bad idea. Gerry." He called out the last part, and the chief steward came over. "Ms. Kaminski here has offered to take over Alice's classes for her. Not this one, I'm sure" — he glanced at Julia, who quickly shook her head — "but perhaps you could work with her to schedule something for later today."

"Of course, sir." The chief steward eyed Julia skeptically, but didn't seem to object. "Come by ...oh, no—" He held up a palm. "Stay here, I'll be back in ten minutes with the day's schedule."

Both men abandoned her, so she let her gaze wander aimlessly around the room, at a bit of a loss. When Hope stepped into the doorway, Julia almost pounced on her.

"Hope." Julia waved her over. "Are you here for the class? I'm afraid it's been cancelled."

"Oh, drats. I was looking forward to it."

"Me, too." Julia opened her mouth to say more, to explain to Hope why the class had been cancelled, then realized that it might be too much for Hope to handle. "Actually, funny turn of events, I've been asked to teach some classes myself."

"You? How fun!" Hope's face lightened up. "Oh, I'm definitely taking any class you're teaching."

"Thanks for the support." Julia laughed. "I'm not sure exactly what yet. I'm waiting for the chief steward to come back with my assignment."

"At least it will give you something to do, to take your mind off whatever your boyfriend and brother are digging into."

Julia nodded. "Whatever they're digging into. Hey, tell me, how well did — I mean, do you know Alice Murphy?"

"Know her?" Hope shrugged. "Not at all. I took a few of her classes, that's all. Why do you ask?"

Julia tried to sound casual. "It's not important, I just wanted to get a sense of what her teaching style was like since I'll be taking over some of her classes."

"I see." Hope's eyes flitted around the room, watching other passengers as they entered only to be waylaid by members of the crew. "And she's not here for you to ask her yourself."

"What?" Julia knew her voice was sharp.

Hope flinched as if she'd been slapped. "What's wrong?"

"Nothing, nothing ... no, Alice isn't here."

JULIA WANDERED out of the dining room, her mind on the classes she'd agreed to teach. Gerry had returned with a proposed schedule, and Alice had not lied — it was a lot of hours. Gerry had only left her with a few hours before her first class.

She vaguely noticed the main lounge as she passed through it, letting her feet simply move as she tried to focus her mind. What could she possibly teach about? She thought about the classes Alice had offered. She needed to provide something similar. Something about color ...how we see things ...how photographs are different from what we see ...The ideas floated loosely around in her mind.

She stopped suddenly. She'd prepared a speech for a conference a year ago and it would be perfect. The challenge now: could she still remember it? She'd spent so long working on it, it must still be there, tucked into the back of her brain.

"Yes," she said aloud.

"Ma'am? Do you need help?"

She blinked and realized there was a young crewman standing directly in front of her. Or had she stopped in front of him?

"Oh, sorry, no." She mumbled her confused response.

"Need to get in here?" he asked, gesturing with his head toward a door whose dark purple glass blended smoothly with the walls around it.

This was one of doors that led to the first-class section of the ship. She hadn't even realized she'd stopped in front of it. It was so subtle, most passengers probably didn't even know what it was. No point rubbing it in their faces, she guessed.

The crewman winked. "I know you're helping with the investigation. No worries."

"Uh, yeah. Thanks." Her own keycard wouldn't have unlocked that door, only those with access privileges could pass through.

He slid his card over the lock and held the door open for her. She nodded her thanks as she passed through to the other side.

That was easy. Too easy. She'd been assuming the killer had to be someone with their own access to the first-class area. Which, unfortunately, ruled out Bill. But if she could get through this easily, then surely so could he.

That was two counts against him.

She passed along a wide hallway, up a few broad steps to a spacious room that opened up onto the pool. A buffet lined one wall of the room, but it couldn't be compared to the buffet near the public pool. This one offered silverware instead of plastic forks, china instead of paper plates, and it didn't look like most passengers were getting their own food. A steady stream of waitstaff passed back and forth, carrying plates out to passengers lounging in the sun.

She snagged a luscious looking strawberry as she followed one of the waiters out to the pool, then stopped to get her bearings. This pool was smaller than the one she was used to, but it offered a series of semi-private spaces around it, each boxed off with low bamboo walls. Beyond the pool, to the left and the right, wide hallways narrowed toward what must have been private cabins, though the doors were spaced so far apart she couldn't be sure.

She recognized a robed figure, even from the back, and walked in his direction. Brad had stopped by the pool, but as soon as she walked toward him, he moved away. Had he seen her? Or was that coincidence?

She wasn't following him, exactly. She just let herself wander slowly after him, curious where he was going.

She felt a bit of a fool when he entered the third cabin door down one of the halls. He was clearly going to his own cabin. Nothing too shocking there.

She glanced around, feeling out of place, and hurried back to the pool. Leaning far over a railing, she shut her eyes and lifted her face to the sun. She could hear the drone of the engines from a distance, the sound of people shouting and laughing coming from the sports deck a couple of flights down.

She needed to get a better sense of who was in which cabin. It had been so easy for her to gain access to this area — could someone like Bill have got in as easily? Or was the killer someone who'd walked Arthur Claypoole back to his cabin, then killed him? Someone he knew and trusted enough to let them stay in his cabin while he went to bed. Or maybe Bill was staying in first class. She wasn't even sure about that.

She shook her head at her own ignorance as she opened her eyes. She had more questions than answers. That wasn't going to help anyone.

She sighed and turned her back to the railing, letting her arms stretch out beside her. As she glanced to her right, she jumped.

Captain Harding was passing by, only inches away. "Oh —"She stopped. He hadn't recognized her. She had no reason to stop him. She had clear instructions from Gerry. In fact, she probably shouldn't even have been there just then, she should have been off somewhere working on her lecture.

She stood up, feeling guilty, and saw Harding enter Brad's cabin, swiping his own keycard to get in.

Well. That was weird.

23

Hope's cabin was empty. Or at least, she wasn't answering Adam's insistent knocks and calls. He stepped back from her door as a passing guest gave him a nasty look.

"Sorry," he mumbled, turning back toward the stairs.

"Sir, can I help?" A crew member had materialized out of nowhere, a solid figure in the white shorts and blue T-shirt worn by the activity crew.

"Where ...?" Adam glanced up and down the hall, but couldn't figure out where she'd come from. "Never mind, yes, you can. I'm looking for Hope Claypoole."

"She left her cabin about twenty minutes ago," the woman replied. "I believe she was looking for one of the activities."

"Of course, sorry, I should have realized," Adam chided himself out loud. "Look, I need to talk to her. Can you help me find her?"

"Sure." The young woman smiled brightly, lifting a radio off her belt. She spoke into it briefly, smiling the whole time. She paused, her eyebrows raised. "When we find her, a crew member will let you know where she is."

"Right, of course."

The woman nodded, finished her call and tucked her radio away again. "Message delivered. If a member of the crew spots her, they'll also let her know you're looking for her."

"Great, thanks." Adam paused before leaving. "How did you know who I was?"

The woman smiled again. "Oh, we all know that, sir. The chief steward asked us all to keep an eye on you."

Adam couldn't help but wonder if he'd meant a helpful eye or a watchful eye, but he didn't ask. He thanked her again and headed for the stairs that would take him down to the main lounge.

Paul was right, he did need to learn more about Arthur Claypoole. Understanding the victim in any murder was as important as understanding the killer — in fact, it was often the best way to find the killer. Pete could focus on the method of the murder, but Adam would always do best focusing on the people involved. And their motives.

His path brought him to the main lounge from the front of the ship and he paused, looking down from a vantage point he hadn't had before. He stood one level above the lounge, on a balcony that ran around the edges. Narrow but elegant stairs curved down toward the lounge, where a large number of passengers gathered, as usual. Marcus must not have been teaching, because the large screen at the front of the lounge showed a silent film of underwater life, coral, plants, and colorful fish floating in crystal-clear waters.

The guests dotted about the lounge ran the gamut from clusters of white-haired retirees enjoying a relaxing trip to groups of young children gathered together, heads bent intently over electronic devices. Couples cuddled quietly in dark, romantic corners of the room while to the far right, customers at the bar that lined one wall created a more raucous scene.

The room seemed to capture the diversity of the cruise itself. A place for everyone, where anyone could be whoever and whatever they wanted.

Even a murderer.

Adam's glance fell on a familiar face at the bar, and he crossed the balcony to take the stairs leading directly there.

"Gerald." He spoke as he leaned in next to the middle-aged man. "How are you feeling today?"

Gerald turned red-rimmed eyes toward him and offered a lopsided smile. "Have we met?"

"Adam Kaminski, we met yesterday morning in the bowling alley. You were ... distraught."

"Ah, yes." Gerald laughed grimly. "Distraught. Sounds like you've been talking with Betty."

Adam nodded and leaned in closer, having confirmed that Gerald was at least mostly sober. "I have. But I could tell you were upset. We all have our own ways of handling that."

Gerald raised his eyebrows and lifted the glass in front of him in a toast toward Adam, then downed the rest of the clear liquid.

"What're you drinking?" Adam asked.

Gerald inspected the glass in front of him. "Rum. Coconut flavored, very tropical. It seemed appropriate."

"I think most people would mix that with juice, though, wouldn't they?"

Gerald shrugged and gestured to the bartender for another.

"I can see you're still upset. Do you mind talking to me about it?"

"You? Why?" Gerald asked, sipping from his new glass.

"I'm looking into Arthur's death. It seems like you knew him pretty well. Part of the family and all."

Gerald took a deep breath and let it out, his eyes roving over the room in front of them, not settling on any one spot. "I'm part of the family, yes. You could say that."

"What does that mean?" Adam asked sharply.

Gerald's head jerked toward Adam. "What do you want me to say? What, you want to dig up bad memories? Like what's happening now isn't bad enough?" He downed the rest of his drink and waved the glass toward the bartender.

Adam knew he had better talk fast, before Gerald wasn't able to respond.

"What happened in the past? What's so bad that you don't want to think about it?"

Gerald closed his eyes, his head slumped over his shoulders. The bartender glanced at Adam as he slid a fresh glass toward them. Adam rolled his eyes, but didn't stop him.

"Our sister." Gerald finally spoke as he opened his eyes. "My other sister died."

"I'm sorry," Adam said. "That must have been difficult. Was she sick?"

"Sick?" Gerald laughed out loud. "She was the picture of health. Sick, phht." Gerald blew his breath out as he was taking a sip and rum sloshed out of the glass. He blinked and put it down. "She was not sick. She was killed."

"Killed? How?"

Gerald threw an arm up. "No one could figure it out. Police decided it was natural causes, but it wasn't. It couldn't have been."

"I don't understand."

Gerald looked Adam in the eye, and Adam was taken aback by just how sober he looked. "No, you don't."

"So why don't you tell me?" Adam waited, then added,

"Do you think Arthur was involved?"

Gerald nodded. "Of course. Arthur was always involved. In everything. He was in charge."

"In charge of what?"

"Like you said." Gerald shrugged, his hand moving along the bar to his glass. "The family."

Adam recognized the inflection of Gerald's voice. He also recognized the familiar term. "You think Arthur was involved in the Russian mob? Are others in your family involved?"

One side of Gerald's mouth lifted in a small grin. "You tell me. You're the cop. But I'll tell you what, after Nancy died, Arthur suddenly decided to let Hope run Nancy's gallery." He slammed his hand down onto the bar. "That was Nancy's business. She'd built it herself. Using her contacts, her own money. He had no right."

"Then how could he do it?"

Gerald shrugged again. "So there was a loan. A small loan. But it was enough. It gave Arthur control. He gave it to Hope. Nancy didn't have any kids, any partners. No one to complain about it. Hope just took over. This new interest of hers in being a patron of the art."

"So you think Arthur was involved in Nancy's death, and he did it to help Hope?" Adam shook his head. That didn't sound like any mob activity he'd ever heard of. He watched as Gerald took another drink, his head beginning to rock back and forth on his shoulders. "You take care of yourself, Gerald. Don't kill yourself."

Gerald didn't respond.

Adam left the man to his drink. Was Arthur involved in the Russian mob? Maybe. It was certainly possible. But he didn't buy Gerald's story for a second. The man had his own issues, clearly.

But he couldn't discount a rumor like that.

And where did Paul fit into this? Was he part of the mob, too? Or, given the warning Pete had received on digging into his past, was it more likely Paul was working undercover to stop them?

"Adam," Pete called out as he worked his way across the room. Adam pushed himself off the bar and moved toward him.

"Pete, I just got some interesting background from Gerald over there."

"Gerald?" Pete looked skeptical. "Do you trust him? He's already three sheets to the wind."

Adam looked back at Gerald, who did indeed look the worse for wear.

"Hey, I got some info on the poisoning, something concrete we can look into. Come on."

"Where're we going?" Adam asked as he followed Pete through the lounge.

"The kitchens."

"What? Why? You want to talk to Guzeman again?"

Pete glanced back at him. "Not necessarily. But he's definitely top of my list of suspects. Think about it. He's got a grudge. He's got access to all areas of the ship. And he's the only suspect who couldn't have done away with Arthur in any other location. He's got access here, but not at the Claypoole home."

"True," Adam had to agree. "So then why not talk to him?"

"I want proof first, and I've got an idea of what we can look for."

―――

"So a liquid, is that it? One that turns into a gas when heated up?"

"That's right," Pete answered Adam's question. "And there wouldn't need to be much of it."

"Hydrocyanic acid. Got it."

Pete's inquiries with his connections back home and in D.C. had produced viable information on how Arthur Claypoole could have been poisoned, and inhaling HCN, or hydrocyanic acid, vapors seemed the most likely. The absence of vomiting made it less likely the poison had been ingested. The fact that the man had succumbed too fast to get out of bed, convulsing where he lay, suggested inhalation.

"But why not use the same method on Alice? That's what I don't get." Adam grunted as he bent low to reach behind a stack of bowls in a ground level cabinet. The kitchen they were searching now was a maze of metal cabinets at all levels. Every inch of space was used efficiently, nothing standing loose, free to slip or slide as the giant ship shifted in the water.

"I don't know. Maybe he ran out."

Adam straightened up. "If he ran out, then what the hell are we looking for?"

Pete stood as well, stretching his neck from side to side as if working out a kink. "The vessel. He had to hold it in something."

Adam shook his head. "He would've gotten rid of it. Tossed it overboard."

"Yeah, probably. But we're hoping he made a mistake. We know Arthur enjoyed Guzeman'sdesserts, it's plausible he brought it to him personally. As a way to thank him for the reference letter, maybe.It would have been so easy for Guzeman to heat up the poison along with the crème brûlée, he was using a torch on it already. And if he did, he might have left the container somewhere in the kitchens or storage area. I already searched his cabin and came up empty."

"That's what we always hope, that stupidity saves the day," Adam grumbled and kept looking. After a few minutes, he turned back to Pete. "I just can't help thinking about that adoption."

"Like how could Brad not know?" Pete didn't stop his search as he answered and his voice was muffled, his back still turned.

"For one. And if he did know, how did that affect him?" He shook his head as he spoke. "But then we're back to means ... how could he have administered the HCN?"

Pete finally looked at Adam. "There's nothing here, we've looked everywhere. There are still two more kitchens, then the storage areas."

"If he knew he was adopted, he might not have known he was inheriting the bulk of Claypoole's fortune," Adam said.

"So that eliminates his motive, then."

"But if he didn't know, then he still has motive."

"Or, he found out and hated the old man for not telling him. That's a whole 'nother motive."

"True. But—" Adam cut himself off when he heard footsteps coming down the hall. Bill turned into the room, followed by Chef Guzeman.

"What are you doing in my kitchen?" Guzeman demanded, grabbing a nearby pan and holding it in front of his body as if it were a sword.

"Mr. Guzeman, calm down. We have the captain's permission to search here."

Pete gave Adam a quizzical look, but said nothing. He

knew as well as Adam that Harding had pulled them off the investigation. "Why are you here, Bill?"

"I overheard Chef Guzeman telling his staff he was coming to find you, so I thought I'd join. See if I could help."

"You do overhear a lot, don't you?" Adam asked. "I've told you before, I appreciate your offer, but we can't use your help."

"Fine, your loss." Bill scowled as he backed out of the room.

"You think I'm hiding something in my kitchen?" Guzeman glared at them both.

"It might not be you, but the kitchen is an obvious place to hide the kind of thing we're looking for," Adam explained.

"And what is that?" Guzeman asked.

Pete and Adam both kept their mouths shut.

"I came to tell you Hope Claypoole is in the main lounge. I understand you want to talk with her," Guzeman said, then added, "I should not be helping you." He stormed out of the room with a loud grunt.

"He clearly has motive and opportunity, given his run of the ship and his history with the Claypooles," Pete said.

"But unless we find a weapon, he has no means, no clear way he could have done it," Adam replied.

"So we keep searching. There are other kitchens."

Adam put a hand on Pete's arm. "Let's take a break from this. I want to talk to Hope again."

Pete sighed. "But we need hard evidence. If we can find proof someone used liquid HCN, we'll be a lot closer to catching our killer."

"Fine, you keep searching. I'm going to do what I do best."

24

"This is a waste of time," Pete said as he followed Adam back to the main lounge. "We can't just keep talking to people. We need evidence."

"Yeah, you mentioned that." Adam didn't look at Pete as he responded. "But we're on our own here, we don't have a police force backing us up, teams of uniforms doing the searching. You're the one who chose to come with me instead of continuing your search."

"So, what, you're too lazy to search yourself?"

Adam spun around to face Pete. "Seriously?"

Pete stepped forward and opened his mouth, but then seemed to think better of it. He took a step back and let his voice drop. "No, not seriously. Look, let's not go at each other. We need to work together."

Adam nodded and looked around the lounge. "There."

Hope sat in the middle of a deep-gold sofa, her legs crossed and angled across her body, one arm stretching along the back of the sofa. In her other hand she held a champagne flute and she sipped from it as she kept her eyes on the room. She looked the most relaxed Adam had seen her yet, as her shoulders moved subtly to the rhythm of the ever-present music. She saw Adam just as he saw her and raised her glass toward him.

"Come on."

Pete followed Adam as he wove his way across the room, navigating a path through the field of chairs and sofas, partying passengers, and roaming crew.

"I hear you were looking for me," Hope said with a smile as soon as they were within hearing range.

"Yeah." Adam perched on a seat opposite her, where he could look her in the eye as he talked to her. Pete sat on the sofa next to her, leaning back against the far arm to avoid Hope's expansive reach. "I appreciate you being willing to talk to us, with everything you're going through."

For a fraction of a second, Adam could swear Hope looked confused, but it passed quickly, her smile replaced with an expression of sadness. "Of course. You know I want to find out what happened to my father."

"I'm trying to learn more about your father. What he was like, who his friends were, what kind of ... activities he was into."

"Activities?" Hope asked. "I wouldn't know about that. He worked. I told you, I wasn't involved in his work."

"OK, then. Tell me about him as a father."

Hope's smile returned, but this time she had a faraway look in her eyes. "He was a great dad. He really was. He took care of me. Always."

"Like how?"

Hope shrugged and pulled her arms back together in front of her body. "What do you mean? Like how fathers are. He raised me. He sent me to school. He gave me a beautiful home, a good life. What else is there?"

Adam took a breath, thinking. "OK, then tell me about the charities he supported."

Hope glanced at Pete, then back at Adam. "Why?"

"We're trying to paint a fuller picture of who he was, that's all," Pete answered. "Get to know him a bit."

"I don't see how that will help," Hope said. "Aren't you trying to find out who killed him?"

Adam smiled. "Yes, of course, but there may be a connection."

"Oh, no, there isn't."

"How can you know that?" Adam asked.

"Because he was a great father. And that's not why he was killed." Hope spoke firmly. "Trust me."

Now it was Adam's turn to be confused. "I'm not suggesting he was killed because of what kind of father he was, Hope. I'm just trying ... oh, never mind. Was your father ever involved with people who were ... questionable?"

"Questionable? As in, illegal activity?" Hope laughed gaily. "Oh, dear, you've been talking to Gerald, haven't you?"

"So you've heard his ideas?"

"Everyone has." Hope waved her free hand. "No one listens to that drunk. Going on about his sister dying mysteriously. It was sad, tragic even, but not mysterious. And nothing to do with the Russian mob." She snickered again.

Adam looked at Pete, who shrugged. "Then tell me about Paul, you seem to be getting to know him quite well."

Hope smiled, a surprisingly girlish grin. "I guess." She looked down at her glass and blushed, pale pink blossoming across her cheekbones.

"So that's going well? Glad you met him?"

"I don't see how this could possibly be related to your investigation, Detective. Yes, it's going well. I'm happy I met him."

"And how much do you know about him?"

Hope's eyes widened. "What on earth are you asking me?"

Adam put up a hand. "About his character, his background, that's all. Nothing ... too personal."

"Well, I guess he's in business. Like Dad."

"Just like Dad?"

Hope frowned. "What does that mean?"

"How much do you know about him, really? Like where he really works, for example."

Hope blushed again, but this time it showed up in angry red blotches across her pale forehead. "What are you saying, that I don't really know him?"

"I'm asking what you *do* know." Adam spoke comfortably, realizing he'd pushed her into an embarrassing admission. "It's not bad that you just met, that's fine."

"You know what?" Hope stood, dropping her glass carelessly onto the ground next to her. "First Alice makes all these ridiculous assumptions about me and Bill. Now you're saying things about me and Paul."

"What did Alice say about you and Bill?" Pete asked, standing also.

Hope threw her hands in the air just as a passing waiter bent to retrieve her dropped glass. The waiter stepped back with a grunt and an apology when Hope's hand came back down, smacking his back. She ignored him. "Why does everyone think I'm having affairs with my cousins? That's .... Well, it's gross. I mean, they're not even rich."

Adam blinked at that but didn't respond. "I'm sorry, Hope, I didn't mean to upset you."

She closed her eyes and lifted a hand to cover her mouth in a delicate, graceful gesture. "Thank you," she finally responded, "I appreciate that. This is a very difficult time for me, you understand."

"Of course, we both do," Pete said.

She took a few deep breaths, her skin returning to its usual porcelain color. "I don't know what I'm going to do now, too. With Brad getting the inheritance ..." She blinked away tears.

"You said you knew that was coming."

She lifted one shoulder. "Knowing and accepting are not the same thing, are they? Plus, I thought my dad knew about Brad, that he'd change the will."

"Knew what?" Adam asked gently, afraid of spooking her again.

"Oh, it's nothing. Just that he's not exactly who everyone thinks he is. But like you said, I knew what to expect. No surprises here."

She glanced at a thin gold watch that twisted around her narrow wrist.

"I'm going to sit in on Julia's class. I don't want to miss it." She smiled at each of them, then slipped away.

"Wow, that was something." Adam blew out a breath.

"She's all over the place. Her emotions must be going crazy," Pete said. "But it's a tough time for her. Look, I need to see Julia teach, too. You coming?"

Adam glanced around the room, not sure what he'd accomplished by talking to Hope. There must be something useful he could pull from that conversation. He just needed to figure out what. "No, you go ahead. I'll keep searching the other kitchens."

"You?" Pete asked with surprise.

Adam shrugged. "You were right, talking isn't getting us

anywhere anyway. Come find me when you're done."

Julia let her mind drift as she looked around the small dining room. It wasn't a standing-room only crowd, but packed enough to make her nervous. Each of the twenty or so round dining tables had at least one student, some looking at her expectantly, others chatting away with each other over cocktails.

She took a deep breath and thought about her talk, the one she'd preparedfor a conference last summer, a talk about form and structure in photographs. It seemed the perfect topic when she thought of it earlier — a subject appropriate for the class and easy for her to cover, since she'd prepared so thoroughly.

Now, looking around the room, she was a lot less sure. Hope caught her eye, gave her a friendly nod and a smile. Another supportive — and sexier — grin from Pete at the back of the room, and Julia was ready. She let her breath out and started speaking.

An hour later, she was walking on clouds. She passed between the tables, looking at the sketches her students were producing, offering them advice and guidance. Or sharing a joke, when appropriate. She hadn't realized how much time had passed until she saw Gerry standing at the doorway tapping his watch.

"Oh, right." She moved back to the front of the room. "Sorry, I think I've gone a little long here. I hope that exercise was useful for you all." One party of six women was already standing and chatting, moving on to their next activity. "I'll be teaching another class this evening, if anyone's interested."

A few students stopped to offer their thanks. Julia hadn't realized before how much those little words of thanks could mean to a teacher. Letting her know they'd enjoyed the class. That they'd learned something. She was going to have to stop teasing Adam for missing teaching.

Finally, only Hope and Pete were left. Julia grabbed Pete's hand and turned to Hope. "Hope, thank you for coming. This was kind of nerve-wracking."

"You couldn't tell, believe me. You were great."

"Ms. Kaminski." Gerry approached, along with Chef Guzeman. "I watched your class, it was exactly on tune. Just what we needed. I hope you're still available to teach again later today?"

"I am, thanks." Julia looked back and forth between them.

"Good. I'll put you down for the five o'clock art class." Gerry jotted a note on his clipboard and walked away.

"Don't worry about him." Guzeman patted her arm. "He's all business. He doesn't have much choice. I just wanted to tell you that I saw the last few minutes of your class, and it really was quite good."

"Wow, thanks."

"I know it can be daunting, teaching to a group like this. Most of them aren't really interested at all, your hardest task is just keeping their attention."

"It was tough, but they were a good group. They seemed genuinely interested."

"That was down to you, don't doubt that." He nodded at Hope and Pete. "I can see you have other plans. Look, I'm always available, if you have any questions, or if you run into any problems."

"Problems? What kind of problems?"

"Nothing, nothing. I tell all the staff, you have problems,

you come to me."

He patted her arm as he left.

"Hon, you are a fabulous teacher. That was awesome." Pete squeezed her tight as he spoke and she coughed out a laugh. "Listen, I have to run meet up with Adam. But seriously" — he lifted her chin so she was looking him in the eye — "I'm so impressed."

Julia couldn't wipe the smile off her face as she collapsed into a nearby chair next to Hope.

"Wow. He's a keeper."

"I know." Julia nodded, then frowned. "That was weird, though, wasn't it? About Guzeman, I mean."

Hope just shrugged. "He was certainly nicer than he ever was when he worked for Dad. Who knows, maybe he likes you."

Julia glanced at her friend. She'd recovered surprisingly well from all the emotional blows she'd been suffering. "How's Brad holding up?"

"Brad?" Hope glanced up at her. "I don't know, we don't really talk about things like that."

"About your father dying?"

"About our feelings." Hope laughed.

"Was he very close to your father?"

"I suppose. I'd been spending more time with him recently, but I guess that was just because Brad's been busy. They were close."

"He seemed to really love you, Hope. I hope you know that."

Hope shrugged again. "Maybe. He never hid the fact that he saw Brad as his 'son and heir.'" She raised her fingers into air quotes as her voice changed to repeat the familiar phrase. "He was old-fashioned that way. He always said it was a man's world." She rolled her eyes. "I never let it bug me, not really. I know I'm more competent than Brad. I'm more like our dad, frankly."

"In what way?"

Hope took a moment to respond, as if considering her words. "He was a realist. A good man, really he was. But he was realistic. About what he did for people. And what he expected in return."

"I guess that's a good thing," Julia said uncertainly.

"It can be," Hope said. "Like I said, competent. Brad's more ... I don't know, idealistic."

Julia liked Hope but she wasn't sure about how competent she was, and couldn't help but think that of the two of them, Brad was the only one with an actual career. Now wasn't the time to point that out, though. Instead, she said, "Do you talk to Bill about feelings?"

Julia thought she was being subtle, but Hope laughed out loud. "Yeah, you picked up on that, huh? I know he has feelings for me — or at least, he thinks he does."

"What does that mean?"

"They're not real." Hope toyed with the edges of her notebook as she talked, flipping up the corners. "You can tell, you know? When a man is really in love with you?"

Julia, who could still feel the tingle from Pete's touch, knew exactly what Hope meant.

"So I treat him with kindness," Hope continued. "I want to stay friends. And I know that eventually he'll find someone. The right someone."

"Who do you think that will be?"

Hope shook her head, as if at a loss. "It's just ... he's got a different way of looking at the world. A little cold, to be honest. I need someone with more warmth in his heart."

Again, Julia bit her tongue as the words "someone with more money in his wallet" came to mind. Why was she being so catty? This wasn't like her, and she didn't like it. "Look, I need to go grab my things. But thank you again for coming to my class, I can't tell you how much I appreciate it."

She hadn't gone far when she turned at the sound of voices behind her. Hope was talking with Molly. Not yelling, not pulling away, just talking. Julia could hear their voices from where she stood, but she couldn't understand what they were saying. It was a good thing that Hope was giving Molly a chance to explain herself. Wasn't it?

25

Their search of the next kitchen proved as fruitless as the last.

Adam had just swung the final cupboard door closed when Captain Harding stormed into the room, followed closely by Bill.

"What the hell do you think you're doing?" Harding's voice was calm but his face was red.

"We're searching your ship for a potential murder weapon, sir," Pete answered just as calmly. "We suspect Arthur Claypoole was poisoned by inhaling HCN vapor. We're looking for a vessel that could have held the gas."

Harding spoke through gritted teeth. "I made it very clear to you both that I no longer require your assistance with this investigation. We'll be docking in less than twenty-four hours. The FBI will investigate then."

"What are you trying to hide, Captain?" Adam was finding it a lot harder to stay calm. "Why not let us investigate?"

"Hide?" Harding actually laughed. "I'm not trying to hide anything. I'm trying to protect the investigation, not hinder it. You two are obviously useless, letting poor Alice die under your watch."

"Our watch?" Pete's anger level was joining Adam's. "You're the captain of this ship."

Harding stepped up close to Pete. "Don't you dare accuse me."

"Gentlemen." Bill was almost simpering. "Please, we're all on the same side here. Looking for a killer, remember?"

"We're done here anyway." Adam left the room and Pete followed.

"What was that all about?" Pete fumed as they passed through the narrow hallways that led them back to the public area of the ship.

"And what's Bill's role in this?" Adam wondered.

"Bill? I'd say he was the calm one there."

"Sure." Adam turned abruptly to face Pete in the narrow hall. "But Harding only knew we were there because Bill told him. Why?"

Pete shrugged. "He thought we had Harding's permission, remember? We told him that."

"Maybe." Adam continued through the hall, pushing through to the public hallway.

"He's just trying to help," Pete said. "To do his job. He has no means or motive, remember that."

"There's always a motive." Adam shook his head. "We just need to find it."

"What does that mean?"

Adam slowed his pace, Pete stepped into pace next to him, and they lowered their voices as they entered the main lounge. "I need you to get back in touch with your contacts in New York. See what you can find out about our friend Bill Langtry."

"I guess," Pete said. "If he works with law enforcement there, I should be able to find some people who know him."

"Good. Maybe Julia's right about him."

Whatever Pete's response would have been to Julia's opinion, he had no chance to share it.

"Pete!" Julia's call caught the attention of a few other passengers, and if that hadn't worked, her running across the lounge waving her arms certainly clinched the deal. "I've been looking for you."

"What's up?" Pete greeted her with a quick peck on the cheek.

"Pete, I need to talk to you. It's about ...well ..." She looked at Adam.

He put his hands up in defeat. "I get it, I know when I'm not wanted. I'll try to find out what other spaces Guzeman has easy access to that we should search. You two ... talk. But Pete, do look into that, like we were talking about, soon, right?"

"Sure, soon." Pete kept his gaze on Julia as he replied.

Adam turned away from them and walked right into Karen, who had been approaching from behind.

"You're searching the ship now, is that what I hear?" she asked with a smile.

"Sorry, we shouldn't be talking shop out here. It's nothing, I promise."

"Mm-hmm. OK. I believe you. So does that mean you have time for a drink?" She linked her arm through his. He glanced over at Pete and Julia sitting so close together on a sofa across the lounge, their faces almost touching.

"Sure." He tightened his arm around Karen's. "Why not?"

"It was such an amazing feeling. Like ...I don't know, like I'm proud of myself. Is that wrong?" Julia asked, looking into Pete's eyes.

He laughed. "Of course it's not wrong to be proud of yourself. You're a good photographer, we both know it. Turns out you're a good teacher, too. Not everyone can do that, you know."

Julia knew she was glowing. She couldn't keep her smile down. "Sorry, I shouldn't be so happy. I know I'm only doing this because Alice was killed." She shut her eyes. "I'm a terrible person."

"Stop it." Pete leaned forward and kissed her forehead. "You're an amazing person. Clearly, I should tell you that more often."

She opened her eyes to see Pete's kind face, his eyes reflecting her own pride. She knew how lucky she was to have him. And she had no intention of giving him up. She just had to find a way to have her cake and eat it, too.

"You know the thing about this job ..." She paused, trying to figure out what she wanted to say.

"Yes?" Pete prompted her.

"It's just on board the boat."

"Right. But hey, now we know how much you like it, maybe we could find some teaching opportunities for you at home, too."

"Right ... but that would be different." She hesitated again. "A really different environment, you know? Different kinds of students."

"And you're worried you won't be as good?" Pete took her hand. "Don't even think about that. You'll be fine."

Julia shook her head. She wasn't being clear. She wasn't

even clear in her mind what she wanted to say. "No, that's not it. I just wonder ..."

Pete let her hand fall and leaned back in his seat. "What's going on, Julia? What are you trying to tell me?"

Damn it, she wasn't getting anywhere with this. "I don't know, forget it." She grabbed his hand. "You know I love you, right?"

Pete's smile grew wide. "I know. Whatever you're trying to figure out, we'll figure it out together."

"Hey." Wayne's voice interrupted them, causing Pete to jump up. "I heard you've been all over the ship. Looking for something, is that it?" Wayne didn't seem to care that his voice was loud enough to be heard on the second level.

"Keep your voice down," Pete said. "What's got into you?"

"I'm still in charge of security on this ship. And this investigation. You need something, you go through me." Wayne poked his finger into Pete's chest.

Julia stood now, too. "Calm down, guys. You're making a scene."

Wayne seemed to realize that she was right. He looked around the room and dropped his hand. "Right, sorry." He looked at Pete. "But you need to understand, if you want to go rifling through stuff on this ship, I have to be with you. Got it?"

KAREN HAD JUST ORDERED their second round of drinks — a mimosa for her, Irish coffee for Adam — when Julia and Pete joined them at the bar.

"Everything sorted out?" Adam asked.

"Sure, I guess," Julia replied. Adam recognized her evasion, but said nothing. "I thought you should know, I've gotten to know Hope Claypoole a bit, I thought you might find it helpful."

"Great." Adam took a sip of coffee. "Because I didn't get very far with her. What've you learned?"

"She's got dreams, that's for sure. And she's got problems." Julia spoke while they waited for the bartender to bring her a Bloody Mary, filling them in on Hope's dream of going to Paris to study art, of her challenge of dealing with Bill's feelings toward her, of meeting new family members through this trip, and of missing her father, the only father she'd ever known. "Like Paul." Julia wrapped up her story. "She just met him and is thrilled."

"Unlike Bill?" Pete asked.

"Yeah, and it seems like Bill is always around when there's some kind of family tragedy, offering a shoulder to lean on, that kind of thing. He's so good to her, I think she feels guilty not sharing his feelings." Julia focused her attention on the mug-sized glass that had been placed in front of her. "Though I have a feeling she might be more interested in money than love."

"I get that," Karen said. "Not knowing everyone in your family, I mean," she added quickly, "not the money part." She laughed. "We all have distant cousins, don't we?"

"We do indeed." Adam frowned, trying not to think about the family secrets he'd inadvertently unearthed recently. "But that can cause problems sometimes, too."

He paused, not sure if he wanted to say anything more. Did he want his relationship with Karen to involve sharing intimate stories? It might be a lot more fun to keep it simple — and a lot less like the kind of choice he usually made. Marcus chose that moment to interrupt them.

"Ah, there you are. Missed yet another of my classes. If this keeps up, I'm going to start taking it personally."

"We're talking about family," Karen said, giving Adam a sideways glance. "The good and the bad."

Pete and Julia exchanged looks that even Adam could read. They knew how vulnerable he was right now and clearly didn't want him delving into old troubles. Pete spoke up. "Let's not get into this now, huh?"

"What are we avoiding talking about?" Karen asked, her smile sweet as could be.

"It's OK, bud, don't worry about it." Adam glanced at Pete. "I can talk about it." He turned his attention to Karen. "It's my grandfather. I already told Marcus, I spent some time trying to learn about him, and it didn't go well."

"You weren't able to find what you were looking for?" Karen asked.

"Sadly, I was." Adam finished off his drink. "But it's time for me to move on. Right, guys?" He turned to Pete and Julia for support. "I'm giving up looking into that particular history."

"Don't you want to be sure? To know the truth?" Marcus asked.

"I'm letting it go. Moving on. Sometimes you don't need to know the truth about yourself and your family. Why does it matter?"

Marcus' face lit up. "I know, what about—"

"Adam's right, it's better to let it drop," Pete cut him off, sounding annoyed. "We've gotta get back to work, Adam."

"Sure, let's go."

"Where?" Marcus asked.

"I'll fill you in later," Karen whispered.

26

ADAM SLIPPED SILENTLY into the library and took a chair by a window. Their search of the remaining kitchen had again turned up nothing. This type of door-to-door work was a lot easier when you had the staff of a police district to help. With just him and Pete, the searches were taking far too long. He understood Pete's position. This was what police work involved most of the time, boring, tedious searches. But this situation was different. They couldn't search the whole ship. They needed to consider the facts, narrow down the search.

He pulled out the papers Pete had given him and started reading about murder by cyanide. He still hadn't pieced that puzzle together. How had Paul known about the murders in New York? And why had he brought them up?

He'd started back with the first case for the third read-through when Bill burst into the room. "Adam, there you are."

"Shush." Adam stood as he spoke. "This is a quiet space."

Bill glanced around at the other people reading or playing games quietly, but didn't seem to care. "I need to talk to you."

"Fine, out here." Adam grabbed Bill by the arm and pulled him into the hall. From their left came the sound of splashes and yells from the pool area. To their right, the soothing music and therapeutic aromas of the spa. "What do you need, Bill?"

"What is your sister doing with Hope?"

"Doing with Hope? What the hell are you talking about? What are they doing?"

"That's what I'm asking you." Now Bill's voice came out as a whisper. Great timing.

"Look, Bill, I have no idea what you're asking me." Adam leaned back against the wall and folded his arms, portraits of previous ship captains looking down on them from the wall.

"Hope told me that she's been spending time with your sister. I saw them together myself. And I want to know why."

"They've become friends. Is that so hard to understand?" Adam tried to keep his voice patient, but it wasn't easy. "Why are you so worked up about it?"

"Are you using your sister to get close to Hope?"

"To get close to her? What do you think Julia is, some kind of bugging device?" Adam had hoped to be making a joke, but Bill didn't crack a smile.

"If you suspect Hope, you talk to me."

Now Adam straightened up. "Why would I talk to you, Bill? What do you have to do with Hope? You're not her guardian."

"I'm her friend, that's what."

"OK, then, as her friend, why do you think I'd be so

interested in Hope? Is there something about her you don't want me to find out?"

Bill's mouth was a straight line, his face set like stone. "You don't need to find out anything about Hope. You leave her alone. I will do whatever it takes to protect her."

Adam stepped closer to Bill, hoping to rattle him, but Bill didn't flinch. "What do you need to protect her from, Bill? Or should I say, who? Who are you worried about?"

"Right now, I'm talking to you. You stay away from her." Bill did nothing more than blink once, but his anger was clear — a calm, white hot anger.

Adam watched him go, trying to figure out what all that meant. As Bill turned a corner out of sight, Adam leaned back against the wall again. What had gotten Bill so worked up?

Adam glanced to the right to see Brad coming toward him from the spa. The skin on his face practically glowed from whatever services he had just experienced. He looked relaxed. Happy. That wouldn't last long.

"Having a good day?" Adam said as Brad approached.

———

"Having a good day, Brad?" Adam repeated the question when Brad responded with nothing more than a blank look. It must have been a very good massage indeed.

"Detective." Brad finally spoke. "Yes, I am in fact. Do you need something?"

Brad kept walking as he spoke, so Adam stepped into place beside him, following him around the pool, up to the next level, then along the deck toward the first-class section of the boat.

"I wanted to ask you a few more questions about your father."

"Ask away." Brad didn't seem to have a care in the world. He certainly wasn't acting like a man whose father had been murdered the day before.

"So you know."

"Know what?" Brad waved at a small cluster of people playing shuffleboard.

"About your father."

Brad finally stopped walking and turned to Adam with a huff of frustration, his hands gripping the towel slung nonchalantly around his neck, his robe at risk of coming open. "Yes, of course I know about my father, Detective. What, specifically, are you asking me?"

"Do you know your real father?"

"My real father? What does that even mean? Are you suggesting my father had a hidden persona?" Brad giggled as he asked, then started up his march around the ship again.

"I mean your birth father. Or birth mother."

Brad stopped again, but this time he wasn't giggling. "What on earth are you talking about? My father and mother are — were — my 'birth' mother and father."

"Ah. So you don't know."

"You've lost me again, Detective."

"You might want to have a seat, Brad." Adam gestured to a group of lounge chairs set up along the railing and Brad took the suggestion.

"Now, what are you going on about?" Brad asked.

"I learned something about you today, Brad. And about your father."

"Yes?"

"Did you know that you're adopted?"

Brad looked at Adam without blinking. Adam wasn't sure if he was even breathing. For a moment, Adam wondered if he'd have to perform CPR.

Finally Brad moved. "You're insane. I don't know where you get your information, but you're way off base. If I was adopted, I'd know."

"Betty Richards told me."

"Aunt Betty?" Brad was incredulous. "I don't believe it."

"She's got photographs, Brad. Of your real mother — I mean, your birth mother." When Brad still said nothing, Adam added, "She told me how much your adoptive mother and father love you. They were thrilled to adopt you. But your mother couldn't have children. That's why they adopted you. And Hope."

Brad slowly shook his head. "That's not true. I would've known."

Adam sat back in the next lounge seat, giving Brad time to absorb the news.

Brad jumped up. "You're an asshole, you know that?"

Adam sighed and stood up again. "I'm sorry to have to tell you like this, I really am."

"Oh, yeah? If you're so sorry, then why'd you do it? Why go prying into my business, pushing my poor Aunt Betty to say things that aren't even true?"

"I needed to know if you knew. I needed to see your face when you found out."

"My parents — my two, only parents — are dead. And they are none of your business." Brad's voice rose as he spoke, and by the end of the sentence he was practically yelling.

"In a murder investigation, everything is my business." Adam used a line he'd used so many times before. Far too many times before. He hated how much darkness he uncovered in every investigation. How much hurt murder caused, for so many people. But he also knew it was the only way to get at the truth. To find a killer.

Brad was gulping air now, reaching behind him for something that wasn't there. Adam put a hand out to steady him and Brad swatted it away.

"Don't you touch me. Don't you come near me. You hear me?" He was yelling at full voice now. "You stay away from me and from my family!"

Brad stormed away, but he looked unsteady on his feet and every now and then almost fell against the railing.

———

ADAM WATCHED Brad swaying up the deck. He'd been surprised by the news, of that there was no doubt. So he didn't know. But what did that tell him?

Nothing.

If Brad didn't know he was adopted, then it couldn't have factored into his motive. And motive he had — several million dollars' worth. It was hardly a secret within the family that Arthur saw Brad as his heir, despite his strong relationship with Hope. Brad was the boy, and for a man like Arthur, that trumped every other consideration.

Adam let out a muttered curse under his breath. The idea of having children and not loving them both equally was foreign to him. Then again, Arthur was foreign. If Adam had been lucky enough to get married, to have children, he would've raised them so differently.

"Penny for your thoughts?"

Adam brought his gaze from Brad's unsteady form to Karen's sexy form, which was leaning close to him.

No way he was going to tell her he was thinking about

raising kids. In fact, one look at her banished all thoughts of children from his mind. "Just working on this case, that's all. Where are you off to?"

She wore a robe that matched the one threatening to slide off Brad. Though in Karen's case, Adam wouldn't have minded a little slippage.

"I was on my way to the spa, but it's not urgent. I can change my plans. If you have anything in mind?"

Adam grinned, but then shook his head. "I don't know. Pete's probably waiting for me."

"I don't know about that. I just saw him and your sister heading off together."

"Oh, yeah? So what, he's abandoning me?" Adam rolled his eyes. "Nah, he's probably going to gather information on Bill, he said he was looking into it."

Karen ran a finger up his arm. "So perhaps you should abandon him."

He averted his eyes from her face, trying to refocus his mind on Brad's outburst.

Karen persisted. "Come on, I know you need some time to figure things out. Not just about this case."

"What do you mean?"

"Oh. Well, Marcus and I were talking about what you were doing. You know, trying to find some things out about your own family. Your grandfather?"

"Marcus talks too much. That was none of his business."

"I'm sorry if I'm out of line. But perhaps talking about it will help."

"Help what? There's nothing to talk about. I wanted to learn more about my grandfather. I didn't like what I learned. So I've stopped looking. That's all."

"OK, then. We can talk about something else. Or we don't have to talk at all." Karen smiled wickedly.

Adam was sorely tempted. To go with Karen. To walk away from this case. But last time he'd let himself relax, let his guard down, Alice Murphy had died. He couldn't do that again.

He bent down, kissed Karen lightly on the cheek. "I'll see you soon, I promise."

27

"Wayne?" Adam tapped lightly on the door to Wayne's office. "You in there?"

"Come on in," Wayne grunted in reply.

Adam walked into the open workspace. Wayne looked up expectantly from his desk.

"You were right before, I'm sorry," Adam explained. "We should've talked to you about what we planned to do."

"Damn straight." Wayne turned his attention down to whatever was on his desk. At least, he turned his head down. The hand holding his pen wasn't moving.

"So I'm here now."

Wayne looked up again. "Why?"

"Trying to figure out our best next step. And I think you can help."

"You think?"

"All right, we need your help," Adam said.

Wayne nodded and dropped his pen, leaning back in his chair and looking up at him. "What do you need?"

Adam slid into an open chair. "We have an idea of the type of weapon that was used on Arthur Claypoole."

Wayne raised his eyebrows expectantly.

"It was a liquid version of cyanide," Adam explained. "HCN — a liquid that can be turned into a gas when it's heated up. And we have one suspect in mind who has easy access to heating things up." He paused, then added, "Who has the most reason of anyone to kill Claypoole while he's on board."

Wayne shook his head. "No way. I told you before, it's not a member of the crew."

"We want to search the areas of the ship that Guzeman has easy access to, places he could hide the weapon."

"And what's the weapon?" Wayne asked.

Adam shrugged. "It could be a number of things. Right now, we're probably looking for a vial that held the liquid cyanide. Not sure yet how he heated it up."

Wayne shook his head again. "You're way off base here. And you're also wasting your time."

"We know you think Guzeman couldn't have done it."

"Not just that," Wayne said. "You've been searching the kitchens, right?"

Adam nodded.

Wayne laughed. "If Guzeman's trying to hide something, he wouldn't leave it in the kitchen where anyone could find it. He has access to parts of the ship's hold that other people don't. There are hundreds of square feet of storage space he could use to hide something."

Adam sighed and dropped his head into his hands. This was futile. "Then help me. We need to find that weapon."

"No way you'll find it. This is a big ship. And even if you do"— he held up a hand to forestall whatever Adam was about to say — "Even if you do find something, how will you link it back to Guzeman?"

"You just said he had access to parts of the ship that other people don't."

"Yeah, but—"

"Look, short of a confession, hard evidence is the only thing that will get our killer convicted. It's not enough for us to figure out who might have done it. We need proof of who did." Adam spoke calmly, making an argument he'd heard so many times before from Pete as he stood up slowly. "So we need to search the hold."

"Wait, no way." Wayne shot out of his chair. "You'll be down there for the rest of the cruise."

"And that would bother you why?"

Wayne frowned but Adam could see from his eyes that he realized the comment made sense. At least with them in the hold they wouldn't be annoying Captain Harding any more.

"Fine." Wayne crossed the room to a file cabinet, rifling through it for a few minutes before pulling out a folded map. "Here. I'll mark the areas designated for the kitchen staff."

JULIA HELD her camera a little more tightly than necessary as she reviewed her mental notes. Her eyes shut, she went back over the additions she'd made earlier that afternoon. She did not intend to simply give the same lecture again. But she hadn't had enough time to come up with something new. So she was aiming for old with a twist.

"Julia?"

She opened her eyes to see Hope watching her.

"Are you feeling OK?" Hope asked.

"Yes, sorry, thanks," Julia replied sheepishly. "I thought

I had a few more minutes before the class started. Just going over my thoughts, that's all."

"That's great. I'm glad you're so calm and collected."

It wasn't hard to pick up on the sarcasm in Hope's voice. "What are you talking about?" Julia asked.

"Just that it's so easy for you to stab me in the back with one hand and craft lecture notes with the other. I hope your class goes really great. Just great."

Hope looked like she was going to say more, but instead slammed her mouth shut, took a deep breath through her nose, and spun around.

Julia chased after her. "Hope, I really don't know what you're talking about."

"Oh, no?" Hope faced her. "Bill told me everything, Julia, you can drop the act."

"Again, still no clue. What did Bill tell you?"

"Just that your brother now suspects me of killing my own father. And the only way he could think that about me is if you told him. He's hardly talked to me at all, but I've been naively chatting away with you. Thinking you were my friend."

"Hope, stop. I am your friend. I mean, Adam is my brother, and to him, everyone is a suspect. But I really don't think he suspects you. At least, not because of anything I told him."

"I don't know what you told him. But now he thinks I'm a killer. And my dad just died ..." Hope's voice swelled and Julia thought she was about to burst into tears.

"Oh, Hope. Let me help. What can I do?"

Hope bit her lips and ran a hand across her eyes. "Nothing. My dad was ... he was always there for me. Not like other people. He did whatever he had to do to take care of me. Even my mother tells me that."

"Your mother? You talked to her?" Julia asked.

Hope nodded. "I did. Finally. And she was actually kind of nice. She explained why she had to leave me. That she knew my father would take care of me. And he did, he really did. He didn't care what he had to do. He always gave us everything we wanted. My mother knew he would, that's why she was able to let me go. She said she wouldn't have been able to, otherwise." Hope looked at Julia, and the tears, if there had been any, were gone. "She's a good person. Not like you."

"I didn't say anything bad about you to Adam, I didn't." Julia put a hand on Hope's arm as she defended herself.

"I don't believe you, Julia. I just don't."

Hope pulled free of Julia's hand and ran out of the room.

"Damn it!" Julia stood staring at the door even as a few potential students came in. She'd really screwed up. Pete and Adam's job was hard enough as it was, they didn't need her antagonizing the witnesses. Stupid of her to think she could even contribute.

She shook her head and made her way back to her supplies at the front of the room. She should focus on her photography and teaching this class.

———

"OK, so you take this side and I'll take that one."

Adam and Pete were in one room of a warren of storage areas in the bowels of the ship, rooms lined with metal shelves and cabinets, each room connected to the next by a bulkhead door. Everything stored here was secured in bins. Nothing would get loose or slide, no matter how rough the waters got.

"There are pockets of space behind each bin." Pete grunted as he reached an arm deep into one shelf. "I'm just doing this by touch."

"And hoping that Guzman was right about not having rodents." Adam wiped his hands together, then started in on his search.

An hour later, the two of them had worked their way through two more identical holds. Adam's back was stiff from bending and a dull pain was forming at the back of his head. He stood and, holding his hands together in front of him, turned from side to side to stretch out his back. "D'you know how many more of these holds we have to go through?"

"There are dozens of them." Pete's response was muffled. "And those are just the rooms Wayne recommended to you."

"You're kidding me."

Something about Adam's tone caught Pete's attention and he looked over, still kneeling in front of a low shelf. "What do you want to do, just let this go? Assume there's nothing to find?"

Adam could hear the frustration in Pete's voice, and that worried him. Pete was always the calm one. The rational one. "Of course not, but ... seriously, man, we'll be down here for days."

"Well, we don't have days, do we? We dock in Bermuda tomorrow." Pete stood, wiping nonexistent dust from his pant legs. If nothing else, at least these holds were spotless.

"Maybe we can think of a way to narrow it down." Adam tapped the fingers of his right hand against his leg as he thought out loud. "All we know is we're looking for some kind of vial."

Pete nodded, one eyebrow raised. "That held either a gas or a liquid that could be heated into a gas."

"Are these storage rooms all the same temperature?" Adam asked.

"No." Pete shook his head as he checked Wayne's map. "The temperature in each hold varies depending on what's stored there. The engines are at the bottom of the boat and they generate some heat, so the refrigerated and frozen holds are on this level. The next level down is storage where the temperature isn't as vital."

Adam leaned heavily against the shelving he'd just finished searching. "That doesn't help us at all. If the poison's all used up, the killer won't care what temperature the hold is." He took a deep breath and let it out in a sigh that sounded more like a growl. "OK, on to the next one."

"Hey, why don't I see if I got anything back yet on my inquiries about Bill Langtry? If we can keep putting all the pieces together, maybe we can narrow this search down, like you said."

Adam felt his brow release and realized he'd been scowling. "Sounds good, partner. Anything to speed this up." He put his muscle into turning the wheel to unlock the next bulkhead door, stepping through into the next, identical hold. He was going to have to start dropping bread crumbs or something, to make sure he didn't search the same room twice. He laughed softly to himself. At least he still had his sense of humor.

Working on his own was even slower going. He was only doing a superficial search, he knew that. Something in his brain was trying to tell him that they really needed to open up each of these bins and search through everything stored there, but there was no way they could do that. The FBI could do a search like that once they came on board.

For now, Adam only wanted to make sure they didn't miss anything obvious. As ridiculous as it made him feel, he needed to know he wouldn't be the cop who missed the vial of poison just lying out on a shelf somewhere, simply because he couldn't be bothered to look.

He was moving by rote, letting his mind wander as his fingers moved behind each storage unit, on top of and underneath each shelving unit. If nothing else, he could verify Guzeman's claim: he hadn't found any evidence of vermin or an infestation. Which made Harding's decision to fumigate even stranger.

He shoved the next bulkhead door closed behind him and moved to the shelf closest to the entrance, his mind still on rats and the embarrassment of missing the obvious. He was obviously missing something here, because for all the secrets he'd uncovered, his best theory was still the most obvious: the chef who'd made the crèmebrûlée.

He was so focused on his thoughts, it took a few seconds for him to realize that a shadow at the far end of the room was moving.

28

Julia saw Pete hovering by the door, but took her time gathering her materials. Her third class had gone just as well as the first two. She was really getting the hang of this. This time, she'd gone beyond simply tweaking her first lecture, talking extemporaneously about her personal experiences with structure and color in her photographs. The students had been happy to watch as she used the big screen to show a series of her own shots from this cruise.

She was surprised by how much she was enjoying this: the back and forth with students, the words of appreciation, challenging herself to think about her own work in different ways. She was getting more out of this experience than she'd expected. And she didn't know what to tell Pete.

"You ready?" Pete approached while she was lost in thought.

"Sure." She swung her bag over her shoulder.

"I told Adam I wouldn't be long, but we have time for a quick drink. I mean, if you're interested."

"Yeah, sure. Sounds good." Julia felt her forehead furrow and forced a smile. "Maybe some dessert, too."

"Great. Hey, you need me to carry that for you?"

Pete reached for her bag but she put a hand on it at the same time. "No, I got it, thanks." She'd meant the response to be light, but she saw Pete frown.

She stuck her free arm through his. "Come on, let's get that drink. I think we both need it."

After they'd settled down at a table in the all-night cafe, sweet drinks and a piece of cake with two forks in front of them, Julia broached the subject that had been on her mind.

"I can't believe how much I've enjoyed this teaching gig."

"You're good at it, too. A natural."

"You came to more of my classes?" Julia asked, pleased.

"I caught the tail end. I could tell how engaged everyone there was. You really are a good teacher."

"Just like my brother, huh? Maybe it runs in the family."

"So maybe you can find a way to teach a class or two when we get home?"

"Maybe ..." Julia used her fork to pick at the cake.

"Why wouldn't you?" Pete asked. "You were saying how much you got out of it."

"I do. I love that my students are just normal people, not art students exactly. Not fanatics." She laughed. "I'm sharing ideas that are completely new to them. Opening their eyes to new things, you know?"

"So ... what are you saying?"

Julia took her time, putting extra care into scooping up a forkful of cake, savoring its sweetness. Finally, she put down her fork. "You know I told you the cruise line is hiring. They're looking for someone to replace Alice."

"Yeah, you mentioned that. It seems kind of fast to me."

Julia shrugged. "It's not that they don't care she's dead, but they have a job to do, that's all."

Pete took his own forkful of cake, then stopped with the fork still in the air. "You mentioned this earlier, now you're bringing it up again. What am I not getting?"

Julia smiled at him and shook her head. "Nothing. It's nothing. It's just ..."

"Wait. Did you apply for the job? Is that what you were trying to tell me earlier?"

"No. I mean, not yet. I am thinking about it, though. That's what I was trying to tell you earlier."

"You want to stay on this boat?"

Julia could see Pete trying to control himself, but his hand was shaking with the effort. "I don't know, it's just a thought."

"That's some thought." Pete placed his fork down carefully. "Why didn't you come out and tell me this earlier, instead of just hinting at it?"

Julia reached across the table to rest a hand on his arm. "That's what I'm doing right now. Discussing it with you."

Pete kept his mouth closed tight as his gaze moved around the room.

It took a minute or two, but eventually he spoke. "Look, I gotta get back to Adam. You do what you have to do."

29

Adam paused and listened. At first he heard nothing but the creaks and groans of the ship, the faint tinkling of music from afar, from those public places where innocent passengers still danced and laughed and enjoyed themselves.

Then he heard a shuffle. A quiet sound, easily missed, but Adam recognized a footstep.

He moved toward the sound, stepping as softly as he could. Was that a person? He stepped through a bulkhead, its door hanging open. "Police," he called out. "Whoever's back there, identify yourself."

A shadow on the far side of the room he entered shifted, then moved. Adam sprinted toward the figure, but it was faster, sliding through a far bulkhead door, then pulling it shut behind him.

Adam spun the wheel that would open the door, cursing the whole time. By the time he got it open, he saw the figure at the far end of the next room, climbing a ladder that took him down to God knew where.

Adam ran to the ladder and looked down into darkness.

Some type of lower level storage room. The lights were off and he couldn't see far into the gloom. Adam grabbed the top rung of the ladder and lowered himself into the bowels of the ship.

He heard another step as he climbed. When he dropped to the ground, he found himself in a long hallway. Which direction had the sound come from?

He paused again. Listened again. He felt the heat rising from the engines just below him. He could no longer hear the muffled sounds of the cruise ship above, as all other noise was drowned out by the droning of the engines.

He took a breath and made a choice. He saw no other doors in his sprint down the hall and soon found himself at another ladder, this one going up.

He swore under his breath, knowing he'd lost his prey, and began to climb.

He was cursing again by the time he reached the top, ending up in a well-lit store room that looked familiar. It might have been one he and Pete had searched earlier. Or maybe they all looked alike.

Then he heard it. The definite sound of footsteps from a door across the room.

He dashed across the room after the shadowy figure, but when he ran through the door, it was a much more solid figure he ran directly into.

"Watch it." Pete stepped back. "What's going on?"

"Damn in, Pete."

Pete took a step back, hands in the air. "Sorry, I thought I was coming to help. What the hell are you doing?"

The hallway stretched beyond Pete, ending in yet another identical bulkhead door, securely closed. No sign of whoever he'd been chasing. "Nothing," he said with frustration. "I'm not doing anything."

ADAM SLUMPED on a stool at the coffee bar, his espresso getting cold in front of him. Coffee wasn't what he needed right now. Whiskey would hit the spot a whole lot better. He glanced again at the readout Pete had just handed him. The reason he'd been chasing Adam down through the ship's holds. They finally had some background information on Bill. And it wasn't what he expected.

Glancing up, he saw Marcus crossing the room toward him. He raised his hand to wave, then froze with his arm half-lifted. Something about Marcus' appearance was off, though Adam couldn't immediately tell what. As Marcus approached, he seemed to see Adam, but instead of acknowledging him, he turned as if to walk the other way. Had he not seen him?

"Marcus," Adam called out to his new friend.

Marcus stopped, paused, then continued the few steps to where Adam sat. His face was red and Adam could tell it was starting to swell, as one side of his face looked just a little larger than the other.

"Man, what happened to you?" Adam asked. "You look like you were punched in the face."

Marcus laughed, but Adam sensed no joy from the sound. It was a harsh, nervous laugh. Unnatural. "Nah, nothing like that. I walked into a door, if you can believe that. I mean, seriously, who'd want to punch me?" He offered Adam a lopsided smile. The smile promptly turned to a grimace and he let his face drop. It must have been painful. "Listen, I'm gonna go see the ship's doctor about this. I'll talk to you later."

"Sure, yeah. You take care of yourself." Adam reached

up to pat his friend on the shoulder, but he'd already stepped away.

His mind was still running through the possibilities of what Marcus wasn't telling him when he saw Karen across the room. Another friend who hadn't noticed him sitting there, apparently. What, was he invisible now? She stood with a group of three other passengers, holding cocktail glasses and laughing, big smiles plastered on all their faces.

Pete slid onto the seat next to him as Adam was debating going over to say hello. "What's with her?"

Adam shrugged.

"Well, Julia's still OK, I think. She's talking to me, anyway."

Adam didn't want to get involved in whatever was going on between them. It was none of his business. Or maybe better to say, it was too much of his business. He waved the paper he was holding. "So Bill isn't who he said he was."

"Not exactly."

"He claimed to be a cop."

"Did he, really?" Pete asked. "He said he *worked* with cops."

"Then he let us believe he was a cop. Just as bad."

"Yeah." Pete chewed on his lip. "But what does that tell us? We're docking in twelve hours, and we've still got too many suspects."

Adam watched Karen as she laughed with another group. Was she looking at him out of the corner of her eye? He couldn't tell.

He slid off his stool. "Let's go talk to Bill."

30

THE SOUNDS of hundreds of diners, chatting, laughing, silverware clinking, came at them from the left as they approached the main dining room. A large group had gathered at the steps leading down to the hostess stand, clogging the hallway. Adam and Pete tried to be as gentle and polite as they could while pushing their way through, in a hurry to get out to the deck where Bill was supposedly playing shuffleboard with some of his cousins.

"Stop!" A beefy hand grabbed Adam by the arm and he swung around, his fists raised for a fight, adrenaline pumping.

"Chef Guzeman, what are you doing?" He tried to sound calm, as if the large man hadn't just scared the wits out of him.

"Come, in here." Guzeman gave him a not-too-gentle pull on his arm before letting him go. Adam and Pete followed him through a door he hadn't noticed next to the staircase. The door blended with the wood-paneled walls around it, not hidden, exactly, but not inviting for any guests tempted to push through to the other side.

They found themselves in a tiny office space, barely ten feet long and five feet wide. A metal door at the far end of the room stood open when they entered, and Adam caught a glimpse of waitstaff hurrying past it in either direction, heading toward and away from the main dining room. As soon as they entered, Guzeman reached over and slammed the door shut, making the small space feel even more confining.

Neither Adam nor Pete was small, yet Guzeman managed to give the impression of towering over them. His shoulders hunched forward as he turned to face them, his hands balling into fists at his side. Adam tensed for whatever was coming next.

"I did not kill Claypoole. Or Alice Murphy." His voice was low, more of a growl than speech.

"Can you prove that? You haven't told us where you were when they were killed," Adam replied.

"Hmph." Guzeman snorted. "I will tell you. But only so you know I did not kill anyone. The last thing I want on this ship is an investigation."

Pete raised an eyebrow and took a step forward. "Interesting comment. Go on."

"I know some things about what goes on aboard this ship, gentlemen." Guzeman's shoulders relaxed as he talked, as if relieved to be telling his story. "Not all of it is, as you would say, above board." He laughed at his own joke.

"What are you talking about?" Adam asked, not breaking a smile. He didn't have time for this, he needed to find Bill.

Guzeman lifted one meaty shoulder. "Smuggling, of course. Surely you know."

The sound of voices carried from the kitchen beyond

their little room, reminders that life was going on as usual on the rest of the ship.

"Know what?" Adam asked, his voice quiet.

"Your new friend. The professor." Guzeman's Spanish accent, the way he rolled his r's, made even the word professor sound ominous.

"What about him?" Adam asked.

"He doesn't tell you everything, then?"

"Enough of this," Pete said. "If you've got something to say, say it."

Guzeman pursed his lips. He looked around the room as if looking for the words he needed. "I smuggle. I will admit this. Nothing big." He waved his hands in front of him and Adam and Pete both took a step back.

Adam felt like smacking himself for the small movement and intentionally leaned forward. "You're admitting to smuggling?"

"It is not a big deal, as I say. Ask your friend, the professor. He will tell you."

"What will he tell me?"

"He is involved as well. So many crew members are. You must understand, I tell you this so you will believe me, the last thing I want on this ship is a murder investigation."

"That doesn't mean you didn't kill anyone," Pete said.

"No, but I have alibi. For Claypoole's death. I was with your friend, the—"

"Stop calling him that," Adam blurted out. "What the hell are you telling me? Marcus is a smuggler? You're a smuggler?"

Guzeman shrugged one more time. "We are not working together, if that's what you mean."

"So what, he's your competition?" Pete asked.

Guzeman smiled, baring large teeth browned with years

of coffee, wine, and God knows what else. "Competition? Him?" He barked out a laugh. "I am in control of my business, Detective. I have nothing to fear from him."

The big man's hands had once again balled into fists as he talked about Marcus, a nasty gleam in his eye. Adam thought about the bruise slowly sprouting on Marcus' face. Maybe he had more to fear than he was letting on.

"Did you punch him? Show him how little you have to fear from him?" he asked.

"Hit him? The professor?" Now Guzeman really laughed. "Why would I do that? He's so tiny, so puny. I hit him, he goes flying off the ship." Guzeman fluttered a hand in the air as he laughed some more. "No, he has nothing to fear from me. Not him, not Alice Murphy, not any of the crew."

Adam watched Guzeman's smile slowly fade, as if it took more effort than it was worth to keep it up. He'd check with Marcus about Guzeman's alibi for the time Claypoole was killed. Maybe this meant he was innocent of the murders. But maybe it meant he was hiding something even worse.

———

"Fore!"

The high-pitched, fluttering, unexpected cry did not prepare Adam for the shuffleboard disk flying toward him along the deck. He swore as it smacked him in the ankle.

"What the—?"

"Sorry about that, dear," Betty trotted over to him. "I did warn you."

"Of course, sorry about my language."

Pete laughed. "Is that a technical shuffleboard call, then?"

Betty grinned at him and took another sip from the slushy-sized plastic cup she held. Adam could smell the rum and sugar from where he stood and it helped explain Betty's wide grin. And those of her companions. All except Bill.

The youngest of the group that hovered around the shuffleboard court, Bill stood somewhat apart from the others. He leaned slightly on his shuffleboard cue and glared at Adam and Pete as they approached him.

"Can we pull you away for a sec?" Adam asked in as polite a voice as he could muster. "We've got a few questions for you."

"Whatever." Bill rolled his eyes and followed them to the edge of the deck.

Adam looked out at the ocean, organizing his thoughts. The rough seas they'd passed through the previous day were gone, and he now looked out over calm, deep green waters. He waited as Bill leaned his cue against the railing.

"You told me you were in law enforcement."

Bill lifted one side of his mouth in a sneer. "No, I didn't."

"You said you were a crime scene tech, and I know that in New York, that means you're a state employee. That means you go through all the rigorous background checks of the state crime lab. But you're not. You didn't."

Bill shrugged, glanced at Pete, then faced the ocean. "I told you I'm a crime scene tech, and I am. I've worked a lot of cases with the NYPD."

"You're a contractor," Pete said. "That's a little bit different."

"No, it's not." Bill's words could have sounded like a

whine if it weren't for the way he lifted his voice at the end of each sentence. "Look, the state and city PDs use contractors all the time. It's pretty standard. I thought you knew that."

"So you think you've been upfront with us?" Adam asked. "Nothing else you want to share?"

Bill grabbed his shuffleboard cue. "Forget I ever offered to help you assholes." He took one step away, then stopped. "And just in case you haven't figured it out yet, I'm not the only person in this family pretending to be something he's not."

"What's that supposed to mean?" Pete asked.

"You really think Arthur Claypoole — multimillionaire immigrant businessman — was such a sweet, charming, giving person?" Bill snickered.

Adam had handled enough investigations to know that people who felt pushed into a corner were most likely to lash out. Usually, with lies. But sometimes with a truth they wouldn't otherwise have shared.

"Why do you say that?" he asked.

"I heard him speaking Russian. All the time, when he thought I couldn't hear."

"So?" Pete shrugged. "He was from Russia. I'm sure his company does a lot of business in Russia. That couldn't be unusual in his line of work."

Bill nodded, grinning. "In his line of work. Exactly. And what do you think he did?"

Adam had had enough. He stepped close to Bill, their faces inches apart, his fists balled. "Bill, if you've got something to say, you need to spit it out."

Bill took a step back. "I'm saying that Arthur was involved in a lot of different businesses, some legit, some less so. And a lot of his work involved exchanging information."

"Are you talking about blackmail?"

"God, no, nothing that crude." Bill laughed. "But he knew how to monetize information. If he had something he thought someone else wanted to know, he'd name a price."

"How did you understand what he was saying if he was speaking in Russian?" Pete asked.

Bill shrugged. "I couldn't, not really. But I can pick out a few words here and there. You don't grow up in Brighton Beach without learning a little Russian. Arthur gave a lot of money to politicians, to entrepreneurs, to Hollywood. And he never gave anything — anything — without expecting something in return." Bill shuddered. "And you never knew what he was going to want from you."

"What did he want from you?" Adam asked softly, stepping away from Bill again.

Bill looked up at him. "He wanted me to stay close to Hope. But he didn't need to ask me that, I enjoy spending time with her. I want to be with her."

"That's what he wanted from you?" Pete's disbelief was evident on his face.

"Yes," Bill said, "don't sound so surprised. He knew she needed extra attention. That's what he asked from me. No problem, I said."

Adam and Pete shared a look. Ignoring the many questions that came to his mind about why Arthur Claypoole would want Bill Langtry hanging around his daughter, Adam focused on the more important part of Bill's news. "So Arthur sold information. But you have no way of knowing if anything he did was illegal. Or even unethical."

"Hm, no. I guess not." Bill picked up his cue to return to his game. "At least some good will come of this whole mess," he added as he walked away.

"What's that?" Pete called after him.

"At least now Hope won't be running off to Paris. I can take care of her, like she needs me to."

"What a jackass," Adam muttered, loud enough that Bill probably heard.

"We can't take anything he says as fact, we both know that," Pete agreed.

Adam nodded, but couldn't help wondering. If Arthur had been trading on information, like Bill claimed, and willing to trade with the Russians, what kind of trouble was he really in?

THEIR DINNER TABLE that night was pushed up against one wall. Adam kept his elbow tucked against him as he ate to avoid bumping into it. Pete sat to his right, Julia on the third side across from him. He tried half-heartedly to start a conversation, but gave up when neither of his friends was willing to pick it up. A few polite comments were all they could muster, and even those seemed strained. Despite their proximity, they were miles apart. No smiles were passed with the salt and pepper.

From where he sat, Adam could see Karen enjoying herself with a group of people he didn't know. The boisterous party occupied a large, round table in the middle of the room. Their laughter carried as their wine flowed. A group enjoying the cruise exactly the way it was meant to be enjoyed. He recognized the bitterness in his feelings. He was being a jackass.

There was nothing wrong with Karen enjoying herself. He was the one with the problem. He had to admit, he was clearly not suited to a casual fling. Was it too late to shift their relationship back into friendship mode? Even the fact that he thought of it as a relationship proved his point. This casual thing was stressing him out. He just wasn't the type of person who could let himself go while on a cruise, let himself be someone different. He could only be himself.

Adam glanced around the rest of the room, but Marcus must be dining elsewhere, if at all. Tonight was certainly a far cry from their collegial and admittedly more optimistic gathering the night before.

"It was nice," Julia was saying as Adam turned his attention back to the table.

"Mm-hm." Pete nodded as he chewed.

"What was nice?" Adam asked.

Julia rolled her eyes. "Are you ignoring us?"

"Sorry." Adam focused his attention on his plate, but even the juicy steak wasn't bringing up his spirits.

"I just asked Julia what she thought of the spa yesterday, that's all." Pete's voice carried more than a note of anger. They were taking pains to be polite, but there was a tension below the surface — and not too far below the surface.

"Oh, right. Look, I'm still concerned about Brad. We don't know why Paul was in his cabin." Adam tried to refocus on what really mattered.

"We should ask them. Each of them, separately. See what they say."

"I agree. Want to find them now?"

"Now?" Julia asked. She glanced at Pete, but looked quickly away. "Is that what you want to do now?"

A waiter passed by carrying a tray of desserts and Adam sighed.

"Why don't I do it. You two can spend some time together." He gave them each a meaningful look. "Talking. Right?"

Julia shrugged and Pete just looked away.

A noise near the front of the restaurant caught his attention. He looked over to see Molly getting up from a table, sharing cheerful goodnights with her dining companions. Adam dropped his fork on his plate and stood. He wasn't in the mood for dessert anyway.

"I'll catch you both later, OK?"

"Be careful," Julia said as Pete waved without a word.

He didn't need their problems right now.

Adam caught up with Molly as she neared the low staircase that led out of the room.

"Molly, hi." She turned as he spoke, then grimaced when she recognized him. "I'm glad I caught you. I never asked you where you were on Sunday night, early Monday morning."

"You're asking me for an alibi? I don't have one." She smiled sweetly. "But why on God's green earth would I kill Arthur?"

"Because he didn't want you seeing Hope." Adam smiled back just as sweetly.

"That's simply not true." Molly dropped the smile. "I mean, it's true he didn't know I was on this cruise. But he knew I'd been trying to see her. He wasn't helpful — that really wasn't his style. I had nothing I could offer him in return. But I think ... I don't know ..." She grabbed the railing as she took the few steps up and out of the room, Adam next to her. "I think he really loved her. I got the impression that he didn't mind my seeking her out, getting to know her. Maybe he thought she needed a mother."

"Needed a mother?" Adam let his confusion show on his face. "She's an adult, why would he think that?"

Molly nodded to a couple entering the dining room. They smiled back. A few paces more and she took the hand of another gentleman in greeting. "I don't know," she finally responded. "It's just the impression I got. Like he felt she needed protecting, she needed someone to take care of her."

"Surely he could've done that himself."

Molly shrugged in that familiar gesture. "Maybe he was too busy. Work. Whatever."

Adam was curious about what Molly was hinting at by that "whatever," but instead he asked, "If he was so protective of her, why did he leave his estate to Brad?"

"That was typical Arthur." Molly snorted out a laugh. "It was always about the men. Women needed protecting, men needed to be in charge. I'm not surprised by that at all."

"What do you think Arthur did with his time? What did he work on?"

"Arthur?" Molly seemed genuinely surprised by the question. "How would I know?"

"Earlier you hinted he had other things keeping him busy besides work."

"Oh. That." Molly let out a deep sigh. "I have no idea what he did with his time. I just know how we were put in touch with each other, that's all."

"And how was that?"

She cast a sideways glance at him. "It was a long time ago."

"Sure, I get that."

She tilted her head to one side with a frown and waited a beat before answering. "It was a Russian tea room. I knew people who hung out there. Not the ...well, not the best kind of people."

"What kind of people were they?"

She shook her head. "I really don't know. I knew enough not to ask too many questions, that's all. I didn't want to know." She looked directly at him. "I didn't ask, got it?"

She smiled and waved at another group coming down the hall toward the dining room. Adam knew he'd got all he could out of her on that subject.

"You seem to have a lot of friends on board," Adam said, truly curious. "How do you know so many people here?"

"Just people I've met. Cruises are very social places, aren't they?" Molly's saccharine smile was back. "It's so easy to meet people."

31

Adam found Paul in the Champagne Lounge, so named because of the neat champagne bar that lined one wall. While Bill was fraternizing with the old ladies of the family, Paul was doing a different sort of fraternizing, it seemed.

He paused at the bar and watched as Paul leaned over to the young woman sitting with him at the low table. They shared a laugh about something and she let her hand fall onto his arm for a moment. As she shifted in her seat, her face turned toward him and Adam recognized her. She'd been running one of the family-oriented games on the pool deck earlier. One of the activity staff on board.

So they did get downtime. And this was how she spent hers.

Another crew member stood on a small stage at the front of the lounge, playing the guitar and singing a song that had been popular about ten years earlier. A whiff of smoke escaped from the shaded door in the corner of the room that blocked off the ship's only smoking lounge. Waitresses in black moved silently between the low tables and armchairs that dotted the room.

The musician wasn't bad, actually. Finishing up the oldiebutgoodie, he'd switched to something a little more contemporary. A blend of traditional Caribbean with modern beats. Adam let the music wash over him as he waited and watched.

The young woman at Paul's table gave him one last smile and touch on the shoulder as she stood. She leaned over, pecked him on the cheek, then moved through the tables toward the hallway that led to the bar next door, turning at one point with a little wave to Paul.

Adam waited until Paul had watched her wiggle through the tables, then silently slid into her vacant chair. Paul didn't blink an eye, just spoke as if Adam had been sitting with him all along. "Can I order you a drink? They have some good whiskey onboard."

"Sure." Adam tried not to let his surprise show. "I usually drink Tullamore, but I'm willing to try something else if you recommend it."

Paul nodded with a small smile and gestured to a waitress. "Bold and willing to take risks, I like that."

When the whiskey arrived, Adam had to admit it was excellent.

"They do offer some decent luxuries on this ship, that's for sure," Paul agreed, cupping his glass in his palm as he looked around. "Like the spa. Seriously, have you been to the spa? Wonderful facials."

Adam laughed out loud and leaned forward to place his glass on the table. "Not really my thing, you know? That's my sister's kind of place."

"I see." Paul pursed his lips. "So if you hadn't been thrown into this investigation, what would you be doing with your time on board?"

"This, probably." Adam laughed again. "Sitting here,

drinking a good whiskey, listening to some good music. Probably spending more time sitting by the pool reading." He let out a breath. "It would've been nice."

"I noticed that you liked music."

Adam gave him a curious look.

"Well, I should say I noticed you've been very friendly with the man who leads the lectures on music, what's his name ... Manny or something?" Paul's grin didn't fool Adam for a minute, but he got the impression it wasn't supposed to.

"Marcus, yeah. And I noticed that you like to be in the know, to have all the right information."

That time Adam was sure he saw a flicker of surprise in Paul's eyes, though it didn't last. He took a moment to try another taste of his whiskey before responding. "Now, who's been talking about me out of school?" Paul asked.

The music had shifted again, this time to a tune that sounded a little more country than rock and roll. Other guests in the lounge were keeping their voices low, but Adam heard laughter carrying from the pub past the champagne lounge.

"Why are you sitting in a champagne bar drinking whiskey when there's an Irish pub down the hall?" Adam asked.

Paul waved a hand toward the musician. "I like the atmosphere in here. Plus, just because I'm drinking whiskey now doesn't mean I won't be drinking champagne next."

"Like if Hope joins you, you mean?" Adam asked.

No reaction at all that time.

"What are you fishing for, Detective?" Paul asked.

"How much do you know about Brad Claypoole?"

"Brad?" Paul frowned, looking out across the room. "I don't know Brad well at all."

"That's not what I asked."

Paul turned to face Adam, a broad smile creasing his face. "Brad. Seriously? That's who's got you asking me questions?" A few guests at the next table glanced over as Paul's laugh grew louder. "Brad, that is too much."

Adam waited until Paul's amusement had settled down. "And why is that so funny? Like I said, how much do you know about him?"

"More than you, apparently, Detective." Paul finished his whiskey and handed the empty glass to a passing waitress, shaking his head when she offered another. "I know he doesn't always follow the straight and narrow path."

"Why were you in Brad's cabin earlier?"

Paul raised his eyebrows. "Now how did you know that? Are you following me, Detective?"

"Just answer the question."

Paul glanced at Adam, then back at the musician. "I think that's my business, I'm afraid."

Adam felt his anger rise, but recognized he wasn't likely going to be successful if he tried to beat the truth out of Paul. At least not here, in a champagne lounge. He laughed at the incongruity of the thought, and Paul glanced at him.

"You said I like to be in the know. Well, I know that Alice Murphy saw Hope with something she wasn't supposed to have ... or maybe with someone she wasn't supposed to be with. Not sure exactly."

"If you're not sure, then how do you know?"

"I heard them talking about it. I was getting a facial — did I mention the excellent spa services here?"

Adam took a breath. "Yes, you did. What did you overhear?"

"Oh, Alice apologizing, 'not trying to suggest anything ...' Something like that."

Adam couldn't resist smiling as Paul mimicked Alice's nervous voice. "Were they arguing?"

"Hm, I wouldn't say arguing, exactly. Hope didn't seem overly upset. Alice was more concerned than she was, to be honest."

"About what?" Adam asked, thoroughly confused.

Paul just shrugged. "I can't tell you that. All I know is that Alice took pains to assure her no one else knew." He let his gaze travel around the room again as he spoke. "Do you think that's important, Detective?"

Adam bit back his retort that of course it was important. He recognized a rhetorical question when he heard one. He decided not to follow Paul's lead and waved to a waitress for a second whiskey. It was good, after all.

Paul blew out a loud laugh and changed his mind, having a second as well. "We are on vacation, after all." He smiled as he held his glass toward Adam. "Cheers."

"Cheers. To finding the truth and exposing a killer."

"I'll drink to that." For the first time since they'd been talking, Paul sounded like he really meant what he said.

"So, anything else you want to fill me in on?" Adam asked with a smile, trying to sound friendly. "Any other secret conversations or goings-on I might want to know about?"

"Quite a few, actually." Paul paused so long Adam thought he was going to leave it at that, but eventually he continued, "Your friend Marcus has his own secrets, you know."

"If you know about them, they can't be all that secret."

Paul grinned and ducked his head in acknowledgement. "I am pretty good at finding things out."

"Go on."

"Chef Guzeman," Paul started, then looked at Adam. "Ah, yes, you've talked to him."

Adam had a pretty good poker face, but Paul seemed to see right through him. "He's got form, yeah."

"Yeah, well. He's not really the small bit player he claims. He's got a lot more going on than you all know about."

"Smuggling?"

Paul nodded. "I'm sure he owned up to something, right? A little bit of innocent trade under the table to avoid taxes? Bringing in small quantities of minor drugs?"

"Something like that."

"Don't let him fool you. He's not what he seems." Paul pursed his lips as he sat back more comfortably into his chair, his attention fully on the music.

"What do you have against Guzeman? Did you know him when he worked for Claypoole?"

Paul smiled and shook his head. "No point telling him your information comes from me. He doesn't know me."

"You want your name to stay out of it? Why, are you afraid of him?"

Paul shut his eyes and shook his head. He didn't answer.

Adam mimicked Paul's pose, leaning back into the chair, his head resting against the soft back. Paul didn't strike him as a man who was afraid. Of anyone. That meant he'd be perfectly capable of killing someone and pointing the finger at someone else. And Adam still didn't know who he really worked for. If he worked at all.

On the other hand, if his tips panned out, they were certainly useful. Maybe he should revisit the details of those cyanide poisonings in New York after all.

ADAM'S WHISKEY glass sat on the table in front of him, now holding no more than fumes. He was tempted to order yet another. He glanced at Paul, but Paul's attention was on the musician, his fingers tapping along with the music on the arm of his chair.

He needed to think through what they already knew. Somewhere, he had a fact that he was overlooking, or not realizing its importance. Means, motive, and opportunity, right?

It seemed like a lot of people had opportunity — too many people with easy access to Claypoole and not enough alibis to go around. Access to Alice Murphy was different, though. So who was close enough to both of them to have that access?

"Adam."

He started at the light touch on his shoulder as Marcus leaned over.

"Adam, I'm sorry about earlier. Can we talk?"

"I think that's my cue." Paul sighed heavily as he lifted himself out of his chair. "Gentlemen." He nodded at them both, then left them alone.

The bruise on Marcus' face was worse now than it had been earlier, unsurprisingly. Adam knew from experience it still had to go through several shades of purple before gradually turning yellow, then fading away completely. Of course, he wasn't sure what other injuries Marcus had sustained.

"What happened to you, man? I mean, what really happened?"

Marcus laughed, then grimaced in pain. He slid into the seat Paul had just vacated.

Adam waved over a waitress and ordered another whiskey. Why the hell not.

"I walked into a door. Seriously. I did," Marcus told him as the waitress brought over Adam's drink.

"No, that's what people say when they don't want to admit they've been hit. So who's hitting you?" Adam tried to keep his voice gentle, to coax the truth out of Marcus.

"No one hit me. But if you must know, you're to blame."

"Me?" Adam's head jerked back in surprise. "What're you talking about?"

"That person you were chasing down in the hold?"

"How the hell'd you know about that?"

"Because it was me. And I'm not kidding, I really did run into a door. Damn." Marcus touched his face gingerly. "Does it still look bad?"

Adam sipped his drink. "It's going to get a lot worse before it gets better. If that was you, why'd you run from me?"

Marcus pursed his lips and nodded, not making eye contact with Adam. "I didn't want you to find what I had hidden."

Adam shook his head. "Just spit it out. What're you hiding?"

"Drugs."

The musician hit a long riff on his guitar and Adam slid back into his seat, whiskey glass in hand, as he contemplated Marcus' admission. "You're a smuggler."

"Nah, it's not like that. I mean, technically, yeah, OK, but not like you think."

"Does Karen know?"

Marcus looked as surprised as Adam that that was his first question. He just shook his head, his eyes wide.

"It's medical marijuana, Adam. That's all."

"If it's medical, why do you need to smuggle it in? I don't understand."

"It's legal in New Jersey, sure. But not in Bermuda. I have a brother, Adam. In Bermuda. He's not doing well."

"Cancer?" Adam asked.

Marcus shook his head. "Parkinsons. The marijuana really helps. I can't even describe to you the changes it makes in him. For him. Without it ... well, he wouldn't be able to get by. But with my help, he can."

Adam felt his hands tighten around his glass and quickly put it down. He'd trusted Marcus, grown to like him. Finding out he was hiding something like this was painful.

Marcus waited a moment before continuing, and Adam was grateful for the opportunity to wrap his mind around this. Even if it was for a good cause, he was still breaking the law. Smuggling was smuggling.

"How did you get involved in this?" Adam asked.

"I bring a little bit in with each trip I make. Nathaniel knew it would help, he'd been able to try it before. Once it became legal in Jersey, he asked me for help. I had to help him, you understand that?"

"I do," Adam said grimly. "I understand the desire to help. But you're breaking the law."

Marcus frowned. "I got the idea from the news. I remembered reading, years ago, about a drug smuggling ring on cruise ships to Bermuda. The cops had busted it, it was a big deal. But I thought, if they could do it, why not me? I already had access to the ships."

"You had it hidden in the hold? How did you get it past Captain Harding?"

"Pfft." Marcus made a dismissive gesture. "Harding thinks he's so strict, but he doesn't know what's going on on his own ship. He's too busy doing his own thing."

"What's that?"

Marcus shrugged, shook his head. "I don't know. I'm just glad it keeps him out of my business. Out of my luggage."

"You moved it when you thought I'd find it?"

Marcus nodded again. "It's in my cabin now. But I don't like to keep it there, it would be too easy for one of my bunkmates to come across it. I'm sorry I ran from you, Adam, it was stupid. I just kept thinking, if you found it, I didn't know what I'd do."

Adam let out a long breath, finished off his whiskey. Really wasn't going to get another.

"So you're the mystery figure in the hold. You and Guzeman are running drugs while Captain Harding is doing something else, we don't know what. Bill is hiding the truth about himself and Paul is spinning one lie after another."

Marcus offered a small smile as he raised an eyebrow. "You need to find the truth."

"That's what I'm trying to do."

"No, I mean for yourself. About your family. That story you told me, about your grandfather. It got me thinking."

"About what?"

"About family. About what I'm doing for my brother — despite the price I could eventually have to pay."

Adam thought about his own family. His desperate need to find the truth.

"No, I'm done with that. Maybe you should be, too." He looked at Marcus pointedly.

"I can't. Not as long as Nathaniel is suffering and I have the ability to help. You shouldn't give up, either. It's clearly important to you. And I already told you, you've got a good chance of finding something out about the past right here in Bermuda."

Adam leaned his elbows forward on his knees. "No one is suffering. No one needs me to find the truth. Unlike this case, which is a lot more pressing."

"Well, life is short," Marcus said. "We do what we must do — to make it worth living."

"I get that, Marcus. I do," Adam said. "I support doing what's right. And I know that's not always about the letter of the law, it's about knowing right from wrong."

Marcus frowned as he nodded. "I believe you have a pretty good sense of that, Adam. You should trust your instincts."

32

That fifth whiskey probably wasn't a good idea. Adam sat up and rubbed his hands over his forehead, trying to clear the blur of sleep. It hadn't been a good night. He'd tossed and turned, not knowing what his next step should be but knowing he was running out of time. The boat would dock that morning and the Feds would take over. He'd failed.

He lay back down and his dreams came back to him in flashes — shadowy figures in trench coats and fedoras, women in sleek dresses with cigarette holders smiling at a bar in a Bermuda hotel, vicious drug smugglers running the high seas, a still-alive Alice Murphy befriended by Hope and Julia then laughing fanatically as Bill chased after Hope, fumes of gas being inhaled by an old man, a serial killer hiding on the streets of New York, a feeling of being lost in a maze of right and wrong.

He had to focus on the case. He lay still, letting his mind work through the facts that he knew. And that he didn't know. Something about Paul was off, that was for sure. But for some reason he couldn't entirely understand himself, he trusted him. So what had he been doing in Brad's cabin? Of course, everyone else seemed to have something to hide as well. Everyone except Brad and Hope, the only people who benefited from Arthur Claypoole's death. Brad, who Bill described as a floppy noodle, and Hope, who everyone seemed to think needed someone to take care of her.

He sat up abruptly, then regretted it as his brain took a fraction of a second longer to right itself. No time for self-pity. He knew who he needed to talk to.

Pete wasn't in his cabin. Julia suggested Adam might find him in the breakfast buffet, but he wasn't there, either. On his way from the buffet to the pool deck, Adam avoided the crowds on the main deck by cutting through one of the passenger hallways, narrower but empty.

If he didn't find Pete at the pool, he'd go ahead without him. This couldn't wait. He could tell his adrenaline was egging him on, and he knew how valuable Pete was in keeping his cool, but he also knew the clock was running out. Marcus' voice rang in his ears: trust your instincts.

He turned a corner in the narrow hallway and walked right into Captain Harding, just pulling a cabin door closed behind him. "What the hell are you doing down here?"

"I ... uh ... nothing."

Adam stopped and glared at the captain. "Tell me the truth. The real truth this time. What's going on between you and Brad?"

Harding fidgeted with the collar of his shirt, though it was already perfectly straight. "How did you know about that?"

"You're hardly discreet."

"Oh." Harding turned pink. "I actually thought we

were. I always try to be. If the others knew, well ... that could be a problem."

"Others? What others? Who are you talking about?"

Harding shrugged. "Not everyone is so understanding about someone like me. Surely you understand that. People can be judgmental. That includes people on the cruise line. I could lose my job."

"People like you? Harding, I don't know what you're telling me."

"I get involved with passengers sometimes. All the crew does it. They just ... they expect the captain to have a little more discretion."

"You're having an affair with Brad? That's what you're trying to hide?"

Harding nodded.

Adam thought back about the interactions he'd seen between them. "So the attention you pay to the female passengers, that's just for show?"

"Oh, no." Harding laughed. "Some of them are so eager. So willing."

Adam looked at Harding blindly, knowing he was being slow-witted but not getting the pieces to fit together.

"I'm bisexual, Kaminski. That's what people wouldn't understand. Gay, maybe. You can put that into a neat little box and tie the string. But people like me? Not so easy to get."

"Jesus, Harding. Why didn't you just tell me that?"

"You don't understand. Life is so simple for people like you. But for me ... in this job..." Harding lowered his eyes.

Adam controlled his anger. It was no good taking his frustration out on Harding. At this point, he needed his help. "By keeping secrets, you made this harder, the truth more difficult to untangle."

"I have my secrets that I protect like everybody else. You think when you're investigating, people are just going to walk up to you and confess all their dirty deeds?"

Adam laughed. "Of course not. But every secret I don't know can pull me in the wrong direction. Can distract me from seeing the truth. So is that all that Brad's hiding, too?"

Harding shrugged again. "How should I know? We're just sleeping together, not making a lifetime commitment. Look, this was one of the reasons I wanted you to get involved in the first place. I knew the faster this murder was wrapped up, the less likely anyone would be digging into my private business."

"Your private business?" Adam fumed. "What about the spouses you're hurting? Brad's married, probably others are too. And what the ... just tell me this, what does this have to do with the fumigation?"

"Nothing!" Harding threw his hand up in frustration. "That really was a coincidence. Guzeman can deny it all he wants, but some of the crew complained about vermin so I stepped up the schedule. That's all. Nothing nefarious, I swear."

Adam didn't even try to hide the annoyance he was feeling. "Frankly, if I were you I'd be more worried about getting complaints from a passenger who thought he or she was more than a one-time fling. Right now, I need to get into Bill's cabin. Can you get me in?"

"I don't know why I'm doing this." Harding spoke through gritted teeth as he slid his master key card over the lock to Bill's cabin and pushed the door open.

"Like you just told me, you have your own reasons for

wanting me to get to the bottom of this case," Adam replied as he stepped into the room.

The cabin was almost exactly like Adam's. An ocean view, but with a square window, not the wide sliding doors he'd seen in the first-class cabins. A bed took up most of the room, with small tables for writing, food and toiletries tucked against the wall.

"What exactly are you looking for?"

"I'll know it when I see it." Adam wasn't willing to share his idea until he'd checked it out. At least not with Harding. "Your crew said Bill was settled at the breakfast bar, right?"

Harding nodded. "But I don't know how long he'll be there."

"Adam." Pete joined them in the cabin, making the room feel very tight indeed. "Julia said you'd be here."

"Glad you're here, Pete. Captain Harding, I appreciate your help." Adam looked Harding in the eye, waiting.

It took a few seconds. "Oh, I see. Right. Let me know if you need anything else." Harding shut the door behind himself.

"I'm wondering why Bill has been so adamant that he didn't bring his tool kit with him on this trip."

Pete shrugged. "Maybe it's unusual for him. He usually has it with him, so he keeps reminding us — or himself — that he doesn't have it this time."

"Maybe ..." Adam drew out the word. "But I was thinking about the cause of death. Claypoole, not Alice Murphy."

"Cyanide poisoning. Could be gas."

"Right. And I was remembering back a few years when the department prohibited the use of mobile wands for identifying fingerprints. Remember that? Now the technicians have to use other techniques."

"Sure. The wands were found to be too risky. Too much chance of releasing hydrogen cyanide gas." Pete laughed in disbelief. "Seriously? You think a fingerprinting wand is our murder weapon?"

"Why not?" Adam knelt and pulled a suitcase out from under the bed. "I know Bill uses one. Let's see if he has it with him, anyway."

Pete acquiesced and turned his attention to the wardrobe built in along a part of the wall, moving his way along it. In a cabin this size, the search didn't take long.

"I think I got it." Pete stepped out of the closet-sized bathroom carrying what looked like a black toiletry kit. He'd unzipped the top and now reached in and pulled out a thick black metal torch.

"What do you think?" Adam asked, stepping over to look closely at the device in Pete's hand. "You've had more experience with these than I have."

"Only because I pay more attention to the details of the reports we get from crime scenes while you're off trying to assess suspects."

Adam grinned. "Guilty as charged. So what can you tell me about this one."

"It's possible ..." Pete said, turning the wand around as he examined it carefully.

"I'm not the expert," Adam said, "but this doesn't look right to me. Look." He indicated a scar where the metal had been soldered.

Pete nodded and pointed to the elements of the tool as he talked his way through what he was seeing. "The wand is made up of a butane burner here, with a cartridge on top. The cartridge holds a hard capsule of solidified cyanoacrylate along with a fluorescent dye."

"A brightly colored super glue."

"Exactly. When ignited, the torch heats the cartridge, and cyanoacrylate vapor is rapidly released. The fumes are directed onto the item to be processed until developed prints become visible to the naked eye."

"But they're dangerous, that's what we were told. The glue can be heated up to levels that release hydrogen cyanide gas."

"Yep. HCN. Which is what we think killed Arthur Claypoole. The wands are designed not to get that hot, so they're not supposed to be deadly, but look. This one has been modified."

Adam looked as Pete pointed to the device. "He's replaced the nozzle with a wider nozzle to make the flame larger. He separated the cartridge from the flame so that he could run the flame for longer before pushing down the cartridge into the heat, making the initial heat higher. With a larger flame that burns longer, it makes it hotter and easy to reach the danger zone for cyanide gas."

"So Bill's carrying around a perfect cyanide gas weapon." Adam thought about Bill's actions. He'd offered to help with the investigation. He'd tried to convince Hope to stay with him instead of going off to Paris. He'd been friendly and supportive to his extended family. "We need to figure out his motive. He doesn't inherit anything and couldn't have expected to."

"And the connection with the other cyanide poisonings in New York?" Pete asked.

Adam shook his head. "I don't know. I don't want to assume anything. Could be a coincidence."

"Or could be we have a truly crazy man on our hands willing to kill anyone to get what he wants, walking around with a perfect killing tool."

"Then why not kill Alice Murphy the same way?"

Pete and Adam both stopped to consider this.

"Is the cartridge empty?" Adam asked.

Pete hefted the item in his hands. "Could be. Could just be not enough's left. Simple as that."

"We need to find Bill. Fast."

"I have a better idea," Pete said. "We need to find Julia."

33

Hope slouched in a plastic chair on the outdoor deck near the breakfast buffet. She stared out at the sea but didn't look like she was watching for anything in particular.

"Hope." Julia spoke softly so as not to surprise her. "How are you?"

"Oh, hi." Hope straightened herself up in her seat. She glanced around, then waved at the waiter standing in the tiki bar. As he brought over a mimosa and took the empty glass from Hope's table, she looked up at Julia.

"What are your plans for the day?" Julia asked. "Now that we're here, I mean."

From her seat, Hope could only see the water, but standing next to her, Julia could look behind her to the gray rocks of Bermuda's wharf. The boat was still moving slowly in and figures on the dock ran alongside, calling to one another as they helped the boat sidle in or set up temporary booths to greet the hoards of tourists.

"Um, I'm not really sure. I might go onto the island later. How about you? Do you have something fun planned?

Or are you working on the paperwork for your new job onboard?"

"Ah, that." Julia sighed with a smile. "I can't believe I seriously considered leaving my home to work here. Something about the open sea, isn't it?"

Hope laughed drily. "I guess so."

"No," Julia continued. "No, I realized that's not for me. I have too much I love back at home to give that up."

Hope looked up at her, her eyes full of sadness. "I'm glad for you. Pete must be, too."

Julia gave a quick smile as she slid into the seat next to Hope's. "I didn't expect his reaction. He caught me by surprise, you know?" Hope nodded, so Julia continued. "He's really committed to this relationship, and I only realized that when I threatened to pull away from it. I can't believe how much I hurt him." She laughed bitterly. "Now I just need to tell Pete. If he's even talking to me."

"We always hurt the ones we love, Julia. It's how life works." Hope spoke the words in a flat tone, as if she were just stating the facts, not making a truly depressing observation. "You didn't mean to hurt him. And I'm glad it helped you sort out your own feelings."

Despite everything she was going through, she meant it, Julia could tell. "Oh, Hope, how about you? Will you be OK? Can you do something relaxing today, just to get away from all this?"

"I can't relax." Hope shuddered and took a sip of her drink. "I understand some investigators are coming on board today. They might want to speak with me, I need to be available."

"Hope, I need to tell you something. About Bill."

The look in Hope's eyes as she turned to face her almost made Julia give up on Adam's plan. What was she doing, dragging Hope into this? This woman had lost so much already. Did they really need to take away her last shred of faith in humanity?

She only faltered for a second. If Bill was a killer, then the answer to that question was obvious.

"Hope, we need your help. Well, Adam and Pete need your help."

"What can I do?"

"Can you talk to Bill?"

"Of course I can. They need his help? They could just ask him themselves, you know. He's so sweet, always willing to help."

Julia frowned and shook her head. "No, I need you to talk to him about your father. About how he died."

"I don't understand." Hope's voice dropped and she pushed her glass away from her across the table, leaving a wet trail in its wake.

"Bill has access to a tool — something he uses in his job — that could have been used to poison your father. To kill him."

"That can't be right. Bill said he doesn't have his tools with him on the boat."

"But he does. Adam and Pete found it, in his cabin."

Hope almost seemed to laugh, but it turned into a question. "They searched his cabin? How could they?"

"Hope, they found the tool. A fingerprint wand. It's ... it's a tool that can be used to poison someone."

"That's horrible. I'm sure he didn't do that. Not Bill. Not Bill."

"I know it's hard for you to believe, given how well you know him. That's why we need you to talk to him. To get him to explain. We know he'll tell you. He's not likely to be as open with Adam or Pete, is he?"

Hope laughed mirthlessly. "Not after they searched his cabin, no." She looked at Julia defiantly. "I'll talk to him. I'll ask him about it. But he's not going to say what you expect. Not Bill."

"Thank you, Hope. I wouldn't ask it it wasn't so important. But be careful, please."

Hope got up. "I'll talk to him. Just to find the truth."

———

ADAM STOOD with his back to the tiki bar, his head turned to the side. A passenger waiting for a friend, to anyone who passed by. But his location let him hear every word shared between Hope and Bill, who stood on the far side of the tiki bar.

Special agents with the FBI were standing ready to be the first on board as soon as the boat docked. That was a good thing, Adam knew, but it would be even better if they could get a confession out of Bill before the lawyers got involved.

Pete had been right. It had been almost too easy for Hope to find Bill and bring him to the buffet for a cup of coffee and a chat. He felt guilty knowing they were setting Bill up and putting Hope at risk in the process. But he was standing right there, it was a public space, he was sure she'd be safe. She had to be.

He hadn't let Hope know he'd been listening in, hoping she would sound more natural not knowing he was there. And she'd agreed easily to talk with Bill alone, still trusting him, apparently.

As he listened, he noticed that her words were clipped, tense. There was no way Bill would believe her. Was there?

"I'm glad I don't have to go to Paris," Hope was saying.

"You're so right," Bill agreed. "But I'm a little surprised, I thought you said you were excited to go."

"I was, you know ..." Hope's voice trailed off for a moment. "But now that I think about it, maybe that was more of my father's dream. Maybe it's better this way, now that he's not here."

Adam heard Bill's sharp intake of breath and realized he was holding his breath. Surely Bill knew a lie when he heard one?

Bill's voice sounded high and tight when he replied. "I'm so glad to hear you say that! I was hoping you'd stick around."

"Is that why you did it?"

"I don't understand, did what?"

Hope's voice wavered. "Killed my dad."

"I don't understand, Hope—"

Harding's voice over the loudspeaker blocked out whatever Bill said next. The standard announcement let the passengers know the timeline over the next hour as the boat docked and passengers were scheduled for an organized disembarkation.

When Adam picked up Bill's voice again, he could hear the confusion in it. "What you're asking of me ... Hope, this is crazy."

"I had no choice, you have to understand that. I needed to hide it, and it was yours, after all."

"But ... I don't understand."

"It certainly made dealing with Alice harder. I didn't plan on that," Hope said, annoyance creeping into her tone.

Whatever he'd missed, the conversation had clearly been moving forward fast.

"I still don't understand what you're telling me. Or what you're asking of me."

"Take your hands off of me." Hope's voice was defensive. "He wasn't my father. And I know you care for me, Bill. You said you'd do anything for me. I need you to step up now." Adam picked up the anger in Hope's tone and didn't wait for more.

He stepped around the tiki bar. Hope's face blanched when she saw him. Bill took in her reaction and turned to face Adam.

"You? You were listening?" She took a step backwards as Bill backed slowly away from her.

"I still don't understand what's going on," Bill said, his voice now wavering.

"Step back, Bill. Turns out this isn't about you." Adam put out a hand as he spoke, gesturing for Bill to move away. "Hope. You did this. You killed your father. You hid the weapon in Bill's cabin to frame him."

A crooked smile slid across Hope's face, but her eyes looked like tiny specks of blue ice. "He wasn't my father. Why do people keep saying that? And besides, that was Bill's fingerprint wand. Everyone knows that."

"You won't get away." Adam shook his head as he spoke. "I heard everything."

"You heard?" Hope barked out a laugh. "You heard nothing. And it doesn't matter anyway. You can't arrest me, you have no jurisdiction here."

Adam shifted his weight as he felt the boat slide up against the dock, heard the voices of crews on land calling to each other. He was getting used to feeling the ground shift underneath him, getting better at dealing with it.

He dropped his arms and stepped back. "You're right." He shrugged. "I can't arrest you."

Hope smiled again, this time reaching her eyes. "It was a pleasure knowing you, Detective." She raised two fingers in a salute that ended with a saucy wave. "Good luck to you."

She turned and sauntered toward the stairs that led down to the gangplank. She glanced back as she took the first step down, but Adam hadn't moved. He stood perfectly still, watching her walk away.

She laughed out loud at that point, grabbing the railing and skipping down the stairs. Adam walked forward to watch her progress, following her at a distance. As she reached the narrow deck where a group of passengers had gathered in preparation for leaving the boat, she picked up her pace. Their cheerful chatter and laughing turned into angry shouts as Hope pushed her way through them.

"We're waiting here, lady."

"Do you have a yellow ticket?" A woman waved the golden piece of paper that indicated the next group ready to disembark.

Hope kept pushing forward, like a fish trying to swim upstream. Soon the shouts carried ahead of her and passengers who were in her way stepped aside as they saw her coming. Adam stepped through the group of passengers in her wake.

"Watch out, don't get involved," Adam called out as one man tried to grab Hope's arm. "Stay back!"

Hope laughed and kept moving toward the gangplank, only twenty feet ahead.

When she reached the gangplank, she stopped and glanced back at Adam. She grinned, gave Adam another mock salute, and trotted down as if eager for a day on the island. The gangplank razor-backed off the ship in thirty-foot stretches that folded back on each other, limiting the downward slope. Adam stopped before getting on, leaning over the railing to see the point where the ramp connected with the dock. Two burly men in blue suits glared up at him. He held up his badge for them to see and pointed to Hope, still smiling as she ran directly toward them.

As Hope threw herself around the final turn, she came face to face with the men, in defensive stances, waiting for her. She tried to stop, to turn, but the Feds had her spun around and handcuffed before her feet had stopped moving.

34

"I KNEW you'd get there eventually." Paul spoke softly, but Adam swung toward him as if he'd been punched.

"Who the hell are you?"

"Calm down." Paul glanced around the crowded lounge. Two agents had maneuvered Hope down the ramp to an SUV waiting on the dock while three more had boarded the boat to talk to witnesses, starting with Captain Harding. Paul kept his eye on the group as they talked, voices low, in a tight huddle across the room. "I'm just glad it worked out with no one else getting hurt."

"No one else except Alice Murphy, you mean," Adam said, not bothering to keep the anger out of his voice. "If you knew something that would've saved her, you should've told me."

Paul stared at him. "Told you? I practically handed you Hope's name engraved on a silver platter. The murders in New York? The fingerprinting wand that she had easy access to thanks to Bill's lovesick blindness? What the hell else did you want?"

Adam sucked in his breath and tried to stay calm. "You

dropped clues. Breadcrumbs. Why not just come out and tell me what you knew?"

Paul shook his head and looked away. "Couldn't. Still can't. Sorry, not my choice, I'm under orders."

"Whose orders?"

Paul smiled as he shook his head again. "You know I'm not going to answer that, why bother asking?" Paul coughed. "Of course, if you have ideas you want to test out on me ..."

Adam glared at him, but realized he couldn't miss this opportunity. He didn't know this guy, had no real explanation from him of who he was and what he was doing. Yet somehow, Adam trusted him. His gut was telling him that Paul was one of the good guys. "Claypoole was using his connections as a political donor to gather information he could sell to the Russians."

Paul dipped his head in a half-nod. Adam took it as agreement.

"You were trying to catch him in the act, gather evidence to stop him."

Another half-nod. "Hope had her own plans," Paul said. "Now there's a favor I want to ask of you."

Adam laughed loudly, then turned his head when a few of the huddled group looked their way. "And what's that?"

"Your sister has some photographs I'd rather not get shared too widely." He looked closely at Adam. "Pictures of me."

Adam took a deep breath and let it out. "One more question. Why are you interested in Brad now?"

"Brad?" Paul laughed lightly. "No, Brad's nothing. He didn't pick up his father's interests. I'm pretty sure of that. My work will take me elsewhere now. I suspect I'm done with the Claypoole clan."

Adam studied the secretive man standing next to him.

A man who could easily be ignored, easily forgotten. Someone who could slip in and out of situations without being noticed but who could turn the charm on when he needed to. He nodded. "I'll take care of Julia's pictures."

Agents were moving their way. "I gotta go now. It's been fun, Detective. I hope we run into each other again." Paul took a few smooth steps and slid into a passing group of passengers.

"Detective." The agent who spoke was short but burly, with the chest of a boxer and the eyes of a card shark. "Gota minute?"

It wasn't a question, so Adam nodded and led the way to a group of chairs. "What can I tell you?"

"Let's start with evidence. What proof do you have of Ms. Claypoole's guilt?"

"Her confession. That good enough for you?"

The agent blinked, but other than that his expression didn't change. "You got a formal statement?"

Adam shook his head. "No. But it was heard by others."

The agent glanced at one of his partners, who said, "Bill Langtry, cousin of the deceased."

"The first victim," Adam added.

The card-shark agent paused a beat before speaking. "It's not much."

Adam offered a small smile. "We've got the murder weapon. She'd stashed it in Bill's cabin, but her fingerprints will be on it."

The agent raised an eyebrow, the most expression Adam had seen yet. "That's good. That's very good. Weapon and overheard confession. Motive?"

Adam raised one side of his mouth, trying to conceal his own disbelief in what he knew was true. "Money. She thought she'd get half of her father's estate. She thought killing her father would make her rich. Or at least rich enough to finance the life she wanted in Paris."

"I thought she was already getting that anyway."

"They had an argument just before the cruise. I think Arthur had decided not to pay for her trip, he wanted to keep her close to home. From what I've learned, he was beginning to worry about her, to think she wasn't quite right."

"He realized she was dangerous?"

Adam shrugged. "I'm not sure. Maybe. But he wanted to keep her close. To protect her."

"He should've been more worried about himself." Card Shark made one sharp nod and stood. His colleagues followed his lead. Adam stayed where he was.

"Anything else?"

Adam nodded. He almost didn't want to say it. Because he wasn't sure there was really a connection? Or because the information had come from Paul? "There are other murders you should look into."

An agent checked his notebook. "The photographer. Alice Murphy."

"Not just her. I mean in New York, where Hope lives."

"What murders?"

Adam sighed. "I understand there have been a series of murders by cyanide poisoning and I have a — that is, I believe they may be connected. To Hope Claypoole."

Card Shark laughed softly. "You think this lady is a serial killer?"

Adam raised an eyebrow and nodded once. "I think she's killed before. Definitely worth looking into. Check the M.O."

"Hmph." Card Shark pocketed his notebook and stood. "Maybe we will. Good work, Detective."

"Not good enough for Alice Murphy," Adam said softly.

"No." The agents left him alone with that thought.

———

Two hours later, federal agents had set up a somewhat more permanent interview room in the library. One by one, the remaining family members were being called in to give their statements and whatever other information they needed to share. The rest of the ship's passengers were off enjoying their first day in Bermuda, oblivious to the drama playing out in the small, secluded room just beyond the pool and before the spa.

Adam and Pete took the opportunity to grab a couple of quiet drinks at the bar in the main lounge.

"To another job well done." Pete raised his Bloody Mary towards Adam.

Adam grinned and shifted his whiskey in response. He wasn't really in the mood for celebrating.

"That's not a typical morning beverage, you know." Karen slid onto the stool next to Adam and ordered a Bloody Mary for herself. "If you don't mind me joining you?"

Adam shrugged. "It's up to you. I got the impression you didn't have a lot left you wanted to share with me."

Karen took a sip of her drink before responding. "Well I'm certainly interested in sharing a drink. Maybe even a visit to the island?"

Pete laughed. "Will you two just kiss and make up already?"

Karen's eyes widened. "I don't even know what we're making up from. Did I miss a fight?"

"Detective Kaminski, Lawler." They all turned at

Brad's voice. The man standing behind their bar stools was not the same man they'd met only two days earlier. Now, Brad shuffled his feet as he stood, his shoulders hunched, his brow furrowed.

"Brad, how are you?" Adam asked. "You holding up?"

Brad tried to grin but it looked more like a grimace. "I guess you could call it that."

"Join us?" Pete asked but Brad shook his head.

"No, thank you. I'll survive. But I've got a lot of thinking to do."

Adam thought that might be the understatement of the year.

"I want to thank you, though," Brad continued. "I know I didn't thank you before. But for finding out ... well, for finding out the truth. About me, I mean ..." His voice trailed off and he looked down at his hands. He held his father's heavy gold watch loosely, running his fingers over the engraving. The engraving of the name that, until yesterday, he thought had been his own.

Adam put a hand on Brad's shoulder. "I can't imagine what that's like for you. Learning something like that at this point in your life. I don't know how I'd handle it."

Pete grinned. "I imagine there would be some anger issues to deal with. And whiskey. Lots of whiskey."

Adam raised his chin in acknowledgment of the truth of Pete's statement. He gave Brad one more friendly pat on the arm and turned back to his drink. "So what will you do now?"

Brad tightened his fingers around the watch. "I'm going to learn about my family. My real family."

"Arthur Claypoole seemed to love you, Brad. I can relate to wanting to find the truth about your family. But don't let the facts of your birth color too darkly your memories of your father — of the man who raised you as his own."

Brad nodded slowly and dropped the watch into his pocket. "I'll see you around, then. I just wanted to say ..."

Pete and Adam both nodded and raised their glasses to Brad, who simply nodded once and left them to their drinks.

"Did you mean that?" Karen asked. "About wanting to find the truth about your family, I mean?"

Adam thought about this. He'd convinced himself he'd learned enough. He was sure that if he dug any deeper he'd only find more hurtful information, more reasons to be ashamed of his heritage, of his ancestors.

He finished off his whiskey and signaled for another. "I think I did."

"I'm glad to hear it."

Adam jumped at Marcus' voice. He hadn't noticed him sidling up to the bar next to Pete.

"Yeah, well, I guess I'm not as ready to give up as I thought I was," Adam replied.

"Good. I mean, I know it's not my business, but I did make some calls."

Adam looked at him expectantly. The bruise on his face was still darkening and Marcus touched a finger to it gingerly, as if checking it was still there. Adam felt the pull of his job, the need to see justice served. He could so easily let the agents in the library know about Marcus' small-scale smuggling operation. Would they care? Did he, really?

"I spoke to a friend of mine who knows the head librarian at what was Bermuda Station."

"Why did you do that for me?" Adam asked quietly.

Marcus smiled. "You're a good man, Adam Kaminski. You think I hadn't noticed that? You're like a piece of music with multiple themes. At first glance, when you first hear it, you think you can pick out the main theme easily. But as the music progresses, you realize that another theme, one you thought was only secondary, is slowly raising its profile, becoming the main theme."

Adam laughed. "You lost me on that one."

"You have more good in you than bad, that's all I'm saying. You have a good sense of right and wrong. I want to help you. It's as simple as that."

Adam glanced at Pete, who simply shrugged. "Don't look at me. I only hang out with you because I have to."

"Thank you, Marcus." Adam leaned over to shake his new friend's hand, glad he hadn't followed his overeager sense of law and order. "Thank you."

"It was just a few phone calls. I can't promise you'll discover anything. But Hettie is a great researcher, from what I've heard. If anyone can dig through that haystack to find a needle, it's her."

Adam finished his second whiskey.

"You having another?" Karen asked, leaning into him.

"I think ... no, I'm not." Adam stood suddenly and Karen leaned away again, turning her eyes to the bar. "I'm going onto the Island. To visit Bermuda Station. Want to come?"

Karen smiled broadly and slid off her stool. "You don't have to ask me twice. This could be an adventure, couldn't it?"

"I would've thought we'd all had enough of that on this trip," Pete said drily.

"Hey, we've got five more days on this cruise." Adam put his arm around Karen's shoulders and they headed to the gangplank. "Let's wait and see how the rest of it goes."

ACKNOWLEDGMENTS

Author's Note

I hope you enjoyed reading *A Pale Reflection* as much as I enjoyed creating it. Writing a book is never a solo effort. I am grateful for all the support I received from my early readers, mentors and friends who took the time to read, comment and critique, particularly the fabulous professionals at TanMar Editorial and Bookfly Design.

I'd like to thank the Sisters in Crime and all the Guppies for sharing their wisdom, their experience and, when necessary, their commiserations, in particular Steve Shrott for excellent comments. I am grateful to Dorothy and Kerry Zbicz for their inspiration and knowledge about unexpected adoptions. I'd also like to thank Matty Dalrymple, Jane Kelly and Lisa Regan (our newly-founded Table 25 Club) for their support and encouragement. Most of all, I want to thank Chuck, for his unwavering belief in my writing.

In each of my books, I try to share the experience of traveling to a different place. I add touches of reality to give the setting depth and complexity. To make it more real. But rest assured this story is not real.

Cruises to Bermuda are, of course, real, but the cruise line and crew in this book are not. To the best of my knowledge, most passengers on cruises do not commit or even contemplate murder! With a few notable exceptions.

There are so many books and resources I could recommend, if you're interested in Bermuda, its history, music or culture, but I will limit myself to three (if you'd like more suggestions, just email me!). First, I recommend Mark Twain's Letters, Volume III. Naturally, anything by Mark Twain is always a good read. This volume of letters in particular, however, includes his entertaining perspective of his travels to Bermuda (of which he was a great fan). And if you read that, you might also want to get yourself a copy of Donald Hoffman's book *Mark Twain in Paradise*.

For information on Bermuda's role during World War II and the Bermuda Hotel, I relied on *Bermuda's History from 1939 World War 2 to 1951* by Keith Archibald Forbes, written for Bermuda Online. Bermuda has a fascinating story, and I encourage you to learn more about it.

I also recommend taking a cruise to Bermuda. I took a few (for purposes of research, of course!). I wasn't sure I'd enjoy the cruise experience, but I truly did. Whether you're the gregarious type who'd be playing adult games in the Starlight Lounge or the quiet type who'd prefer a quiet book in the library, my experience has been that there's something for everyone. Bermuda itself has so much to offer, from water sports to music to a complex history.

To keep up on news about the Adam Kaminski books, including the sixth book in the series, please visit my website to sign up for my newsletter or follow me on Instagram or Facebook.

janegorman.com

CPSIA information can be obtained
at www.ICGtesting.com
Printed in the USA
LVHW030621270420
654496LV00006B/1529